Hills Like White Hills

Also by W. D. Wetherell

FICTION
Souvenirs: A Novel
The Man Who Loved Levittown: Stories
Hyannis Boat and Other Stories
Chekhov's Sister: A Novel
The Wisest Man in America: A Novel
Wherever That Great Heart May Be: Stories
Morning: A Novel
A Century of November: A Novel

NONFICTION
Vermont River: Essays
Upland Stream: Essays
*The Smithsonian Guide to the Natural Areas
    of Northern New England*
North of Now
One River More: Essays
Small Mountains
This American River (editor)
Soccer Dad
Yellowstone Autumn

Hills Like White Hills

stories

W.D. WETHERELL

Southern Methodist
University Press / *Dallas*

This collection of stories is a work of fiction. Names, characters, places, and incidents are either the product of the author's imagination or are used fictitiously.

Requests for permission to reproduce material from this work should be sent to:
Rights and Permissions
Southern Methodist University Press
PO Box 750415
Dallas, Texas 75275-0415

Cover art: Winslow Homer, *Sleigh Ride*, c. 1890–95,
the Sterling and Francine Clark Art Institute, Williamstown, Massachusetts.
Jacket and text design: Kellye Sanford

Library of Congress Cataloging-in-Publication Data

Wetherell, W. D.
  Hills like white hills : stories / W.D. Wetherell. — 1st ed.
     p. cm.
  ISBN 978-0-87074-558-4 (alk. paper)
  I. Title.
  PS3573.E9248H55 2009
  813'.54—dc22

                                        2009016925

Printed in the United States of America on acid-free paper

10   9   8   7   6   5   4   3   2   1

For Nick Lyons

Acknowledgments

Some of the stories in this collection previously appeared, in slightly different form, in the following publications: "A Fixture on Main Street for Sixty-three Years" and "Pucker Pie" in *Green Mountains Review*; "Watching Girls Play" in *Georgia Review*; "Hills Like White Hills" in *Virginia Quarterly Review*; "The Master's Hand" in *Boston Review*; and "The Lucy Coffin" in *Take Me Fishing: 50 Great Writers on Their Favorite Sport*.

Contents

That Old Montana Pure

MY FATHER was the best cowboy singer in the state of Maine. *Cowboy*, not country. He would get mad if you called his music country. He dressed like a cowboy, talked like a cowboy, sang like a cowboy, and had a good cowboy name, Jack Stang. At one time in the late fifties he had quite a following, at least in the greater Augusta area where we lived. "Welcome to North Texas," he'd drawl at the start of his show, which every third Saturday filled the social hall of the largest Methodist church in town. "Howdy y'all North Texans," and all the loggers and their wives, the paper mill workers, the lobstermen in from the coast, all these hardworking, salt-of-the-earth men and women would laugh, whistle, and applaud. They were out for a good time, and Jack never disappointed them. He opened with Tex Ritter's "The Wayward Wind," then did his version of "Mule Train" complete with bullwhip, walking to the edge of the stage and snapping it right over their heads. After that it was my turn. I would probably have vomited once or twice by then, gotten one of my sick headaches, and yet I was always pretty calm by the time he actually lassoed me.

Jack would put down his guitar, pick up his lariat, start spinning it around his head, all the while humming "You Are My Sunshine." What's up? the audience wondered, hearing his voice go soft. He absent-mindedly glanced to his right, then, with a sudden quickening, sent the lariat flying off toward the wings. He couldn't actually lasso me—he was good with a rope, but not *that* good—and so my job was to pick up the loop before anyone saw it land, step into its middle, shimmy it up over my legs, then my tummy, then my accordion, smooth my dress down again, and let him tug me out onto the stage.

"You are my sunshine, my only sunshine, you make me happy when skies are blue."

Out I'd come, like a fish on the end of a line. A skinny fish. A tall, awkward, painfully shy ten-year-old, with buck teeth and premature acne and bones that stuck out at obtuse angles, and a face that was the exact opposite of cute. And people expected cute. They expected Jack Stang's little girl to be cute, someone they could ooh and ahh over—all the ladies, that's what they wanted to do. And there were always a few reflexive oohs when I appeared past the curtain. But what my appearance mostly elicited were resigned kinds of sighs, particularly from the old ladies, who knew from experience that hopeless little girls turned into hopeless grown-up women.

This was all lost on Jack. He sat me down on a stool, gave me a hug, and pulled off the lariat, rubbed his hand up and down the accordion keys like he was polishing them for me, getting them ready. This was mostly for the audience, but then he'd bend down in a courtly, old-fashioned bow that was for me alone. *Okay, Sandy, it's just you and me out here and I love you more than anything and betcherlife that's all that counts in life anyway.* That's the look he would give me—and then he would start in on "Cool Water," the Sons of the Pioneers' song he had made into his trademark.

My contribution was pretty modest. Every time he sang the word *water*, I'd softly echo it, *wah-ter*, and then squeeze out a C on the accordion, adding a second echo that was supposed to make it sound like we were singing from the bottom of a canyon. After that it was "Whoopee Ti-Yi-Yo," and my line was "Get along little dogie," which I was supposed to say more than sing, with a pout like Shirley Temple's.

I couldn't do this very well. I could never match his inflection on *water*, the accordion always did opposite of what I told it to do, and the "little dogie" line never got the laugh it deserved. If I looked like a mess, I sounded even more of a mess, and yet Jack would always look over at me not only like he and I were partners, but perfect equals when it came to music. When I mangled my lines he couldn't help wincing slightly, but he never let the wince get control of his face, not once in the three years we sang together.

"That'll do'er," he drawled when we finished. "Isn't she great, ladies and gentlemen? How's about a nice round of North Texas applause?" And they would always oblige.

He always sang the same songs in the same order. "The Wayward Wind." "You Are My Sunshine." "Whoopee Ti-Yi-Yo." "Red River Valley." "Tumbling Tumbleweed." "Do Not Forsake Me." "South of the Border Down Mexico Way." "I'm an Old Cowhand." "The Yellow Rose of Texas." "Streets of Laredo." "Bury Me Not on the Lone Prairie." "El Paso." "I Ride an Old Paint." "Back in the Saddle Again." "Don't Let the Stars Get in your Eyes." "Home on the Range." "Ghost Riders in the Sky."

The list brings it all back to me. How cold the halls always were, at least backstage, and Jack always wore a purple bandanna around his neck to protect his vocal chords until he went on. How tinny and cheap his guitar sounded when he first took it out of his case, and how, to warm it up, he would hold it in close to his chest like it was a woman he was loving up. How he would flirt with anyone attractive enough to warrant it, swagger a bit with the men—this as a kind of warm-up exercise to complete the transition from Jack Stang TV repairman to Jack Stang singing cowpoke. Meanwhile, I was mostly left on my own. These social halls and junior high auditoriums and Masonic temples always had more junk around than you might expect, and I was a great one for tripping over old props or wires, sending crates toppling with a huge crash.

"Hey, don't kill yourself, Sandy!" Jack would shout, in a voice that was all Texas now, not Maine. "Two left feet wouldn't be bad," he'd drawl to his cronies. "How come I ended up with a daughter's got twelve?"

I forgave him that—I had to, or else I couldn't go on. No one in those days despised me more than I despised myself. Once he lassoed me, the humiliation was worth it, just for that one moment to have a father protecting me, drawing me to him, holding me near. I wonder about that now of course—wonder that I was so starved for those things I'd accept that kind of trade.

If you say all those song titles out loud, sweeten up the syllables, add just the slightest amount of gravel, you'll know what Jack's singing voice sounded like. His audience was old enough to remember singing cowboys from the movies, and this is what they expected as regards authenticity; Jack groused about this, but didn't dare make his voice go rough. He refused to dress like a Hollywood cowboy, didn't have a fancy sombrero or rhinestone chaps. He dressed like a working cowboy circa 1888, in dungarees and a cheap flannel work shirt the color of old hemp. He wore his hair longer than men did in those years, and it was even sandier than mine was, so it made it seem he'd been so long in the saddle the color had bleached out. He was short, wiry—his muscles, including those in his face, were all tied up in tough little knots. A working man— the lobstermen, the loggers, the mill hands had no trouble accepting him as one of their own.

No singer ever depended on his audience more than Jack. He needed listeners who could respond to his sweet, lonely sound, and add their own yearning, so the blend, on a good night, could make you smile and sob at the same time. Those people sitting in those social halls on metal folding chairs. Even at ten, I could understand them a little—that what they wanted from Jack was to be freed from their cares for an evening, taken back to a time when men and women were brave, strong, and independent, and maybe still were, out there in that never-never land west of the Mississippi. It wasn't exactly Hollywood they were thinking about, and it wasn't the real West either, but something inside them the music released. Jack had a name for this kind of music. *Montana silver* he called it, or, at other times, *that old Montana pure*—and maybe it wasn't the music he was referring to at all, but that sweet, lonely spot inside people his music was able to reach.

For me, it took being away from him to fully understand this. Why I was away, how it happened, all the details, doesn't really matter, or maybe it matters everything, but in a blur that defeats a simple explanation. That he and Mom went bust was just as much her fault as it was his. When he lost his TV repair business, gave up pretending he was anything but who he was, she took a hard look at their marriage and immediately checked out. I was on my way to my third foster home in three years when my aunt and uncle in Massachusetts decided enough was enough and brought me down to live with them. Slowly, agonizingly slowly, things started to change—and then they began changing very quickly, in all kinds of ways.

Seven years went by, with only the flimsiest of contacts. A Christmas card every year. A record he cut for my fourteenth birthday. A biography of his hero Rex Allen he was trying to write and did I have any suggestions? Twice, calls from sheriffs in small Maine towns after he'd been stopped for DUI. Now and then, a review from some obscure north country newspaper, talking about how he was still a master of the old favorites, a crowd-pleaser from way back.

His only phone call came the summer I graduated from high school. I realized it was him right away, noticed only that his stage drawl had now become his everyday voice. But the funny thing was that he didn't recognize *my* voice; he kept asking for Sandy Stang.

"Hello?" he shouted. "This is Jack Stang calling. What's all that racket?"

"A tape. The Doors they're called. Jim Morrison is the singer's name."

"Jimmy Morrison? Old Jimmy?"

What I didn't say was that it was my boyfriend's tape deck we were playing it on—my boyfriend Neal who lay stretched out on the couch behind me, listening with the amused little smirk I was then in the process of confusing with sincerity.

"How are you, Dad?" I asked, tucking the phone in close.

"How are *you*, Sand? Everything right in your life? No one picking on you anymore? You tell me when anyone does, all right, Princess? You have acres of potential, I always said that, and you just have to tough it out a little while longer. Everyone respects a fighter, always have, always will."

Who was he talking to? *Wrong number* I wanted to say— the little girl you remember simply isn't here.

But I didn't say that. I asked about his career, how the singing was going. There were no other threads to tug.

"Have you been out West on one of your collecting trips this year, Dad?"

"Getting too old for that sort of thing. Stuck pretty much close to home. Bursitis the doctor says and there's this liniment I spread over my wrists. That's pretty near to the reason I called."

He had decided it wasn't much of a life for a man his age, traveling the back roads, singing himself hoarse every night, going out to Montana to collect new songs every autumn, coming back to face the winter. Cowpokes never worked much past forty, three quarters of them were dead before that, and here he was pushing fifty. He was going to give a series of farewell concerts, say goodbye in person to all the places that had been so good to him through the years, finishing things off with a grand finale performance in Augusta at the Methodist church.

"That's where they love me best, Sandy. You know that your-self. I've booked the hall for August 20, and they tell me seats are going fast."

"That's wonderful, Dad"—and I really meant it.

But it was a trap he had set, and now he suddenly sprang it.

"Well, I was thinking about how all those good people re-member you just as well they do me, and how it would be swell if you came along too, and we did it just like in the old days, you and me starting out with that duet they always loved."

Neal was tossing these little pretzels at my back, trying to get my attention.

"You mean when you lassoed me?"

"We wouldn't have to include that part if you didn't want to. But I've still got your accordion. No one ever played it as sweet as you did, Sand. Lots of people, why they'd come right up to me, tell me you had a career waiting if you wanted one, a girl with that kind of talent. We could do a little of that and sing a song or two, and that's all it would be, a regular reunion there on stage. Well sure, the audience matters, all those good people wanting to show they still care. But what I really mean is a reunion between you and me."

"Dad—"

"Remember that time the crow got in the back, and all those lumberjacks went around chasing it with brooms? I never saw men that big laugh so hard; they were swatting and yelling and falling off chairs. That crow could yodel better than me, betch-erlife he could."

"There's college I have to get ready for."

"College?"

"I'm going away to college this fall. I have a scholarship.

My boyfriend and I are going backpacking before that out in Colorado."

"Colorado?"

"Yep. Me, Dad. *Me.*"

He couldn't even bring himself to ask what college, or any of those simple questions even a stranger would know enough to ask. But that only helped his cause, because in the inevitable way of these things, my anger quickly turned to guilt. My absentee cowboy father, my father who never had any time for me except for twelve minutes every third Saturday night, calling out of the blue after seven years—and here I was the guilty one, so it was all I could do not to cry.

"Cowboy music?" Neal said, when I finally came back to the couch. His smirk deepened, turned his chin into a block. "Music for losers."

His saying that infuriated me. More than anything, I didn't want to be the kind of person who totaled up life that way. If he had ever heard Jack on stage, spinning his stories, singing his songs, he wouldn't have said it. Losers? With an audience who loved him? A passion he could pour his heart into? Something that gave meaning and shape to a life? I tore into Neal pretty good, but he wasn't impressed—my father's six-minute phone call, what it provoked in me, turned out to be the beginning of the end between me and Neal.

But it got me thinking, that casual remark. How could someone be a failure who loved something so much? Jack had discovered cowboy music while serving in Korea. He'd seen combat, awful stuff, and the only break they had was an occasional rest behind the lines where they watched movies flown in from the States, including a lot of Gene Autry and Rex Allen.

Jack was nineteen—there had to be something to put beside all the killing. If it was cowboys singing on horseback to blushing schoolmarms, then that was fine by them—anything to pull him away from the cold and the fear.

A corporal from Arkansas sold him a battered Gibson guitar, and he quickly learned the basic chords. Half the men in his company were from the Southwest, so he picked up the drawl just as fast. After his discharge he went back to New England, began singing in bars and at square dances, and he caught on fast. Most of his audience couldn't afford record players or records, but they knew the songs from the radio, and to hear them sung in person was a treat. He would cover half of Maine on a typical weekend, singing in Rumford on Thursday night when the millworkers got paid, driving all night so he could sing in Eastport for the sardine packers or in Houlton for the potato farmers, then driving down to Augusta for his regular Saturday night show, and a brief reunion with his wife and daughter. He was on the radio too, WBFB in Bangor, with a show called "Cowpoke Sunday Night," which for six or seven years in the fifties had a big following, not only in Maine, but over in Vermont and up to Quebec.

Jack's day job was TV repair—a cutting-edge, state-of-the-art occupation, at least in 1959. But he went at it half-heartedly, resenting the time it stole from his music. Whenever I visited him, his shop was crammed full of unrepaired television sets, with more piled up outside under orange tarps waiting their turn. My mother constantly nagged him over his lack of ambition. He would put up with it most of the year, but every September something in him snapped. He would hang a *Closed!* sign on his shop window, cancel whatever singing engagements he'd made, board the train in Augusta, and disappear for two weeks out West—Montana he said, or Wyoming, or once even Utah. These were what he called his "collecting trips," when he went around learning new songs from the few old-time cowboys who were still left—songs I don't remember even making their way into his repertoire. But he always came back invigorated in October, restored, kinder, happier. I remember one miraculous Halloween when, freshly returned from Montana, he remembered my existence long enough to take me out trick-or-treating.

So, between his gigs, his radio show, and his collecting trips, Jack carved himself out a career, even if it wasn't quite the one he dreamed of. That's what I was thinking about, after the partial truth of Neal's remark sank in. How a lot of these cowboy songs, if you really listened, were all about glorifying defeat, failure, and extinction. How that might get to you, sing them long enough. And how much courage it takes in life even to be second-rate.

"I'd love you to be up there with me, Sand," he said on his next phone call, the one that was the clincher. "I'd love one last time us singing those old-timey songs, seeing the look in those good people's eyes when they see us reunited live on stage."

We agreed to meet at a restaurant called Toppler's before the concert, have dinner together, then go over to the church in time to rehearse. I wasn't nervous about seeing him again so much as puzzled. Why was he saying goodbye to his singing? He was only in his fifties. Some people that age seem anxious to wrap up their lives early, but he was never that type. A grand farewell? Maybe that's what I was looking for myself, something that would wrap up an unhappy chapter of my life before I left for college.

And of course curiosity played a part. I hadn't seen Jack in over seven years. Had he changed?

He had and he hadn't. He was still wiry and lean; there had never been enough fat on his body for a paunch, but those knotty muscles in his face had gone slack, and there were puffy rolls on his forehead, flabby indents in his cheeks. He'd always been tanned, but these new wrinkles were pale and splotchy and difficult to accept. They seemed to hide his eyes, or something did. I remember saying to myself, *Well, I'll meet them directly, read what's going on there,* but after we hugged, when we went over to our table and sat down across from each other, bashfulness kicked in and I couldn't do it.

His voice was hoarser than I remembered it being; all the sugar had been leached out, but I liked it better that way, since he now sounded more like Dylan than he did Gene Autry.

"Well then, here we all are!" he said, leaning forward, tucking his thumbs over the table edge in his characteristic way. He nodded to himself in satisfaction, tucked his napkin up high on his shirt, waved over the waiter. "Whiskey!" he growled. Startled, the waiter tried not to smile. "Coke for the little lady"—and this time the waiter laughed.

"Great imitation, man," he said. "John Wayne? Neat."

Jack drummed his fists on the table until his drink came. I got up the nerve to look at his eyes now. They were heavy and motionless, not dancing around like I remembered. His nose too. It had widened, gone flabby, taken on too much red. I remembered those phone calls from apologetic police chiefs in those small, rural towns. Lots of his yodeling heroes drank when they weren't performing; he knew that about them, so was this part of the impersonation too?

No matter how hard I tried to appraise him, it was nothing to the way he appraised me. He ordered another drink, took a long swallow, then stared over at me in obvious disbelief. I had looked like a chipmunk when I was little, an emaciated chipmunk with buck teeth, bad fur, and a dull-mouthed way of staring—but this is not what he saw now. The clothes test I passed with high marks—this was 1969, and I was dressed like all my friends, in scruffy denim like a working cowboy— but the looks test was tougher. He wasn't prepared for what he saw, blinked hard to snap the homely little girl back into place. When the waiter came over to take our order, lingered longer than he had to, started flirting with me, this confused Dad, so right from the start our conversation seemed off-balance and strained.

"Predicting a full house tonight," he said, jabbing his thumb toward the window. "Lots of fishermen in from Rockport, those that are left anyway. Loggers too, though don't know how they scrape up enough for tickets. Millworkers are out on strike up in Millinocket, so I guess we won't see many of them."

"I'm pretty nervous about this," I said, which God knows was the truth.

"About singing?" He looked at me in amazement. "Well, I've been nervous before, plenty. Once I was invited down to Austin to cut a demo, I ever tell you about that? Record compa-ny big shots, producers, sidemen—they were all there watch-ing me, hoping I'd fall on my kisser probably, and I had to keep sucking on those licorice drops to keep my throat working.

Almost signed a big contract, audition went super, but they were tightening their belts up just then, so they told me the best thing to do was go back to Maine and stay in touch."

"Dad, I'd like to—"

He held up his hand. "Let me order a fresh one first, don't want to interrupt your train of thought."

He slid the new drink between his hands, pushed the half-empty one a little farther off, but still within reach.

"Now, you were saying, Sand? I want to hear all about what's up in your life—boyfriends, college, anything you think your daddy needs to hear."

And so I told him, or tried to tell him. He listened patiently enough, but I could see that most of what I said bewildered him. "Let me ask you something?" he said. "This college in New York. How long you got to go there, couple of months?"

"Four years, though it might be six if I go ahead with engineering."

"Engineer?" He let out one of his low cowboy whistles. "Let me ask you something else then. It must cost some money, six years of college. It ain't free?"

"Uncle Mike and Aunt Barb are taking care of that."

"They are? Well, salt of the earth is what I've always said about Mike and Barb. Salt of the fucking earth." He looked at me, made his eyes dance their old little dance. "Better'n me anyhow."

His wink made it a little easier. Our hamburgers came, the whiskey was starting to work on him, and he did most of the talking while we ate. Some of it was about the concert—how he was getting a little stiff in the hands to throw a lariat, so we'd skip the lasso part. My old accordion he had in the trunk of his car—but no, I told him, I didn't want to play accordion, I was so bad at it. I'd prefer just to sing. Well, that was okay, he said, though I could see he was disappointed. He'd cover me with his guitar if I was a tad bit rusty; he could make sure the melody smothered any lapses. I had nothing to be nervous about; he would watch out for me just like always.

After that was settled, he rambled on about a lot of things. About how corporations were ruining the state, stealing a living out of men's hands. About how we were fighting in Vietnam with one hand tied behind our backs, boys no older than I was getting killed in rice paddies, and what the hell were we doing there anyway? About all these smarty-pants women sticking their noses into places they weren't wanted, creating a ruckus just to get noticed. About how you should never forget those who you met on the way up in life, because you were bound to meet them on your way down again—a young person better understand that if they didn't want to be a snob. About how Maine was a hard place to live, but a harder place to leave ("I'll manage," I snapped). Pretty soon all this came around to his own life, the near misses, the chances he almost had, the broken promises, the slick lying bastards who always stood in his way. He'd almost had his own radio show down in Boston. He'd almost been given a record contract with Decca. He'd almost opened for Eddy Arnold at the Maine State Fair. With each new sip of whiskey, another *almost* came out, and that's what I found most painful, the part that was so different.

"Time to go now, Sandy," he said when the waiter brought over our check. "We'll try the stage out, see if we can find those dead spots that used to sink us."

I nodded, but made no move to get up.

"Can I ask you something, Dad?"

My tone caught him—he sat back down.

"Why sure. Ask away."

"When I was little and you used to go out West every fall. We'd be at the station and you'd have your blanket all rolled up and your knapsack and your sandwich. I used to ask you why you were going out there, and you used to smile and say it was to get a fresh helping of that old Montana pure. I still wonder about that sometimes. What you meant. What you meant by that old Montana pure."

He looked at me hard, seemed trying not only to brush away the years but to see into a part of me that wouldn't require any words to understand. Understand what he found out there, the spirit that inspired him, all the space, freshness, and freedom he couldn't even find a name for, but which he had seen and learned from and almost grasped. It was huge, it was something he couldn't get his soul around—or maybe that was me wishing it was huge, because he didn't answer me, or he did, but only by letting his eyes slide down from mine, drop toward the table again, sink to where his hands, his shaky hands, clasped the whiskey glass and the warm amber fluid that remained.

I nodded. He nodded. That was what we turned out to be good at, my father and me. Nodding at truth when there wasn't any other way around.

"I have another question," I said.

"Shoot."

"How come you're retiring from singing?"

"It's just," he mumbled. "It's just . . . trouble with the lyrics."

"Remembering them?"

"Believing them."

He downed the whiskey. We paid our bill. The waiter held the door open for us with a courtly flourish; we crossed the street to the social hall, found the closet that passed for a green room, got ready to go on.

A man in a string tie came to wish us well—an old friend of Jack's, loud and profane, and I didn't like it when he claimed to remember me and gave me a big hug. He brought a bottle with him, poured out a couple of tumblers. I mumbled something about wanting to watch the first few songs from out in the audience; the two of them were laughing pretty hilariously by the time I left.

Jack was wrong about it being a sellout. I stood in the back row and counted and there were plenty of empty seats. I hadn't seen any posters outside—had he even bothered to advertise? The people sitting there weren't old yet, but getting up there; the men wore nylon jackets with the names of their fishermen's cooperative on the back, or their union, but the women had made an effort to dress up, and looked like they were on their way to a square dance.

Out Jack came, to a warm, welcoming round of applause. He started them out like he always had, with "The Wayward Wind," then without pausing went into "Mule Train," only that wasn't quite as successful, since he couldn't get the bullwhip to snap. But the audience loved it anyway—they remembered all his tricks—and those strong faces now all wore contented smiles.

Jack talked more between songs than he used to. It was a strange mix of stuff, from the kind of free-flowing monologue he'd given me in the restaurant to long introductions to whichever song he was singing, as for instance the story of how a handsome young farmboy named Leonard Slye from Duck Run, Ohio, joined the Sons of the Pioneers in 1937, and changed his name to Roy Rogers. He moved to the edge of the stage, looked right down at his audience and addressed them directly, telling them they were the salt of the earth and they better not forget it, because if they forgot it the bosses would stomp all over them. Trapping lobsters wasn't that much different from punching cattle. Straddling a saw log wasn't that much different from straddling a good quarter horse or a strong woman, and that's what they were, the strong and enduring salt of the good fucking earth.

I could see the women, even some of the men, grow uncomfortable with that kind of talk—and not just the profanity. They didn't feel sorry for themselves, and they didn't want anyone feeling sorry for them, or maybe they did, but it was only acceptable if it came in songs. They were impatient for him to start singing again—couldn't Jack sense that, or was he too far gone?

"The Whispering Wind," he sang. "The Yellow Rose of Texas." "I'm an Old Cowhand." "Tumbling Tumbleweed." "Ghost Riders in the Sky." They were all laments now; no matter how hard he tried putting bounce in them, every note came out slow, deep, and mournful. All his cockiness was gone, the little strut that made him seem taller than he really was—and yet I could tell the audience still hung on his every word. On the slower songs, the ones that really were laments, people dabbed at their eyes with their sleeves. Cowboys were gone, forests were cut, factories were closing, the seas were fished dry—and there Jack stood yodeling away.

"Here's a little tune I'd like all you good people to help me out on. I had the honor of being the first one ever to sing this in the state of Maine, this was back in, oh, 1953 I think it was. It's called "Home on the Range," and we'll have you pretty fillies take the first verse, and we'll bring the broncos in on the second, and if we're lucky, finish damn near all together, how's that?"

If I was going to find the strength to go up on stage, now was the time, with that plaintive sound filling the hall. Jack saw me take my position in the wings, nodded briefly, but there was still one more chorus left to go. Some out in the audience closed their eyes, letting the words, those never-discouraging words, sink in so deep they could never be lost. Jack held his guitar vertically, put it right against his ear, made that last note last longer than the audience could sustain, so the echo helped ease the song away to wherever such songs wait when no one is singing them.

"Thank you, folks, sounded really fine on that one, betcherlife you did. Now's about the time in the show I'd like sharing a little surprise with y'all. Remember how we did it in the old days, me and my little girl Sandy just the two of us up here on stage? Life can play tricks on you sometimes, life is one hell of a cruel trickster, and here I used to imagine we'd be partners always, only someone put notions in her heart and that's not the way it turned out. But that's okay now, because she's here with us tonight all the way from Boston, Massachusetts, just to share my farewell concert. She never stopped being an inspiration to me all these years, and so let's bring her out here with an old-fashioned North Texas kind of welcome . . . my little cowgirl, Sandy Stang!"

What was funny was that it was harder without the lasso, there was no encouraging tug, I had to find the nerve to go out there on my own. Jack was singing "You Are My Sunshine," and I could see right away there were people in the audience who recognized me, or seemed to, squinting up at me like Jack had back in the restaurant, surprised that the years could play the reverse kind of trick it was playing on them. Did some of the women actually gasp at the change? No, it was my imagination, but that was okay. I took some satisfaction from that, my deserved thirty seconds of revenge.

That's all it was. I sensed something different about how Jack sang to me, but at first I couldn't focus on what the difference was, I was too busy dealing with my own emotions. He finished "You Are My Sunshine," and the audience gave us the big round of applause he had asked for, but "Cool Water" didn't go anywhere near as well. He always sang the first verse alone, and I wasn't due to join in until the chorus, my simple echo note, but before I could, I suddenly understood what was different. He was singing to the audience, not me—facing them, not getting real close to sing to me alone like he had when I was ten. His lassoing me with the lariat had been a sort of joke; it was nothing compared to the way he really lassoed me, wrapping his voice around my embarrassment so nothing could hurt me or make me sad. But he wasn't doing that now, not even trying to do that, and it threw me badly. It was my turn to repeat his *wah-ter*, but I spoke it rather than sang it, spoke it flatly and ironically, with the smirk Neal had taught me, the smirk of our generation.

Jack caught it right away of course. He didn't stop playing, didn't act surprised, but merely nodded, as if he knew this was coming, had anticipated it all long.

"A little rusty on that one, Sandy. You don't want to sing like you're some smart-ass frog."

There were some hesitant laughs from the seats closest to the stage. I don't think I quite believed what I heard, because I didn't run off the stage in tears or yell at him or any of the things I could have done. He sang the last verse, I mumbled out another dry, echoless wah-ter, and then we went right into "Whoopee Ti-Yi-Yo," only this was worse, and when it came time to sing "Get along little dogie," I said the words fast and ashamed in little more than a whisper.

Jack's guitar made a twanging sound, an ugly twanging sound that was meant to imitate my voice, and then he just stopped playing altogether. He leaned his head back, rubbed his hand up and down his grizzled neck like he needed a shave or needed a drink or was appealing to heaven.

"You'd reckon someone who claimed they loved something would really mean it, wouldn't you now? You'd reckon someone who said they loved someone and wanted to go partners would feel obliged to pay attention to that claim. Someone who before they got uppity and smarty-pants had a real special quality about them, I always felt that, and you know what, ladies and gentlemen? I was dead wrong."

He twanged his guitar, made his voice go falsetto. "Get along little doggie," he said in an effeminate lisp. "Get along little doggie, along now stupid fucker, haul ass."

He rambled on like that, playing that mocking voice, mumbling, until no one could follow the music or his words.

I couldn't see very far out into the audience, but then something dark and oval rose against the spotlights, and something else farther to the right, and I realized it was people getting up and leaving, one after the other, the women first and then the men . . . and then finally there was no one sitting in the social hall at all, just me and my father up on the stage in the blue of the spotlight, and then I turned and left too, and so it was Jack Stang alone, hunched over his Gibson guitar, the shiny black one he had traded for in Korea, floating out those sad, drunk notes there was no one left to catch.

I know what you expect me to say—that the farewell concert was our farewell too. Another six years went by, and except for a brief meeting at my mother's funeral, I never had any contact with Jack at all. That changed after I graduated from med school. I had met Alex there; we were in a special program for rural practice, and after Erica was born we moved to a small town farther up the Maine coast than the tourists had yet penetrated. So I saw Jack fairly often during the last three years of his life. It wasn't like he was my father—neither one of us bothered pretending that—but more like a no-obligations friendship with an interesting old man. He lived in a rooming house in Bangor, and still sometimes sang, mostly to senior citizens or at hospitals. But all the sparkle was gone. He would complain about how even the old folks only wanted country now, didn't understand that cowboy was entirely different. In the end, he didn't so much die of anything specific; like the lyrics of his songs, he simply pined away.

There's a sequel to this. A few years after he died, by who knows what connections, I got a call from a bus driver over in

Bar Harbor. He was there driving a seniors group on a foliage tour around New England, and one of his passengers wanted to speak to me, if I was really Jack Stang's daughter. Her name was Laura Grimaldi. She came on the phone and what she said made me agree to drive down to meet her at the hotel before the bus tour moved on.

She was a woman in her sixties, white haired and pleasant looking, with enough left in her looks to see she must have once been stunning. She had met Jack in Buffalo, New York, in 1959, she explained. She was working behind a candy booth at the city's central station when a wiry-looking man came up and asked her where he could find the train to Montana. This made her laugh, him asking her like Montana was just one stop down the line. They talked for a while, flirted. Instead of him going to Montana, she brought him back to her rooming house, and he stayed there for two weeks. They fell in love with each other—she wasn't shy about admitting that. She never married anyone else, Jack was so special to her, but things being what they were, he could never be with her more than for those two weeks every autumn, weeks she eventually came to live for.

What would they do with their time? She blushed—it was charming to see a woman her age blush—then tried to explain. Well, they took a lot of walks together. They visited the falls, went to minor league baseball games, sat on her porch watching the cars go by. Jack enjoyed cooking hamburgers on the little grill she had. Toward the end of his stay, he liked to lay out on her patch of lawn working on his suntan. The great thing about Jack was that you didn't have to do very much; he seemed content just to be with her, and their two weeks together always went by too fast.

"Did he sing to you much?" I asked. Outside the lobby the bus driver was beeping his horn, and she was hastily grabbing up her things.

She looked puzzled. "Sing? Why would he sing?"

"He never said anything about singing?"

She tilted her head to the side, tried hard to remember. "We used to listen to my Perry Como records, and he always said he liked him. Other than that? No, I don't think so. He wasn't even a very good whistler."

I shook hands with her—but that wasn't good enough, we threw our arms around each other and hugged. I've thought about what she said a lot in the years since, in trying to understand Jack's puzzle. I always return to the same place, throwing the question he threw at me at his farewell concert back at him. How could he love someone as much as he loved Laura and never share with her the greatest passion in his life? How could he not do that? By what trick of the mind, hocus-pocus of the heart? Jack Stang, for pity's sake. How not sing to her? How not sing?

The Master's Hand

NO ONE BOTHERED telling her he was a good man deep inside. The dozen that came to the grave site were not the kind for evasion, and even if they were, the November grayness was too bitter for anything besides truth. They stood in a ring, the men in hunting clothes except for Mr. Andrews and the minister Ted had found through the VA, the women in woolen coats that seemed spun from the same stark fabric as the sky. They bowed their heads, mumbled to the minister's prayer, then came up to shake her hand—people her age, forty and fifty; people who had lived in town as long as she had; people who had few illusions about life, and none whatsoever about him.

"I'm sorry, Linda," is what they said, bobbing their heads with shyness, moving on. Only a few added anything to this. Mary Demarest from the post office said, "It's a blessing" the way people did after someone had taken years to die, not seconds. Tom Clarkson of the road crew made a grabbing motion with his fist, managed a half-hearted grimace. "He could

smash a softball, jeezus he could." Mr. Andrews told her there
was no hurry getting back to work, even with Christmas coming and their being busy. Her job at the craft center was to take
a burning iron and write *From the North Country with Love!*
on the back of all the souvenirs, and there had been a moment
in the service when she weakened, felt herself being drawn
down the open hole after him, and the strength that saved her
came from closing her eyes, imagining the words seared on
the red battering ram of his forehead: *From the North Country
with Love—straight to hell.*

Afterward, after Ted had paid the minister, told her he
would come on Sunday to check up on things, given her the
appraising glance that was all twins ever needed, she drove
alone to the house, feeling a fatigue that surprised her more
than anything else had all week—that she was turning out to
be an amateur in exhaustion, she who had always thought herself a pro. She was half asleep just driving the county road,
and even the ruts and bumps of the washboard that led the
final yards to the house her grandfather had built did little to
jar her loose. In the early darkness all she was aware of were
scattered sights tied to scattered feelings. The salty pattern the
snow made on the circle of surrounding hills—how she was
free to love it now, the terrain that had turned out to be too
hard and tough for even Earl to ruin it. The way Paco howled
when he heard the car—how tired and heavy the sound made
her feel, hammer blows driving her lower toward the ground.
The heat of the woodstove when she opened the front door . . .
the heat from the fire he had kindled just before storming out
of the house Monday afternoon . . . and how it seemed to mock
her with its illusion of comfort, safety, and welcome.

She groped in the darkness for the light switch, then stumbled toward the kitchen past the carton of Christmas lights she had been taking out when the call came from the state police. As heavy as her fatigue was, there was one task waiting before she could give way. In the drawer by the refrigerator were dozens of old pens, stubs of pencils, even some paintbrushes left over from the days when there had been a child in the house, their tips dabbed with red and blue crust. She rummaged through these until she found a pen that seemed light and delicate enough to do what she asked of it, then went to the phone book for the writing paper pressed in back.

Sitting under the kitchen lamp, it took her only a few seconds to write the lines she had been composing in her imagination for the past twelve years. *Dear Ellen. He's gone. You can come home now if you want. Today is the first day of the rest of our lives. Your loving mother.*

She read it over, wishing her handwriting was less cramped, more open, then found an envelope and printed the address she had memorized when it came on the birthday card last spring. Finishing, she went into the parlor and stood by the stove, staring down at what lay scattered across the dirty bricks of the hearth. Chunks of firewood; a rusty poker; the blackened, gauntlet-sized glove. And then, with nothing more to test herself again, she climbed upstairs to her bedroom, bolted the door shut, and collapsed into the stupor that was her due.

She woke to the sound of Paco's barking out by the barn, the echo making it seem farther away than it really was, less ugly, less mean. That was all she expected from life now anyway, to have the worst of it off her shoulders, have its rawness come muffled, but even this wasn't going to be accomplished without effort. The house was stained with his things; he wouldn't be gone until they were gone, and so after a lukewarm cup of coffee, an untasted plate of eggs, she started in.

She worked all morning, making a pile in the parlor, then carting it out to the woodshed where Ted could come and load his truck. She started with the military magazines, the dirty videos, the homemade cigarettes, and when they were gone, she went into the back room for the archery equipment, the bows with their complicated levers and pulleys, the arrows that seemed tipped with deer blood the way Ellen's brushes were tipped with paint, the decanters shaped like race cars he bought empty at yard sales and filled with grape wine, the posters and certificates from the secret militias he was always joining through the mail—breaking the arrows over her knee, ripping the camouflage off the hangers, dashing the decanters against the floor. And yet none of this helped; the pounding on her head was worse than before, not better; and she felt herself falling deeper into the hole his living had dug for her, and this time there was no way to keep out.

There was only one surprise—a flimsy shoebox with a collection of lead soldiers he must have had when he was a boy. Some were painted, but most were not. She held one up to her face, squinted at the features . . . bland, serene, lifeless . . . and for some reason this wearied her more than any of his other possessions, and she threw the toys into the woodshed with the rest.

Finished, she went outside to stand on the frozen ruts of her garden, stared out toward where the tree line supported hard flowers of cloud. It had snowed again during the night, and the rim of hills that encircled the farm was covered with something that was more sugar than salt, fluffier, more soothing. A crow flew across the whitest patch, underlining it with black, and a moment after that came enough sunlight to set the ground dust to sparkling, everything right up to the stubborn dark border of her boots.

"Goddamn," she said, biting her lip. "Goddamn it to hell."

Turning, she walked quickly up the gravel path toward the ruins of her grandfather's barn, drawing strength as she always did just to stand in its presence. She had gotten as far as the sliding door, had bent to pry some ice away, when something caught her attention, and she walked carefully around to the silo side, leaning forward from the waist to see better, not be surprised.

A metal cable extended from the barn fifty yards to the old Porter apple tree her grandparents had planted to celebrate her birth; attached to this cable with a swivel was Paco's wire leash. He was straining at the farthest end, forepaws in the air, dancing like he was trying to tow the barn to safety. His barking was louder than she'd ever heard, crazier, wilder, and she realized this was the pounding noise that had pressed on her head ever since waking up.

She backed off slightly so the dog couldn't reach her if he turned. That was the extent of their relationship in the four years he had been chained there—in giving him distance just like she gave all the other hazards of life distance, and otherwise ignoring him altogether. He was a wolf-hybrid; "Just like me," Earl would say, laughing with a snort that turned his throat the same red color as his hair—only snake-hybrid would be more accurate. The dog was spindly and gaunt, and walked sideways with his nose coiled back in toward his tail. There were black splashes over his eyes and flanks that made it look like he was dressed in camouflage; the eyes themselves were white and empty, and it was clear he saw life mainly through his teeth.

The fifty yards of his run crossed the small terrace of lawn that rose from the garden—the prettiest spot on the farm, the place she brought her dolls when she was little—and it had been Earl's habit to go out there after dinner, sit on an upended gasoline can, and simply stare at him, never petting him, never even calling out his name, just staring toward the coiled spring of his ferocity the way she herself stared toward the hills.

Paco. Paco the wolf-hybrid. Paco her husband's joy in life. Paco, who with the knives and the filth and the camouflage was now hers.

She saw what he was dancing toward: the porcelain mixing bowl that served as his dish. Empty, he must have nuzzled it during the night until it rolled out of reach; now, frantic from hunger, he was lunging toward it again and again, neck straining, legs spread open to pull, his stubby white cock straight out in furious wanting.

That close, his barking was easier to tolerate than it had been in the house. It wasn't a bark anyway, not the begging you got from a dog, but something shriller and more insistent, like commands shouted from a boss who was hoarse. She listened for a minute, then reached her hand up and pulled on the cable—once, then a second time much harder. Feeling this, Paco sat down and looked back toward the barn, head bent to the side, eyes narrowing into a squint. Expectation set him panting, but then he went belly down in a crouch, his lip curled back over his teeth, growling, with his jaw pressed against the dirt like he was sending his hatred to her through the ground.

He didn't leave the bowl, didn't rush her. Backing slowly from the barn, she went to the kindling piled on the scrappy pavement left over from the days when they were young and stupid enough to still work the farm. The first stick she pulled out was too thin, and she had to squat down to find one better suited to her purpose. What Paco was used to seeing in people's eyes was fear, but he wouldn't see it in hers, not if she could help it. Holding the stick by its middle, she took up a position just a little way beyond the bowl and started very softly to hum.

Paco spun around to face her, his eyes going from the stick to her face, then back again, trying to understand the connection, reading by her tone what lay in wait. "Hungry?" she said. She reached with the stick until it met the bowl's rim, pressed down so it rolled over, then scraped it back over the dirt toward her boots.

"Poor dog. No one left to take care of you? Left alone all by your lonesome? I'll get you your food."

She bent to pick up the bowl, turning slightly as she did so, just enough that Paco saw his chance. It was over so fast she didn't have time to be frightened. There was a shadow crossing the gray saucer of sunlight that underlay the white bowl, a warm push of air, the pinging sound of wire going taut, and then she looked down to see Paco on his back, squirming desperately to right himself, gnashing his teeth as if they held between them a corner of her flesh.

No time to be afraid. No energy for that anymore. Nothing to do but stare down at him with a look colder than anything in that hard and hopeless November light.

"You want it, don't you?" she said, imitating Earl's flat, weary intonation she had heard too many times. "You want a feel of the glove."

Paco was back on his feet, pawing furrows into the dirt with his flattened claws. She reached again, this time facing him, then backed away with the bowl toward the house. By the time she was inside, his howling was excruciatingly loud, and she had to turn on the radio to drown it out. In the refrigerator was the frozen rabbit that was his favorite food. She boiled it, watching the pot until the pinkness turned brown, then mixed it with kibble from the bag in the pantry and brought it back outside, still steaming from warmth.

"What was it, Monday since you been fed? Here. Wild game dinner fit for a king. All yours."

She put the bowl down on the ground in the exact spot she had found it, then stepped back to watch him battle with the wire leash. He pulled hard enough that the cable bowed out, but it was still too short, and the tension snapped him on his back. He jumped again, then a third time, then a fourth, the smell making him wild, the intervals between flying through the air, landing on his back, coiling himself together again, coming so fast there was no separating them, and all she saw was the crazy blur of his desperation.

"Needs seasoning, does it? You never learned how to cook the way I liked anyway. Trying to poison me, that's it huh, Linda? You need teaching, you. You wait here."

She walked to the barn, shoved the door open with her shoulder, kicked through the riddled targets, the broken snow machines, the shredded tires, until she found the can she was looking for, lugged it back again—and all the while she did this, she felt a lightness in her legs and arms she hardly remembered having before, as if all the grimness was draining from her veins down through the screw cap into the kerosene.

There wasn't much of it left in the can—just enough to dribble over the meat. She kicked the bowl so it slid across the ground toward the bare spot where Paco danced. He was on it instantly. He jerked his head back, poked his snout down, pulled it away again, shook his mouth back and forth so hard it set the fatty hump on his neck to rolling, sat back on his haunches, started to howl.

"What's the matter with you? Won't join me in a sociable drink? Think you're better than I am, don't you? Go ahead and drink up. We've got lots of time, you and me. No one can hear us, know that? Yell all you want. Plenty of time. A November day is the longest thing in the goddamn world. Sneering? A snobby one, huh? Think you're better than me just 'cause your father was school principal and dressed you pretty, turned your head."

She remembered feeling ashamed when she first started talking out loud that way, frightened, hardly recognizing the voice as her own. Having the dog to listen made it easier—it wasn't really talking to herself at all.

The cold kept the fumes low over the dish so Paco couldn't get past them to bite in. She could see the confusion in his eyes, the humiliation—recognized these all too well. In her pocket was the match she had been saving for the woodstove, and it occurred to her it would be easy to light it and toss it in the bowl the moment his snout went down.

"You want the glove now? You want the feel of it, just holler."

By the woodshed was a frozen coil of hose. She dragged it

over, breaking apart the kinks with her boot, then went back and turned on the faucet. At first there wasn't much water, but then the ice burst free and it came out in a jet. She filled his water dish, slid it past the food bowl where he couldn't reach it without choking, then put her thumb over the nozzle and sprayed it back and forth along the grooved path his pacing had made under the cable. Slowly to the right, slowly to the left, covering the ground thoroughly, then covering it again, until the brown became wet with blackness and the blackness froze.

"Here, Paco," she said softly, tilting her head back, patting her throat. "Here, come and get me."

He was smarter this time—he pulled to the side, straining, so his feet stayed on the dirt. There was no way to reach her without crossing the ice. He turned in a tighter circle, turned again, squatted and screwed his eyes closed, pressing out a turd. She aimed the water to blow the steamy heap of it away, then raised it the inch or two it took to bring the jet against the ugly black spot on his flank.

It stung him—he hopped to the side, started licking at the fur where it hit, but by now she had the jet going against his shoulders, and it pressed him back onto the ice. He snarled and snapped at it, trying to bite the spray before being hit, but she moved the nozzle faster, hitting his paws, then his tail, then the hollow spots under his ears, then his nose, so he couldn't anticipate where it would go next. He rose tight against the cable like a fish against a line, exposing his bottom, and she instantly turned the stream there, screwing the nozzle tighter so the water drove even harder, hitting him full force against his cock.

While all this went on, he never left off his snapping, never once stopped baring his teeth. She knew that kind of hate, knew it too well. Every reaction to the world, every response, there in the tightness of his jaw, the acid in his throat. A minute of it and she felt exhausted, sickened—the heaviness was getting worse, not better, and with a disgusted motion she looped the hose clear of the dishes and walked through the afternoon shadows back toward the house.

The dark came early, but she did nothing to hold it off. From the couch she could see orange bars thrown by the flames through the woodstove's vent, and it made the black seem deeper, more total, something a lamp could have no effect against. She may have slept for a time, but not so deeply she lost track of Paco's howling, or missed the sound of a car door closing and tires spinning away up the road.

When she did get up and turned the lamp on, it was to find it was snowing out, and someone had left a chicken casserole on the front step. There was no name, even when she brushed the snow off the foil. She brought it inside, feeling strong enough now to turn all the lights on, creating a cream-colored ring in the house that rose like an extra wall.

She took her time over dinner, liking that feel—of treating herself, making things easy. She used paper plates so she wouldn't have dishes, ate slowly, fixing herself a hot mug of cocoa as a reward once she was done. When the phone rang she didn't answer. She heard it again, minutes later, but by then she had her coat on and with a plate full of leftovers was pressing through the door outside.

It was snowing harder now, gritty pellets that slanted through the spotlight and accumulated fast on the ground.

Paco lay curled against the bar near the mound of his own vomit; it was clear he had managed to take a few bites from the bowl, and that the brown stinking wetness was the result.

Keeping back from the ice, never leaving off watching him, she dragged the gasoline can over, brushed the snow off, and sat down so the spotlight was at her back and Paco had to squint to keep her in sight.

"Go ahead and growl," she said. "Good for the soul, growling." She laughed, or at least tried to, but the cold burned her chest and she had to wrap her arms around herself to stay warm. "Not much of a day for you. Nope, not much of a day at all."

She could feel his eyes fixed on the shelf made by her knees. She pushed the plate out in plain sight.

"It must have been something you did to provoke this reaction," she said slowly, trying to remember the counselor's words, the exact tone. "Something in your own behavior; can you search your memory? What we want to do is empower you to take your future into your own hands. Understand me? Empower. It's what we got to do to you."

The snow came down against her neck, even with the collar raised. With the light blocked by her shoulder, only a little made it to the barn; in her weariness, Paco's shape began to blur, so he looked like a pile of rags thrown there to freeze.

"Why don't you just leave if things are so bad? Why don't you just up and fly away like a little bird? Why don't you pretend no one will come and find you and hurt you worse than before? You're empowered just like one of those spacemen with rockets on his feet. Fool for sticking it out here anyway. Snow in June, that's what it'll do to you. Frost in August and flies the rest of the year; only trash would want it anyway, ain't that so? Land of poison. No one's going to hurt you if you just get up and fly away like a little old robin."

The words came easier the faster she talked, so she hunched forward on the can, lost in them, hardly aware now of the dog's presence. "You know what you get for aggravating me? You know what you get, don't you? You know, because you know me, know from last time, and I'm warning you that glove's still hanging right where I left it. Ran from me once—where'd it get you? Treated like dirt in the city, ain't that so? Go ahead and run and then all this becomes mine, even the memories, and when I have those I have you, ain't that so?"

She put the plate of leftovers on the ground, sliding it forward with her boot so it was well within his reach. Paco pushed himself wearily to his feet, taking mincing steps across the ice so as not to fall, his head down into his chest like the snow hurt his eyes. When the chain tightened he looked up—saw the food, saw her leaning over it—and instantly made his decision, springing toward her throat, so she imagined the tearing press in her flesh even at the very second she heard the pinging sound, realized the chain had caught him and thrown him sprawling back.

She shook inside, shook to the point of tears, but she didn't let him see this—knew in that moment she was never going to let anyone see tears again. "All right then," she said, facing the icy patch where he sat howling. She reached with her boot, kicked the leftovers toward blackness. "You're number 257 on our case list. You smart enough to remember that, or you want me to write it down? Women like you are on a line that stretches around the goddamn block. Call our machine in the morning if another incident takes place."

She turned toward the house, stopped, looked back. "Goodnight, Paco dog. Sweet dreams you."

She listened to his howls that night the way people listen to a sound that's been in their life all along, but only now are they really hearing. At times, she pictured it as a siren, imagined ambulances racing to help her; other times it seemed like a hot wind that had spread its jaws around the house and slowly crushed inward, starting on the room, then the beams, then the ceiling. Around midnight she got up, looked out the window, tried staring past the snow, paced for a restless half hour, then fell asleep again curled in the armchair with her robe wrapped around her shoulders. This time she really did dream, imagined Paco with his head pressed on her lap, so they were friends now, survivors, the dog recognizing this, so the howling wasn't howling after all, but the cry of a helpless creature begging her forgiveness.

She woke up later than usual, startled to see the sunlight frosted on the windows, confused for a moment as to where she was. The dream was vivid enough that it still possessed her as she drank her coffee, and it was only the phone ringing that began to shake it loose.

It was Ted. Talking as slowly as ever, putting each word out like it was a concrete block needing much consideration before it moved, he explained he was on his way over—that he'd been getting calls all night from neighbors who heard the howling, neighbors who weren't too scared anymore to complain. It was time to end it, Ted said. He was bringing his deer rifle and he would take care of things himself.

His call only emphasized this new feeling, made her long to make friends while there was still the chance. Without even putting on her coat she went outside, squinting toward the shards of sunlight where they shattered apart on the barn. Paco was huddled against the boards, looking weaker than the night before, his fur frozen in clumps that reminded her of the cheap stuffed animals she had once bought Ellen. He was still howling, or at least trying to; his snout jerked up as before, enough so she could see the tendons tighten and flex below his muzzle, but what came out was brittle and hoarse, as if the night had driven the ice deep into his chest.

When he went for her it was in slow motion, shaking free of the ice, gathering himself, shivering, finally managing a comic imitation of a pounce. She saw all this with perfect clarity, with plenty of time to back off, and yet what she couldn't avoid was the hatred in his muzzle, the growling that came at full strength, redoubled strength, tripled strength, eyes slanted, head down, teeth bared, so it was as if someone had taken ferocity, plopped it down in front of her, drawn its silhouette with an icy black pen. Always before she thought Earl had made up the wolf part just to brag, but she could see it now—how the food didn't matter to Paco, the possibility of warmth or shelter, nothing except the overwhelming need to transfer the tension from his throat onto hers.

And the odd thing was this still didn't frighten her—made her know, if anything, a brief moment of victory and satisfaction, so when she backed away from him it was with a grim sort of smile.

"I had nothing to do with it, just remember that. Your choice, not mine."

No thought was needed anymore, no decision. What was needed was to back away from the ice, press her shoulder against the heaviness of the winter door, walk inside to the woodstove, reach like a robot toward the asbestos mitt hanging from its nail on the hearth—the blackened glove that had hung there even before Ellen left home; the glove she had never put on before; the glove that was the last thing in the house that was his. Always before she had imagined it being unbearably heavy and coarse, a glove of iron, so she was surprised at its lightness—at how well it fit.

She got down on her knees before the woodstove door, opened it with a half turn to the right, then reached the glove past the burning logs in front until it came against the apple-sized coals lying against the base plate, closed her fist around them, brought the three largest ones back out.

They didn't burn, the glove absorbed all their heat, and so she was able to walk back outside holding the coals in front of her the way she had held the bowl of food, the redness flaring at the new touch of air, its smoke coiling backward toward her eyes. Behind her on the other side of the house came the sound of a truck door slamming, but she walked on anyway, not stopping until she came to the spot where Paco crouched over the frozen rabbit.

"Here, Paco," she said. "Here this is for you."

He saw the coals cupped there in the glove, realized at once they were meant for him. He backed up slowly on the ice, the rabbit flopping from his mouth like an extra tongue, arching his back the way a cat would, growling, but this time in confusion, his muzzle trembling. His fear maddened her even more than his hatred; she walked toward him so there was no chance of his sliding past her on the cable, and when he had backed as far as the barn, she stopped and held the coals up toward her face so he could see what had become of her, the liver-white saucers on her cheeks, the dead patches of skin that flaked off in the cold, brought the other hand up to touch them so there would be no mistake. *Here, Paco. Here is what coals do. Here is how he held them before jabbing them into my face.* But his eyes stayed fixed on the coals, so it was like a wire extended from their center to his eyes, one she could pull any direction she wanted and the tightness wouldn't let go.

Behind her she could heard Ted's voice off by the kitchen, but she kept on anyway, and then when she was within reaching distance and Paco had nowhere left to go, he sprung wildly to his right, hard and desperately enough that his weight came sideways against the frozen collar, snapping it open. For the first second he didn't realize he was free, merely cowered there whimpering, but then with her next, much more sudden step, he was off and racing away from her, feet on solid ground now, running toward the field, his speed increasing once he got there, his silhouette flattening, so within seconds he was halfway to the trees.

She turned, saw Ted folded over his truck with his rifle taking aim, a red and black shape of great intentness, and she threw the coals down and ran toward him shouting before it was too late.

"No!"

He heard her—he looked over long enough that she could read the puzzlement on his face—and it was enough time that

Paco was past the first low rise into the trees. She saw him run toward the gap where the hills separated, let go their choke hold on the meadow. The county road was there, the highway, the interstate that led toward the south. Toward the south where she'd fled once herself, so she knew exactly what was waiting for him there. She didn't feel regret at seeing him run, but only satisfaction—felt a second, more violent kind of snapping as the hardest part of her tore away. Ted was taking aim again, there was one last chance to stop Paco as he crested the last rise, but she waved her arms, shouted at the top of her lungs, wanting only to hurry his escape from it—the land of the scarred, the stubborn, the ones meant to stay.

Watching Girls Play

QUICKER, QUICK as he'd been in college, he could have
sped the car up just enough to head the ball off the top of the
windshield and rocket it toward goal. As things are, he eases
into it too slow, the ball coming down obliquely against the
roof, bouncing three times there like an angry fist trying to
get his attention, then rolling back down over the flattened
antenna. The car is instantly surrounded by girls or parts of
girls—brown legs, red knees, pink elbows, reaching for the
ball, laughing, draping themselves over the hood blotting out
the sun, then just as suddenly parting again, the dimpled ball
nudged and herded back to where it belonged by ponytails,
shag cuts, and curls.

Dolger smiles, knowing this is expected of him, but the
girls have already gone back to their field. A funny incident—
well, not so funny, he could easily have run one over—and he
surprises himself by stopping the car and getting out. It's autumn, this is country, and he hasn't been so deep in country

in a very long time. That there is a soccer game about to begin on the village common before a classic New England church has nothing to do with it, not in his opinion. Soccer is a kind of bonus, an extra-added attraction to what is basically a badly needed break from the car.

He locks the doors from habit, then walks slowly toward where the first spectators are arranging their blankets and lawn chairs around the base of a tall, sloppy-looking elm. It's late enough in October the leaves have mostly fallen, and what color hits him hardest comes from the perfect green of the field. Later, looking at it more professionally, he will note the flinty patches scrubbed bare by cleats, the mud there by the south goal, a pronounced dip in the same direction. But that first glance comes to him right through the lungs, as if he's breathing pure green adrenaline, so it's all he can do not to lope to his usual position there at midfield.

Easy fella, he tells himself—he's still at the smiling stage, taking it all in. Above the field the sky is a deep and perfect blue, decorated by a flower or two of broken cloud. No scrub marks there, no dips or depressions. He can remember being exhausted toward the end of hard games, and how he would deliberately blast the ball high toward the sky just to soak in some of that exhilaration, the coach not daring to yell at him because he was the star. The kind of thing you couldn't coach a younger player, but there you are—he knows lots of tricks you couldn't teach. He swings wide around the trees toward the far end of the field, not stopping until his newly polished loafers come against the powdery lime of the end stripe. Knowing it's foolish, unable to stop himself, he glances around at the spectators to see if anyone is watching. Being that close to a field is something of an exile's return, and he can't help expecting someone to acknowledge his presence there, to point, whisper, or stare.

Soccer is big at home, of course. Youth leagues, clinics, everyone playing. Often, driving to the home office, he would pass a game in progress and be tempted to stop. If Andrea were in the car, she would turn and look the other way, unable to bear any reminder of children. There was a time earlier in their marriage when he would have enjoyed coaching, but there was no way around her hurt, and in time he came to avoid the games too, taking long detours just so he wouldn't brush up against the happy blur of color spinning around the maypole of that black and white ball, the dance he had once been so good at himself.

But this is different—he feels he can trust himself here for a few spare moments before continuing toward Boston. Down by the south goal stands the home team dressed in silky red shirts and silky black shorts. These are the girls who had surrounded his car in pursuit of their ball—sixth-graders probably, girls of eleven, womanly in their legs but not much above that, except for one or two overweight ones who can barely touch their toes during drills. They laugh a lot, jump and laugh, and the tallest, a redhead, leads them in a warm-up that involves slapping the inside and outside of their knees like Tyrolean folk dancers. The goalie, the one dressed in an elaborately patterned jersey that suggests camouflage, has a crown on her head, a papery silver one, and everyone takes turns wearing it, like it's part of their ritual.

Warm-ups over, they take shots on goal, fed balls by their coach, who stands to their left with a farmer's patient stoop.

A balding man in his fifties, he wears green work clothes and suspenders, calls out to them to listen up and concentrate, acting as the gentle damper on their high spirits. Dolger approves of him immediately. Yes, that's the way. Let them pour their exuberance out early, then pull them slowly back to the work at hand.

The visitors, the yellow and blue team, are slow in getting off the bus, and Dolger's first impression is that the wrong team has shown up. They're much bigger than the home team, twelve-year-olds at least, and there is one girl, dressed in a purple jogging suit, who looks to be high school age. They run toward the north goal and immediately begin their drills— serious, unsmiling, mechanically filling the goal with balls that, unlike the home team's, are drilled in and hammered rather than tapped, shunted, and nudged.

This doesn't seem to worry anyone but him. The little knot of spectators by the elm has thinned out along the sideline, but they seem more intent on gossiping among themselves than paying attention to the field. Young women in wool shirts putting babies on the ground to toddle toward other babies. Older brothers and sisters kicking beach balls toward the road, getting yelled at. The fathers, the few there are, leaning against the pickup trucks, which make a shiny chrome barrier behind the far end of the field. A much larger group of parents accompanies the visitors. They're older on average, better dressed, more caught up in the game. They slap their hands together, yell out encouragement with what seems to Dolger's ears, given the beauty of the day, a distinct note of discordance, even harshness. One thing is obvious: they have *not* come to see their team lose.

At midfield is a rickety set of risers six rows high. Leaning on the rail, calmly smoking a pipe, is a suntanned man of about his own age, looking out at the field with the careful squint of appraisal you only see in true lovers of the game. "Great day for soccer!" Dolger says, coming to a stop near his shoulder. He is filled with it, all but bursting, and it feels so good he says it again. "Good soccer weather, conditions perfect."

He hopes this will lead into talk about the upcoming game, some inside information as to who is who among the players. Hopes, even, he will have a chance to slip into the conversation the words that are part of what bubbles inside of him: *second-team All-American senior year.*

The man hardly looks at him. When he does turn, it's with a scowl that makes the pipe sag below his chin and almost drop. "Snow tomorrow," he mumbles sourly, pointing nowhere.

"Well, up yours buddy," Dolger wants to say—but even this isn't enough to dent his high spirits. He brushes past the man to where he can get a better view of what is happening. The referee, a bowling pin of a man dressed in black, brings the captains out for the coin toss. The tall girl on the blue and yellow team stares at her smaller counterpart as if she's playing some sort of mind game, trying to intimidate her. She wins the toss, jerks her thumb toward the south goal, the muddy goal, the one where scoring will come easiest.

There is some delay in actually starting—shoelaces to tie, the wrong number of players on the field, a problem with the clock. Dolger thinks about using his cell, then decides against it; he's only going to watch the first five minutes, so it hardly matters. If anything, the delay gives him a chance to appraise both teams, get a better fix on the matchups.

The home team, while small, has distinct possibilities. On the front line are three girls who aren't much more than skinny sticks, but speedy-looking ones, and the girl on right wing, the one with short black curls, looks particularly so, a tomboy who can really scoot. Midfield is shakier. One girl is tall and willowy, someone you could picture being named Ashley or Heather, but she stares dreamily off toward the clouds, hardly seems aware there's a game starting. Her partner on the left wears shorts that flop down toward her ankles and flimsy sneakers rather than cleats. Deeper back are the fullbacks, and they don't seem comfortable. Both are heavy and clumsy looking, buried in back to hide them, and they don't promise much for the defense. At any rate, the goalie, the one in camouflage, has the right look—lean, hungry, and anxious, particularly the last.

The visitors are an entirely different proposition. Their goalie has on a psychedelic sweatshirt and big orange mitts— she cups her hand around her mouth, yelling out a mix of encouragement and scorn. In front of her are two fullbacks who seem actual pillars, so tall are they, so strong—both wear their sleeves rolled up over their biceps. The midfielders, by contrast, are small but clever looking, and one of them, while she waits for the kickoff, juggles a pebble from foot to foot.

It's the front line that really worries him, particularly the girl starting at striker: the tall girl, the boomer, the one whose shots had blistered the net during warm-ups. Her hair falls down her back in an aggressive ponytail, which the pink bow does nothing to soften. Her lips are thin and pressed to whiteness; her cheeks are suntanned, but suntanned hard, as if they had recently gone from porcelain to brick and are now on their way toward something harder. She wears her shorts high, and why not, since her legs are like weapons—long muscled, shapely, her thighs tensing as she stands over the ball waiting for the referee's whistle to start play. Unlike the other girls, she has breasts, matronly breasts, bound and girdled for battle by a jersey that's far too small. Sherry is her name. The parents on her side call out her name, smug at possessing her.

It becomes his last fully coherent thought of the afternoon—how quick is the human propensity to take sides. Who were these girls to him? Nothing, and yet instantly they're everything, the red and black ones, the home team that is so obviously outclassed. His heart goes out to them, to the point where he can hardly focus on the other team at all. He remembers this from being a player—how anonymous a mob the other team always seemed. A mist, a cloud, a maze you had to butt through or glide past or somehow evade, scarcely human, until you saw one of them drop in pain from an injury or cry in despair when Dolger scored.

The delays are finally sorted out, the referee has the whistle in his mouth and his hand on his stopwatch, when there's a movement on Dolger's left where no one had been before, a scent, a woman's soft voice.

"It's George, isn't it? George Simms?"

This startles him, coming when it does, so it's all he can do not to jump. Turning, he sees a blonde, outdoorsy-looking woman in her thirties, wearing a suede coat the same brown color as the fallen leaves.

She smiles at his surprise, in a way that's obviously meant to be disarming. "Oh, that's an old line, isn't it?" she says. "Pretending I know you from way back when. But I can tell you're not from around here." She points toward the field. "We're the hicks. We always lose."

He smiles absent-mindedly—he's still waiting for the whistle. "Great day for soccer, huh?"

"My daughter is halfback. Number seven?"

The Ashley girl—no surprise there.

"Do you have someone playing?" she asks, moving closer.

He's about to bring out his usual line—*No kids, not yet*—then realizes how stupid it sounds, at his age. And besides, the whistle's gone off now, the girls are running around in madcap patterns that make no sense, and he's anxious to be free of this intruder and concentrate on the game.

"Can I just stand here next to you for a little while?" the woman asks. "This thermos? There's schnapps inside if you'd like some. Everyone brings schnapps to the game. That's how we locals cope with defeat."

Is she teasing him, flirting? It's hard to know what she wants, but then she grimaces, brushes back her hair, comes out with an explanation on her own.

"My former husband is that porky one over there with the other team. The cowboy hat? He does that, stands with the enemy just to bug me. Well, I'm bugging him, standing next to a handsome stranger. Bugging him good." She takes a long swallow from the thermos, wipes her lips with her coat sleeve. "Eat shit, Henry," she says, staring across the field. "Eat shit, you cheap ugly mean-hearted son of a bitch."

Dolger mumbles an excuse, then jogs down the line following the play. Losing the first seconds of play makes him feel disoriented, and his eyes race across the field trying to catch up. He had nightmares like this, ones where he was still playing striker and the game started without him and he was dropped into the middle of chaos without the chance to warm up. The ball emerges from a scrum of pink flailing legs over on the far side, and his eyes bore in on it, then pull back to gauge everyone's relationship to that vital black and white core. He squats down on his haunches, plucks a handful of grass, stares.

The play stays ragged at first—it's as if each girl must touch the ball with her foot before being convinced of its reality, and only then can she begin the job of urging it into motion. There are some wild looping crosses, some exuberant headers, the ball skittering away into a mound of maple leaves with the galloping posse in hot pursuit. It doesn't take long for the magic of the game to assert itself, the old familiar geometry. Triangles, squares, diagonals, and the only trick is to anticipate these, arrive first at the point where the diagonal is driving, the apex of the triangle, the heart of the square. These girls haven't quite mastered geometry, and yet for those first few minutes the ball seems content to draw lines on its own, filling him with a gladness that all but makes him shout.

How he loves the game. How he loves it! He would have been content to watch forever under a sky so fine, feels he could do so if only he could draw back far enough, sit up on the highest riser or run into the meadow to climb the tallest tree. He stands up, the better to see past the parents, and he loses the pattern for a moment; the math gets away from him, and suddenly it's all wrong somehow. The home team is huddled over like they've been kicked in their stomachs, while the visitors, the big girls in blue and yellow, are turning cartwheels across the grass.

Sherry has scored the game's first goal. It happened so fast it already seems in the distant past—he's surprised he remembers seeing it at all. The ball had been moving in harmless little skips and bounces, but then a hard shape bulled past the softer ones. There was a stooping motion, a head bent intently toward a foot, the ball rocketing on a perfect line from the far right edge of the penalty area toward the lower left corner of the goal. *Missed*, he decided, relieved, but his angle was wrong, because the ball curved back again, then dropped vertically past the goalie's desperate and tardy lunge.

1–0 visitors. He would have credited them with a good play if they had been better sports. It's not only the cartwheels, the arrogant high fives, but the way they so obviously sneer at the smaller team, as if this punishment is just the start. He can see their coach on the opposite sideline standing on the bench calling out numbers, wiggling his fingers, giving them a play. The home team slumps back into formation, acting like they're used to this and somehow relieved, as if being zapped is the only geometry they know.

Dolger glances down at his watch. Five minutes gone—time to make his calls. But he's caught up in it now, and instead of heading back to the car he moves on toward midfield. Play has started up again, and for a moment it swirls past where he is standing, close enough he can hear the girls pant and sputter, smell the perfumed sweat of them, hear them in quick little whispers call out each other's names. The ball is squeezed out past the sideline. Instinctively, smoothly, he sticks his shoe out and flicks it up into the ball boy's arms.

"Blue!" the referee shouts, pointing downfield.

More parents arrive. The little pockets on the sideline thicken into a wall that is nearly continuous, so the field now seems more like a boxing ring than a prairie. They seem evenly divided between those who care too much about the game and those who care nothing. The man with the pipe, the one who had looked so phlegmatic, cups his hands around his mouth, shouts the same thing over and over, "Who wants the ball! Who *wants* the ball, dammit!" Just beyond him is the blonde woman, who has found herself a more willing man to flirt with. They stand close enough that the buttons of her coat touch the zipper of his jacket, the two of them smiling and posing toward each other like they're staring into mirrors.

Dolger brushes past them until he stands on the corner of the field where he can see better. They're shutting Sherry down, he decides—but then she winds up and one-times in a shot from well outside the box. A minute later she scores her third, this time on a header, the smaller girls falling away from her, intimidated by her strength. They're right to be scared— had she been left back a year or what?

He has to admit she has talent, if only a fairly basic one. Her trick is to fake left by dipping her shoulder, then go right and shoot—and if the home coach were smarter he would put one of his middies on her with instructions to watch her right foot and ignore the rest of her body. He wondered if he should tell the coach this himself—as pleasant as the man seems, he doesn't know much about soccer. If he did, he would be yelling at the ref, protesting the bigger team's tactics. Sherry has skill, but the others depend on roughness, particularly the fullbacks, the ones with their sleeves rolled up, who like to wait until one of the smaller girls is making a run at goal before pinching in with their shoulders and bringing her down.

It's brutal, seeing this. Even their midfielders, speedy as

they are, have been taught to kick the ball out of bounds whenever they are challenged, breaking up the red-and-black team's rhythm. It's negative tactics all the way, the kind that were ruining soccer, not only on this level but worldwide. It infuriates him, thinking about this. Didn't anyone care for the beauty of the game anymore, the grace?

Against all this the home team does the best they can, especially the little girl with short black curls, whose runs end time and time again when she is double-teamed or deliberately tripped. But she's a determined one, a plugger. After every tumble she picks herself up, rearranges her shinguards, goes off in pursuit of the ball, her skinny legs spinning. Dolger's heart goes out to her. He can picture having the care of a girl like that, giving her just the right amount of coaching so as to harness her speed, the way they would talk about a game afterward, how he would gently but firmly remind her of what she should do.

And his heart goes out to the Ashley girl too, though in a completely different way. She plays with real abandon, her long blonde hair streaming behind her like a decoration left in the air. She has a fluid, gliding sort of quality that takes routine chances and turns them into art—a coltish flourish to her headers, a dancer's follow-through to her kicks. She's the kind of girl he would have been nuts about at that age. Even now, watching her, wishing her on, he can't help feeling that old forgotten need to show off, and it stirs him in a way that seems caught up somehow with the blowing leaves, the wild beauty of the clouds.

It's 4–0 before he decides there is no use punishing himself further. As things stand, the sales meeting is history, and he is already practicing his excuses as he detours back to the car. He's gotten good at this lately, making excuses, dreaming things up. He is trying to think up an excuse for making excuses when something so unexpected happens it stops him in his tracks.

The home team scores a goal. The little black-haired girl, the speedy winger. She had been crunched by the fullbacks on a breakaway, only this time instead of crumbling to the ground she keeps on running, the ball at her feet, and when the startled blue-and-yellow goalie rushes out, she makes a hopscotch kind of motion and tucks it by her into the net.

4–1! He pumps his fist in the air, all but shouts. That's soccer for you, the sudden turns in fate! All the red-and-black girls leap in the air and cheer, but the girl who scored isn't having any part of this, and rushes all serious back to her position, eager to get another one. On the other side, everything is confusion, stunned disbelief, and Dolger realizes this is very likely the first goal they have allowed all year. Their coach stands well out on the field with his hands on his hips, screaming. The goalie, catching his tone, screams at her defenders, who then yell at the midfielders, who turn to scold Sherry, think better of it, then hang their heads in a perfect pantomime of guilt.

This changes things for him, changes them considerably. For all his interest in the game, he had kept a wall between what was happening there and his own involvement, but the goal by the little winger pierces it, lays it in ruin. He finds an open spot midway between the two benches, feeling a surge of adrenaline that makes his earlier excitement seem the merest drip. If anything, it's too much too soon—a sweaty kind of vertigo drenches downward from his head. One of his youth coaches when he first started playing had warned him about becoming too passionately involved, even at eleven, suggesting a trick to sober up. *Become the ball*, he had said, and while the other players had laughed at this, thought it silly, to the young Dolger it made immediate and perfect sense. In extremity, in moments of disorientation, he could become the ball, identify with the solid nylon roundness, its subtle indentation and give, even the pungent smell it would take on toward the end of a game, a compound mix of perspiration, boot polish, dirt, and grass. *Become the ball*, the coach had told him, *because no matter what happens out there, the ball always comes back to earth.*

Sherry gets off a shot from the penalty area, but she's pressing now and it sails over the net. On the return upfield the little winger gets the ball again, and after a long run down the right side she crosses it beautifully to Ashley, who is open. The fullbacks pinch in on her but seem fooled by her flowing hair, because in the next moment she's clear of them breaking in on goal. Shoot, Dolger says to himself, his ankle cocking back. *Shoot!* But before she can, one of the midfielders appears on her right, running for all she is worth, and, seeing she's beaten, launches herself through the air in a feet-first tackle that rakes her cleats against Ashley's knees, bringing her down.

"That's a yellow card!" Dolger screams, thrusting his shoulders over the line. "Hey, ref! What is this, football! For God's sake, give her a yellow card!"

Had he really yelled? The hot ripple in his throat convinces him he had, but that is nothing compared to the angry sensation that runs down his knee in sympathy with the fallen girl. She picks herself up, limps gamely back toward play, while the referee, all oblivious, runs leaden and blind in the same direction.

This spoils everything somehow, his yelling. The burning sensation gives way to a wet circle of dampness on the small of his back. Even the clouds begin to darken, so a matching chill presses down on him from above. He backs up from the line, telling himself this is ridiculous, that he's become too involved, but at the same time there is something tugging the other way, a vacuum left in the air by the soccer ball, the rush of the girls, sucking him in. He moves back to the line, cups his hands around his mouth, yells "Go red!" as loud as he can.

Neither team plays well in the next few minutes. A wimpy header, some sloppy throw-ins, a weak shot, and then, mercifully, the whistle blows for the half.

The home team rushes off the field in good spirits thanks to their goal. They sprawl on the ground around their grandfatherly coach, burying their legs under leaves until each becomes her own tapered mound of scarlet and yellow. One of the mothers has clementines for them—one of the girls sticks a wedge crossways in her mouth like an orange smile—and soon they're all doing this, nearly choking on giggles.

Over by the other bench, all is business. Their coach has them kneel around him in a circle while he draws diagrams on a chalkboard. Only Sherry stands apart from this. A stocky, red-faced woman, certainly her mother, gets right in her face, exhorting her, whipping her on—and then, in the very next second, kneels down and gives her legs a vigorous massage.

As a player Dolger had always tried for a moment of complete oblivion during halftime when he could let his mind and muscles go slack. He seeks this now, turns to look away from the girls out toward the field. Their younger brothers, seeing their chance, boot the ball toward the goal and scream their heads off, scaring away the dogs that are crapping in the penalty area. Dolger watches them, then goes off searching for a refreshment stand, somewhere he can slake his thirst, which is suddenly tremendous. In the grass right in front of him, set there like a stubby little fountain, is a thermos someone has forgotten; for lack of anything better, he squats down, unscrews the cap, takes a long sip. Whatever it is tastes chocolate, and he's surprised and even shocked when the heavier taste of the schnapps kicks in. He takes another swallow, then a third, then screws the cap back on with unusual concentration, and places the thermos in the exact depression where he found it. Feeling stronger, he walks toward the visiting team's bench, stands there waiting to get the coach alone.

He's a young man in his twenties, and between the blazer he wears and the smooth blandness of his features, he resembles the evangelicals who came to their house with religious tracts, though not nearly so polite. Judging by his compact build, he had been a soccer player himself, maybe still plays in a beer league somewhere. Seeing this, Dolger feels a little softer toward him, as if he's a fellow fraternity member; the words *second-team All-American senior year* arrange themselves on the back of his tongue.

The coach gives his players their last instructions, then points them back to their positions on the field. "Say something?" he grunts, noticing Dolger for the first time.

"It's just—" Dolger does his best to smile. "Hey, I'd rest that number 9 of yours. The other side keeps rotating their players.

I see you keep her in all the time. The thing to do is rest her, give the other guys a sporting chance."

The coach stares at him with a bovine kind of shock. It takes seconds to dawn on him, what Dolger is saying, and a few seconds more before he finds the words to fling back. "Fuck you, old man"—and then he turns and spits toward the grass.

And what's odd, the words don't affect Dolger, mean as they are. What affects him are the coach's eyes—how they're like a mirror held in front of Dolger so he can see himself as the coach must have, a funny, flat-headed guy in a jacket and tie carrying too much weight in his shoulders, too much redness on his face. He wilts under this. He tries again to smile, find the words that might bring them back to that fellowship, but the best he can find is "Have it your way, coach." Very aware now of his posture, his stride, he walks down the sideline trying to convince himself the whole episode hadn't taken place.

What is any of this compared to the game itself? It's what he loves above all, how each moment scrubs out the ones that have come just before, the ball rolling downfield in a perpetual, well-scoured present. The home team kicks off, the ball hits a hard spot and bounces, a defender tiptoes around some dog crap and gets left behind, someone else slips, someone stumbles. There's a mad scramble in the penalty area that makes him think of chorus girls engaged in a bitter shin fight—and then the ball is in the net, the score is 4–2, and he can see the field all but tilt in the home team's favor.

"Yes!" he shouts, throwing up his arms.

He can't stand still now—he paces up and down the sideline, unable to stop the motion inside, hunting for a place where he can see past the parents to what is happening. It's obvious the Sherry girl is sulking—what angry thing had her mother said to her?—and without her leadership the big girls play uncertainly, getting mad at each other, colliding, giving up too soon on 50-50 balls and in general falling apart. At the same time the wind comes up, the sky has blackened under some fast-moving scud, and this seems to intimidate the blue and yellow players most, as if they're city kids unused to having the elements breathe so directly on their necks.

The black-haired girl scores next, a neat little header, and before the shock of this fades, Ashley turns a pirouette, reverses herself, then curls the ball in from an impossible angle to tie the score. This wakes Sherry up. Rather than slouching disconsolately after the play, she catches up with the ball near midfield, knocks over three smaller girls, then lofts in a lob, putting her team back on top.

Ten minutes go by, twelve minutes, fourteen, and the game should be over, but the girls show no sign of slowing down. The coaches yell and gesticulate as before, and he realizes it's his own inner clock that has gone haywire, lost in the punishing black clouds, the darkness, these first hard jabs of November. The wind pushes the parents into tight little knots, so they stand like herd animals near midfield, the steam from their thermoses horizontal over their shoulders. The sun, in setting, finds a keyhole in the clouds, and a last shaft of amber shoots the entire length of the field, so it's as if the girls play at one goal, their shadows at the other.

Dolger goes back to find the abandoned thermos of schnapps, takes a hard swallow, hesitates, shrugs, drinks the rest down, then walks in choppy steps two-thirds of the way toward the home team's goal, the one they're defending. The only other spectator there is a short man with a trace of black mustache, pointing a furled umbrella toward the goalie as though it's a gun. For a second Dolger thinks it *is* a gun—there's that look in the man's eye, the squint of a sniper, the loner, the boyish man who suddenly runs amok. He's talking, his rubbery mouth shaping each word with careful deliberation, making sure it flies in the direction he aims.

"You hear me, goalie princess? You suck, you know that? You suck, and the ones in front of you suck even worse. Hey you, goalie sunshine. You suck, and the ones in front of you suck double."

Is he a parent, someone sent from the blue-and-yellows to make her cry? With his cheap black raincoat he looks like a visiting British hooligan. He croons the same words over and over in a soft monotone, just loud enough so the goalie in camouflage can hear. And she can hear. She keeps glancing over at him, then tries hard to look away, moving instinctively farther and farther away from him, so that she stands at the far corner of the goal now, well out of position.

Dolger knows what he should do. Approach the man, yell at him, grab his raincoat and pull it over his shoulders, pummel him until he stops. But his encounter with the coach has made him wary, and after a minute or two of indecision he backs away, ashamed. Who knew who you were dealing with in this day and age? He had read of incidents at Little League games where spectators were sued just for voicing their opinions, and there were soccer riots that had started over just such arguments, wars even, people crushed in stampedes against barbed-wire fences, poor people playing in barrios who shot each other over bad passes—and all these swarmed over him in a nausea that took on the shape and substance of this rain-coated man crooning abuse there in the dark.

Dolger has blown it now, with the missed phone calls, the temporary postponement of his life. But who would care? His doctor would find another prostate to check, Andrea would sparkle even more brilliantly at her party without him, there would be one less aging salesman for his company to lay off. The parents watching the game would have to forget their own problems once it was over, find their daughters and put their arms around them, but who was there he could comfort? And this became another part of the nausea, the pity part, the ache he can't pace away from no matter how hard he tries.

Even as a player he had felt something like this. Yes, he re-members it now, the feeling of disgust that came in the waning seconds of a game, the prospect of having to leave the clear-ness within the lines for the murkiness without. To fight it, he would double up on his concentration, slap himself, draw his muscles into alignment so as to focus on the job at hand. And wasn't something like this his responsibility right now? To pay attention right to the end? Out on the field the players have become nearly invisible, kicking at balls of dark-ness more than at the ball itself.

"Make it happen!" he yells, coming to life.

One minute left now—in the twilight he can just make out the referee squinting at his watch. Ashley collects the ball near the penalty area, makes one of her ballet moves, then flicks the ball to the girl with curls, who slants toward goal, eluding the first tackle and heading straight for the last defender, who has her squarely in her sights. Here it comes, Dolger decides. He can feel the sharp bony thunk of the collision on his ribs, but the defender miscalculates in the darkness, and rather than hitting the black-haired girl with her cleats, she hits the ball, driving it between her own goalie's legs, tying up the score.

The home team goes crazy, hugging one another, shouting, turning cartwheels. A tie is a moral victory, a victory of major proportions, but at the very height of their elation, Dolger recognizes a danger they are blind to. All the while the girls are celebrating, the referee keeps looking down at his watch. Sherry, sensing there is still time, rushes the ball back to midfield and kicks off before the red-and-black girls even line up.

"Get back!" he screams, drunkenly waving his arm.

Too late. Sherry feeds the ball to her winger, who returns it immediately, and then a second later she is around the last defender, the fat girl who makes a helpless stab at the ball and falls down. Alone now, thirty yards from goal, Sherry dribbles down the sideline just inside the chalk, needing only five or six steps more before she's in shooting range.

Dolger, realizing he alone can stop her, advances toward the murky edge of white, then stops as abruptly as a dog hitting an invisible fence, teetering there, caught between impulses. He has the angle on her, the geometry is on his side, all it will take is to jab his foot six inches across the line and in the darkness no one will see. But it's as if Sherry can read his intention, half-formed as it is; she dips her shoulder to her left—and just as he sticks out his loafer expecting her to come back toward him, she dips her shoulder left again, cuts that way, draws her leg back, and launches a vicious kick toward goal.

So hard and fast and sudden is the shot that, in his stupor, he takes the full brunt on his chin, snapping his head off, sending it soaring downfield. *Become the ball*, his coach had told him, and he was the ball now, the seams of his face spinning sideways, the block asymmetry of his features causing him to wobble and crazily swerve. Below him he can see twenty-one girls yearning toward him like flowers toward a weak amber sun, the only motion coming from the goalie scrambling backward to cover the open corner he's flying toward so impetuously, her face a mix of terror and hope, the first white snowflakes laying like crystals atop the pinned coils of her hair. He longs with all his being to soften for her, slow himself down, fold himself into her youth, even as he senses the harsh logic of his inertia. Below him the crowd makes a snapping, sucking sound, then goes silent. He sees the goalie dip her knees slightly, then leap backward and toward the side, but he senses it's too late, too desperate. He closes his eyes, braces himself for impact, expecting nothing more than the cold, sardonic clasp of twine, when he feels girlish hands on his face pressing in on his ears—tentative, grasping, then suddenly sure, yanking him down short of the goal line, pulling him into her, tumbling, grunting, sobbing, but not letting go.

The Rowboat

ALL SUMMER the weather stayed miserable, and now here they were on Labor Day, lying in bed arguing over donuts. Pure fat, Scott said, when she asked him to go get some. Hardly like you, Ticia, hardly like you at all. Well, bagels then, she countered, staring out at the rain. Low-fat muffins. Coffee with skim milk. *Something.* He took his hand, stretched out his penis, grunted his doubtful little grunt. Try the country store, she suggested, the one with the peeling Coke sign and those cute old men buying Budweisers. That dump? he said, pulling on his shorts. His petulance got him moving, but it deepened, turned sour. He called from the store to say they didn't have donuts, then he called from the highway to say Dunkin' Donuts was closed because their grease maker was down, and then the next call came from the interstate; he was on the way to their favorite Italian bakery on West Fourth Street—so what if it was an eight-hour drive, he had work to do in the city anyway, and she could damn well enjoy the rest of the weekend without him.

She hung up, mad at herself for not conveying what she meant. When she was little they had a family summer house on Martha's Vineyard, a ramshackle place with cedar siding, a flat roof the seagulls sat on, a porch that went everywhere. She loved the beach, the ocean, but what she cherished most were all the little routines they had. Going to Gay Head to watch the sunset. Playing softball on their rocky lawn. Her father, before anyone woke up in the morning, driving six miles up island for donuts, so there would be a big warm box of them waiting on the table for breakfast.

It's what they needed at the lake, because little routines and traditions were what got you through a rainy summer when each weekend was worse than the last, all their guests had canceled, and she had celebrated the Fourth of July by having her third miscarriage in as many years.

She made herself coffee, stood drinking it on the widest, highest terrace of their deck. The view is priceless, the realtor had told them, just before putting a price on it. Usually, you could see the necklace of islands that looped the eastern shore, the broadening in the center that was always whitecapped, the long rocky point that remained the only part of the shoreline that wasn't developed. Now, all that came through the mist was the damp, turpentine smell of hemlocks, and though this may have been priceless too, it wasn't what they had invested in, and it didn't do anything to soothe her mood.

The phone rang, she rushed up the steps to get it, but instead of Scott it was the contractor who was supposed to come give them an estimate for a fifth bedroom. He couldn't make it, and that was a little thing, but coming on top of everything else it was too much for her. She changed into a bathing suit, threw on a sweatshirt, ran too fast down to the dock.

There were three boats there, five counting the windsurfers. The newest was a one-person shell she had ordered from New Zealand, and which brightened up her mood just by the purposeful, ready way it swung at its mooring, its glossy green nestled into the softer green of its own reflection. The contractor who built the guesthouse had an interest in boats, and without charging them anything extra he had rigged up a clever pulley system that allowed her to haul the shell to the end of the dock without getting wet.

She slid the cover off the seat, fit the oars into their locks, flexed backward and forward, started out through the mist. By keeping their neighbor's red boathouse directly astern she was able to steer toward the point and the sunken rowboat. She had discovered it on her first row back in May, and she had used it as her turnaround mark all summer, since it made exactly a mile from their dock. It wasn't sunk very deep, but you had to know exactly where to look, and even now, though she had been there a hundred times, it took several minutes of idle drifting before it came into view.

Under ten feet of water, resting flat on the weedy bottom, was an old rowboat, the heavy wooden kind no one used anymore, its boards rotted away, its stern gray and petrified looking, its bow pointing forlornly toward shore—the shore it had been too leaky to ever reach. She pictured an old fisherman sinking it deliberately the way the old-timers abandoned rusted cars in the woods, just to be rid of it. Did it have a name? she often wondered. If she stared down on sunny days there were squiggles along the side that looked like they might spell a name. The refraction of the water put ripples into what was left of its planking, so it seemed to be crawling along the bottom, and she was always surprised, on coming back again, that it wasn't any closer to shore.

She stared down at it for the few minutes it took to fully catch her breath. Through some trick of mist the light seemed brighter on the lake's bottom than it did in the sky, like a weak sun was shining upward through the boat's missing floorboards. Leaves, autumn colored already, had become waterlogged and sank, so there were mottled reds along either side of the boat, a path of gold trailing off the stern.

The rowboat was her secret; she always paused there, taking in the wistful, lost feeling it evoked, then rowed herself out of it on the long glide back to their dock. No day was complete without having stared down at it, and though she worried about her obsession, she defended it too. This included never telling Scott, since he would have been sarcastic. "A loser's boat" was what he would say, though in another mood he was capable of calling up his old rugby buddies from college, getting them involved in a project to raise it off the bottom. He wasn't the type to stare down into the depths, but if he did, he would want what he saw.

The mist made the oars sluggish, but she finished fast—silly, pointless arguments with Scott were good for her time. The bow of the shell touched the edge of the dock, but rather than getting out she sat staring up toward the house. The gray was so thick it doubled the eaves, doubled the siding, so the house seemed twice as big as it really was, twice as appealing. Its silhouette filled the rocky bluff on which it sat, seemed a soft, more fluid kind of granite, enough to make her wonder whether she could get an architect to come and duplicate the effect. A second living room cantilevered out over the cliff might do it, or a tower, a library tower, built to continue the upward line of the spruce. There was a man in town whom the first contractor had recommended, or, failing him, she could bring up someone from New York. On a misty day, that was the thing she must insist on. He had to come in the mist and sit out on the lake looking shoreward, and then he could draw up plans for exactly what she meant.

She had showered and was standing naked in front of the mirror suffering her daily five minutes of dissatisfied self-appraisal when she heard a voice out by the guesthouse. The FedEx man, she assumed, but FedEx men didn't talk that way. "Hot dog, Janet! It's still here! Hot diggity dog diggity!" The shouting didn't move toward the house, but seemed heading into the woods instead, which gave her time to pull on a fleece and her jeans.

A green car, a restored Volkswagen, was parked crossways in the driveway. Beyond it, an elderly man was making machete-like motions with his arm, hacking away at the underbrush as he moved deeper into the woods. A few yards to his right, on the edge of the cliff over the lake, stood a woman with a yellow rain slicker draped over her shoulders—she looked younger than the man, but not by very much. She stared out toward the lake with her hand shading her eyes, though there was no sun, no glare. Her rigid, intent posture made Ticia think of a whaling captain's wife waiting for her husband to come back from the sea; Nantucket had been where she and Scott had looked for a summer house first, and she still sometimes regretted not having bought there.

They were harmless—she took in that much. With that settled, she felt a wave of sympathy for them that all but made her gush.

"Hello!" she called from the deck, as if they were dear, deaf friends. "I'm Ticia van Dorn. Welcome!"

The man did seem deaf. He didn't turn, kept on karate-chopping the vines and branches. He seemed boyish and lithe for a man his age; she thought he might be an old headmaster, or a beloved football coach who was now retired.

"Golly jeepers!" he yelled, coming to a stop. "Come over here you two, get a load of *this!*"

The woman still stared out toward the lake, and only with reluctance turned away. "We always called that camp talk," she said, joining Ticia at the bottom of the deck. "We never used it anywhere but here. We could talk that way all day and never get tired of it; the cornier it was, the harder it made us laugh."

She looked to be in her sixties, with high cheekbones age only emphasized and blue eyes vivid as a girl's. She wore tweed trousers that fit her perfectly, a brown cashmere sweater that hinted at autumn the way the leaves did. Stunning once, Ticia decided. No, stunning *now.*

"Eureka!" shouted the man. "Bull's-eye, I'm positive it was right here."

Getting through the vines to him was difficult, but when they did, he was pointing down to a blackened circle of dirt.

"See it? And look. Those rotted birch stumps were the chairs, and that rock with the scars was the back of the fire ring, and I bet if I scramble around I could find some carbonized marshmallows and rusted beer cans—" He looked up at Ticia and winked. "Too many beer cans, and rolling papers probably, and wine bottles too, mostly Gallo since that's all we could afford back then. This is where it was by golly, yes-sirreebob!"

The wrinkles on his face were so wide and elastic they wrapped themselves around each word. He took his wife's arm, tugged her gently over to the mica-flecked circle, stood watching until at last she nodded too.

"Yes, it was here," she said quietly.

"Chapman National Park we called it. We had benches made out of birch logs and a fireplace we put rocks around, and we'd have campfires here almost every night, and probably my brother Roddy built the benches, and there was a path he cut—see, here it is!—through the woods over to the diving board we had on the cliff. Geronimo! That's what our girls would yell. Geronimo! and they'd hold their noses and jump off."

He smiled at his own excitement, stuck out his hand. "Peter and Janet Chapman. Once upon a beautiful time we used to live here."

"You did?" Ticia's voice rose from wanting to hug them. "Oh my gosh! That's really so sweet. And you've come back to see it again? That's so unbelievably sweet!"

The man, Peter, took a stick and poked at the blackened dirt. "What was the name of those people we sold it to, Janet? Something-sham—Haversham? That was thirty years ago. The girls grew up, the drive got a little long for us, all the way from Ohio, so we sold, though, gee willikers, it broke Janet's heart."

He said it gently, like he was teasing, but his wife barely smiled.

"We bought it from someone else," Ticia said, as they turned automatically to face the house. "It was really cute and all, but it needed repairs; the owners after you must have really let it deteriorate. We tried . . . we put a lot of money into restoration, but in the end we had to tear it all down just to get the cigarette smell out."

This was a lie. They had arranged to rip it down even before the closing, but she couldn't bear to hurt their feelings.

"It was just a shack," Peter said. "It's probably better that way."

"Can I show you around? Can I offer you some lunch? My husband Scott had to go to New York on business, so I'm all by myself. I'm dying for some company."

"We won't stay long," Janet said. "It was just a whim we had, to visit one last time."

Having found the old campfire, Peter seemed reluctant to tear himself away. "Did you ever happen to come upon an old rocking chair while you were doing your site work? It would have had water skis strapped to the bottom, which was an invention of Roddy's before he got killed, strapping skis to a rocking chair so an old man like me—I was eight years older than him—could go waterskiing with the kids."

Before he got killed? Ticia wasn't sure she had heard right, but there was no way to ask.

"Or how about that old pulley system we used to haul supplies from the boat? Any relics of that? There wasn't a road for our first six summers; we had to ferry everything in by water."

He took her arm, led her around the property, turning around now and then to make sure his wife followed. And she did follow, but slowly, gingerly, as if not fully sharing his excitement, but not wanting to spoil it either. Peter pointed to a rock jutting out from the cliff where they flew kites when the wind was right, showed Ticia where they had drilled holes in the rock to anchor the old dock. He explained how Casper their Labrador puppy used to go flying off the end chasing a Frisbee they'd toss out over the lake, and how that would have been the summer of 1968, which meant they all but invented it, Frisbee tossing for dogs.

He showed her the remains of a fallen pine, thick as a redwood, on which one night over Labor Day weekend twelve of their closest friends had sat in a row singing "Yellow Submarine" at the top of their lungs, explained how through the darkness their neighbors out on their porch had joined in, then the people next to them, until the song encircled the entire lake, the cottages and camps, everyone singing. "WE ALL LIVE"—one side of the lake would sing, then there was a pause, then the other side of the lake answered, "IN A YELLOW SUBMARINE!" then there was another pause, and the echo from the hills would sing it on its own, the deep, sluggish echo that never managed to repeat more than the first word of whatever you shouted: YELL—ooo, so wistfully, so soft.

He took her on his tour, Ticia listened patiently, and then, when his stories started slowing down, the things he was searching for became harder to locate, she felt it was her turn. Not abruptly, but perfectly naturally, as if they had come for that express purpose, she began showing them around the outside of the house, explaining what part had been built by what contractor, or designed by which architect, including little stories from the construction, incidents she thought might amuse them or make them laugh. She was on the patio pointing down to her rowing shell and the windsurfers when she realized they weren't behind her anymore, and she looked around to see them holding hands, walking back to the rock they had flown kites off, lingering there, oblivious.

It disappointed her, but she hid it the best she could.

"Come out of this rain now!" she called, in the same firm, coaxing tone she used with her parents. "You've traveled such a long way you deserve a good lunch."

They ate in the breakfast room with its view of the lake. The rain streaked the windows; it was like silver slugs crawling down the glass, and she cranked out the awning, which embarrassed her by squeaking. "You have any sewing machine oil?" Peter asked, but she shook her head no. Of the two, he seemed the most restless, and though he ate two sandwiches and polished off a glass of Merlot, he seemed waiting for a chance to bolt.

"You and your hubby ever climb Big Cock Rock?" he asked.

"Peter!"

"Well, it looks like one, doesn't it? We never minced words around here. Roddy cut a trail to it back of the old outhouse. I'd give a lot to see if I could trace my way back up."

His wife made a half-regretful, half-resigned little gesture, as if she were holding him back and shooing him off at the same time.

"You'll be careful in this rain?"

"Jiminy Cricket, Janet! Of course I'll be careful. My wife's a little shy sometimes, Ticia, but you get her talking, she can tell you much better stories than I can."

The rain came down harder after he left. Both women, once they cleared the dishes away, drifted toward the fireplace and the long, cushion-covered bench that made a half square around the hearth.

"Does it work?" Janet asked.

Ticia wasn't sure; somehow they'd never gotten around to lighting it, but there were logs, a coffee mug full of matches. Janet pulled the screen away, knelt down, expertly poked and prodded, and soon had a fire going, a real fire, one that threw out a delicious warmth.

"It draws beautifully," Janet said, staring down—and though Ticia wasn't exactly sure what she meant by this, she felt absurdly grateful, to gain her approval at last.

The bronze light took years off her face. Her hair, Ticia saw now, had a vibrancy and luster that made the gray seem accidental, something that would soon wear off. There were freckles near her nose, and it was easy to picture her as she must have been when they lived there—a slender, athletic redhead in a black swimming suit standing on the edge of the dock, smiling, laughing, the presiding personality around which the family's happiness spun.

"Our last few summers here were on the sad side, really," she said, as if sensing Ticia's image of her, wanting to dispel it before it got fixed. "The girls were grown up and they didn't get back much anymore. It was harder to round up old friends. The road went in behind the lake and houses were going up everywhere. When we built here in the sixties it cost nothing. It was easy even for schoolteachers like us, but then all that changed."

"You taught school then?" Ticia asked.

"We had an argument, not a real one, a gentle argument, about coming back again. Peter has always wanted to. For me, it was harder. I couldn't tell him why of course. I pretended the drive was too long. All the way from Ohio I kept thinking—we shouldn't do this; we should turn back now. But I didn't have the courage to disappoint him. He wanted this so much."

Maybe, Janet said, they hadn't really conveyed to her what their summers here were like. The sweetness of those years. How the beauty of the lake heightened every human emotion it touched, so love seemed deeper here, friendship, loyalties. Even puppy love, something harmless—it could so easily become something else. Yes, it was the sixties, the country was in turmoil, but history wasn't interested in a quiet lake in Maine. She had been thinking about this on their drive east, and what she decided was that their summers represented the last time a place could exist in secret—and, what's more, they had known this *then*; they hadn't rushed heedlessly through the experience but cherished every second, sensing how soon it would all slip away.

"It was on Labor Day weekend, just like it is now. The weekend we had the big party for Roddy. He was Peter's kid brother, and everyone treated him like that, the crazy kid brother, and yet he was the one who was behind all our best traditions, always inventing things, always thinking up new adventures. He left college to help their father after his stroke, and he meant to go back, but the draft caught him, and instead of sending him to Germany liked he hoped, he'd just gotten his orders for Vietnam. That's what the weekend was for. To give him the best going-away party possible, wrap him so tight in our love he could never come to harm."

That had been naive of them, stupid. But the protests hadn't started yet, the evening news accounts were rosy, and there was no way for two high school teachers from small-town Ohio to know what was really going on. That summer, Roddy hadn't been to the lake, he had been finishing advanced infantry training in Georgia, and it was six months since they had last seen him. He had changed—his spirits didn't bubble up and get him laughing anymore. He smiled and laughed, sure, but it was measured, forced even, not at all like the Roddy they remembered. The house was full of guests, people were sleeping on the floors, and they had invited a college girl named Barbara Conte from across the lake who was absolutely perfect for him, but he hardly talked to her the entire weekend. There were three parties, a party every night, and like old times he would take the lead in grilling hamburgers, tapping a keg, or getting a volleyball game started—same old Roddy!—but then suddenly, with no explanation, he'd break away and go walking by himself to the lake.

Janet paused for a moment, stared down toward the fire's whitest embers, the place her story seemed to rest. In the distance, off by the entertainment center, Ticia could hear the phone ring and the message machine click on. She could tell by the rhythm of the voice that it was Scott, by the softness that he was apologizing, but it seemed so distant, so irrelevant, she couldn't bring herself to move.

"The first time it happened was on Friday night. I was in my bathing suit, there was all this talk about going for a swim the moment the full moon came up, but almost everyone had been drinking, and after I put the girls to bed I couldn't get anyone to come. I remember feeling disappointed at that, like a child gets disappointed. I threw a towel around myself because it was cooler now. I had been watching Roddy, I suppose because

I was so worried about him, and when he left the dancing to walk toward the lake I dropped the towel off my shoulders and went over to join him."

This was at the dock, though in those days it was more like a causeway, it extended out into the water so far. All the people on that side of the lake tied their boats there, and it was a help-yourself arrangement—everyone was free to take out any boat they wanted. Roddy was untying a canoe when she got there; without either of them saying anything, he got in the stern, then held the canoe tight to the dock while she let herself down into the bow.

"It was sweet, that's what I remember thinking—sweet of him to take me with him. He was a lot like Peter in that respect. He was generous with the best part of himself; he didn't hide it away like so many do or dish it out in little drops. He had the same blond hair as Peter did too, only on him it was all in curls that even an army haircut couldn't tame. I won't pretend I could see his eyes, not sitting in the canoe, but when they were on you they were really on you; you would feel, after a second, that they had been staring at you for a long time. It was quiet on the lake, hardly any ripples. The moon came up, so there was a white path we could follow right across to the point. 'I didn't see you dancing,' he said, and I said it right back to him, 'I didn't see you dancing either; maybe we should have teamed up,' and then he made his little laugh that came so rarely now. 'Maybe we already have,' and he dipped his paddle into the lake, held it over my shoulder, twisted it so the water dripped down from the blade onto my skin."

What was odd, until that night he had always acted shy around her—friendly, but shy. Sometimes she wondered if he even liked her, or if he was just being nice to her for Peter's sake. He would watch her as she fussed with the girls or got dinner ready, making sure he knew where she was at all times, and she always read this as wariness, and she had always been too caught up in the summer to find a way around this. So, the canoe ride was important, she knew that much. Important to share the quiet, not ask him any questions, let the beauty of the lake warm away any shyness he still felt, so they could be real friends at last.

"We just ordered a canoe from L.L. Bean's," Ticia said. She made a curvy motion with her hands to demonstrate its shape.

Janet nodded, but hardly seemed to hear. From that far away on the lake, she explained, the noise of the party was little more than a chirping crickets sound. A motorboat must have been cruising across the lake's far end, because the last pulse of its wake lifted them slightly, then let them back down. When they came to the point, its cliff was high enough to blot out the lower rim of the moon, and they drifted on the edge where the black and the milkiness touched. These cliffs made it hard to climb up to the point itself, though the spruce were beautiful there, much higher and wilder than anywhere else on the lake. In all their summers, she didn't remember anyone actually going ashore; it was a point you canoed to, stared at longingly, then came back.

Never had it looked more alluring than on that night. The branches shredded up the moonlight, furled shadows into shafts, so it was like staring up toward a pillared canopy, something out of the Arabian nights. Roddy dug the paddle in, pried them around so they faced shoreward. There did seem one place where the cliff might be climbed, and it looked like there was a small, flat clearing right above. She was going to suggest they try, but now it was her turn to feel shy. "We should go back now," she said, thinking of their guests. "Okay," Roddy said. He turned them around, and that was all either of them said until they got back to what was left of the party.

On Sunday, events conspired to create the same result. There was a mammoth softball game on the rocky meadow they called their lawn, a barbecue, and then cars and jeeps were pulling in from all over the lake for another dance, with an actual band this time, a Bob Dylan wannabe and a girl drummer who shook her hair like Ringo Starr. This was all intended for Roddy, step two in the big farewell, but though he went around talking to people, made an effort, again, he didn't seem particularly interested. And Janet too—she found it hard to take part.

"I was watching Roddy, that's how I spent the day, walking around making sure I could keep him in sight. When you're thirty-four, when your children are beginning to be more in-dependent, a mood comes over you, and like any other mood it comes and goes, only this one lasted longer and came back every time I saw him. It made me feel nostalgic. I kept think-ing about the silly days before I met Peter, and that suddenly seemed like something I badly needed, that I could indulge myself in, that I deserved. There were more girls there than on the previous night, but Roddy stood apart watching, and then it was midnight and everyone was drunk again except us. He caught me watching him this time, and he made a little nodding motion, and without his saying anything I knew he meant for me to follow him down to the lake."

It was reversed from the first night, the way they were dressed. Roddy just wore swim trunks, it was so hot out even at night, but she had dressed in a linen skirt and a loose cotton blouse, the Peruvian kind everyone wore now but was new and daring then. She wasn't sure why she dressed so carefully, spent so much time over her hair. To honor Roddy, she decided. She could remember putting it to herself just that way.

The same canoe was tied to the dock. The moon was late in rising, so Roddy steered by the light of the camps on the opposite shore. Unlike the first night, they talked, Janet turning around in the seat so she could face him. It was confused: he was going on and on about how much he respected Peter even though he was always yanking his chain, how much he looked up to him for all the work he did with kids, and then suddenly it was about the army, how it wasn't as bad as he pictured, there were lots of good guys in his platoon, but he didn't know what would happen once he went to Nam, they would probably split them up, and the worst thing that could happen was getting sent as a replacement to a unit where you had no pals.

"That's what they say anyway. You can't count on anyone but yourself over there."

He was quiet for a time, seemed waiting for his words to disperse through the dark—then, when they had, pointed with the paddle toward where the forest, with the moon coming up now, seemed combed and brushed with white.

"Canada's through there, isn't it? Walk far enough through those trees and you come to Canada."

It seemed such a silly, random thing for him to say. "Canada?" she said.

"Yeah, Canada. You know. The friggin' North Pole."

It startled her, not so much the language as the bitter way it came out—it was like he wanted to nail something sharp and permanent onto the night. He sensed her confusion, seemed to paddle more softly, more carefully, just to make up.

"Know something?" he said, after they had been silent for a time. "The thing I always liked about you is your smile, the way your mouth always seems to be smiling. For other people mostly, but for yourself sometimes; that's what I notice. I always wondered what it would take for that smile to disappear. Nothing anyone could say, I don't think. Nothing that could actually happen. It would take something soft and gentle, a touch probably. A gentle little sideways touch."

He left off paddling and they glided—the water seemed to know the canoe was coming and parted to get out of its way. Above them rose the cliffs of the point. The moonlight played the same trick it had the previous night, coating everything in a creamy luminescence, though this time there was a satiny look as well, a richer, deeper vibrancy in the black the white fell on. It was plain now that the cliffs were topped by a clearing or glade where the trees gave way. It wasn't big, perhaps the size of a small room, but it was perfectly flat. Some trick of light made it appear floating; that was the odd and alluring thing. Made it seem like a rectangle hovering over the forest floor.

Roddy left the paddle crossways on his lap, but there was enough of a breeze to push the canoe in closer to shore. From the distance the cliff had seemed unclimbable, but now, up close from this new angle, they saw something that had been invisible the previous night: a small wedge of beach, not much wider than the welcome mat placed before a door. Beyond it was a long, upward slanting gully as dark and slippery looking as a playground slide. No—gentler than a slide, climbable, if two people helped each other, held hands.

No one had discovered this before them, she was sure of that. In all the summers, no one had discovered there was an easy way up onto the point.

They floated there, the beach almost in touching distance, but Roddy still didn't reach for his paddle and the breeze seemed unsure where to take them. We should go back now, she knew she should say, and then suddenly her voice was saying it on its own. "We should go back now." "Okay," Roddy said, like he had the night before, and it was as if his voice was operating independently of his will, just like hers.

"The next day was Sunday, and none of our guests had left yet, but the mood was flat and sour. It was summer ending, most of it, but it wasn't just the normal bittersweet feeling you got, but something heavier. Everyone started drinking earlier—there was a pyramid of beer cans that got higher and broader all day. Roddy spent the afternoon helping Peter bury one of the water pipes deeper below the frost line. I was busy packing for the long drive home, and so we hardly saw each other. I was impatient with the girls, impatient with everything—by the time it got dark out, I was ready to scream. Things seemed so hateful and complicated and the only way I knew how to simplify them again was to be out on the lake with Roddy, and past that I didn't really think or care."

They played touch football after dinner, and she remembered it being played in complete silence—everyone was too sad to make noise or too drunk. One of Peter's teacher friends punted the ball deep into the woods, everyone fanned out to find it, and hardly anyone bothered coming back. Roddy stood alone staring out into the dark where his team had been, and that made him look unbearably lonely and forgotten. She stood on the porch watching him; she remembered, most of all, how hot and constricting her jeans and shirt felt in the heat—how she wanted to pluck at them, rip them, tear them to shreds.

They met at the top of the steps this time, held hands as they walked together down to the dock. Because it was the last night of summer, all the boats had been hauled out—the canoe wasn't there—but before surprise could set in or disappointment, Roddy tugged on her hand, led her toward the end of the dock.

A soggy piece of hemp was tied to one of the ring bolts. Roddy bent over and pulled, then got down on his knees and pulled harder. It took a long time to haul it in. Attached to the end was a rowboat, a leaky old rowboat crusted in gray algae, its wood all splintered, the boards so rickety that moonlight poured through the sides. *Porky Pig* someone had written in whitewash across the stern, as a joke probably. "An orphan!" Roddy said, that smile of his coming back for what seemed the first time all weekend. "Golly jeepers!" he added, then held it steady while she got in.

Her weight alone was enough to nearly sink it, and when Roddy got in water began lapping over the sides. "Bail!" Roddy told her, and she tried, using a rusty soup can she found sloshing around in the bottom. Roddy was good in these situations, the summer was full of crazy adventures with boats, and he managed to row fast enough that the worst leaks stayed above the waterline. It was exhilarating and funny, at least at first, but then they were out in the middle of the lake and it wasn't that at all, but something more urgent and desperate.

"Take off your shirt!" Roddy said. She tugged it over her head and handed it to him; he stuffed it in the worst of the holes, then took off his own shirt to stop up one in back. This helped, but then a board sprung loose with a slow, splintering, mocking kind of creak, and the water that had made a pleasant gurgling sound now rushed in on them like an angry fountain.

They could see the point now, the hidden beach, the inviting ramp that led up to the clearing—they weren't twenty yards away. She could picture the two of them walking up it hand in hand, picture how the moonlight would look fanned out across the little clearing, like a sheet spread gently across the spruce needles—she could picture that, pressed her eyes shut to put them there, make it come true. Roddy leaned forward on his seat, frantically scooped at the water they couldn't keep ahead of—and never had he looked so young and vulnerable and sad. When the water was up to their knees he left off bailing, struggled forward to hold her—and then it wasn't like sinking at all, but a rising, lifting sensation as the water surged up to take them and they were suddenly in the lake. And it was ludicrous and funny and absurd and comic, and yet never in her life had she cried so hard.

"A fisherman heard the commotion—he was trolling and he steered over to pick us up. It was an old-timer I didn't know, but he turned out to be a shrewd and understanding man. He got us to the boat, neither of us with any clothes on, and he must have leapt to the wrong conclusion—or maybe the right one. 'Act drunk,' he told us, when he dropped us off at the dock. We had been missed this time; there were flashlights shining out over the lake, and then Peter came down with a blanket he immediately wrapped around my shoulders. 'A last row,' he kept saying, like he was explaining for us, using the words to shelter me past all the partyers to the house. Someone else was looking after Roddy by shoving beers at him, and when I woke up in the morning it was late, the car was packed high with things to take back to Ohio, and he was already gone."

In the silence where her words had been came the sound of rain slapping against the roof. It fell harder than before—the teasing curtain of mist now pressed in like a solid wall. Janet turned from the fire, got stiffly to her feet. In the course of telling her story a strand or two of hair had fallen across her cheek, making her look windblown, as if she had just rushed indoors.

"I know what I'm supposed to say. That time goes so fast, that it sweeps all memories before it. But this happened yesterday, that's what I can't get over. It was thirty-six years ago, but that makes no sense to me; I feel like I'm falling when I say that. It happened yesterday, understand that? *Yesterday.*"

She looked out toward the rain, stiffly shook her head. "I shouldn't have come back."

Ticia stood up now, moved toward the older woman with the intention of taking her arm. She wanted to tell her that the rowboat was still there on the bottom of the lake—tell her how she had sensed something special about the point ever since she first saw it, how she had been drawn back to that spot again and again, how she had always wanted to dive down and touch the boat, feel its wood, take its mystery in close to her heart. She was going to tell her this, but there was that one moment of shy hesitation, and then came a loud sound out by the door, shoes stomping on the patio, and there was Peter, her husband, coming in through the screen brandishing a long, blackened piece of steel.

"Gee willikers, see what I found!" he shouted. "Horseshoes! Remember how we used to toss them, Janet? I remember Uncle Buzz getting so mad once when I beat him, he threw his way out into the lake, and there were three matching geysers, one, two, three!"

He held it out to Ticia with a little bowing motion. "A lot of ringers went around this pipe, let me tell you young lady. Plant it in your lawn and it will bring you good luck."

Time to go, he told them, with the same brisk eagerness he brought to everything. He'd get the car running—and he thanked her very much for letting them visit and reminisce. Ticia followed Janet out the door, stood with her for a moment under the protective overhang of the roof.

"You've made a beautiful home here," Janet said.

Ticia nodded. "Scott says we could get two million for it easy."

It was stupid, not what she wanted to say at all, but she couldn't take it back. Janet walked slowly toward the car where her husband stood holding the door open. "Goodbye old lake!" he shouted toward the mist. He took Janet's hand, held it for a moment in his—waiting, listening, finally shaking his head. They were already in the car, it was disappearing down the driveway, when the echo came back again, but only the first word, too late, too feeble, for them to hear.

A Story in the Irish Style

I HAD A VACATION; Carol didn't. Work was slow at my job, frantic at hers. She had been to Ireland; I hadn't. Her life experience—that's the phrase we used—was much larger than mine. She had stories and adventures from everywhere; it's one of the reasons I fell for her, and I think that's what motivated me—the catching-up factor—to take two weeks during the winter before our wedding, pick out a country I'd always been curious about, and come back with stories of my own.

And I found one, very quickly. When the plane landed at Limerick, we didn't taxi to the gate but remained on the runway with the engines turned off. Something shook the fuselage—a boy two seats over made jokes about a monster eating us for breakfast—and when I looked out the window, it wasn't to the usual amber sunrise you get after crossing the Atlantic, but to a darkness that seemed total. Water streamed down the glass, and it took me a while to realize it was snow, melting as it hit. Below us, barely illuminated by a flashlight strapped to his belt, a figure in a chartreuse parka wigwagged signals toward the cockpit. But it was obvious the snow was already layered too high—that having landed, the plane was now stuck.

Snow in Ireland! A heavy gray snow that fell like wet cement. That would be my story for Carol, and if all the other passengers looked apprehensive, I was filled with the kind of adrenaline that makes you want to laugh. After a long wait, announcements were made, a ramp manhandled over—we were loaded onto a caravan of three buses. A woman in a green uniform met us at the terminal, announced that since it was impossible for the flight to continue on to Dublin, we would be taken there by train.

"Snow train?" one of the passengers asked, a cynical-looking man who acted like he'd seen all this before. "We'll never make it, lass; then what will you do with us?"

That train ride to Dublin turned out to be the dreariest ten hours of my life. It was fun at first, exciting, bizarre, but then exhaustion took over, the cold seeped in, and it seemed that we were butting against a solid monotony too thick for the train to pierce. No one had been smart enough to bring any food along; the lights kept going out, the power, so the tea that was brought around was ice cold. No one joked anymore. Babies cried, old people trembled on the verge of panic, businessmen stormed up and down the aisles searching for someone in authority, and always out the window dropped that slurry gray snow.

At one end of the car there were five or six of us, sitting around a metal table that would have been good to play cards on if anyone had brought cards. The man directly across from me was the biggest man on the train and probably the most frightened; he was an electrician from Cincinnati who had been hired to do work at a new building site in Cork on a two-month contract. He'd never been out of the U.S. before, he told us. Judging by his expression and the way he buried his face in his hands, he was sorry he'd ever left. Beside him was a dark-complexioned young priest who was the only one of us with any food—a plastic-wrapped sandwich he nibbled on in stingy bites. He was reading a magazine whose cover story was titled "The New Ireland!!!" Something about it seemed to infuriate him, because he kept slapping at the pages and scowling, finally stuffing the magazine into a crack in the window in an attempt to keep out the draft.

The two women were more interesting. The youngest introduced herself as Kitty. She was in her twenties, vivacious and funny, a flight attendant who was using her free pass to have one last fling before settling down. The snow, being stranded—none of this bothered her, but only acted as a stimulant. She flirted with every male in the car, tried leading a sing-along, and came back from one of her excursions up the train with a bottle of Jameson she was generous in sharing, and which made the last half of the trip somewhat more bearable than the first.

The second woman sat tightest to the window, her hand rubbing little crescents into the steam. At first, I thought she must be fourteen; she wore a white cardigan sweater buttoned at the throat, making her look like a schoolgirl on her way to the convent. But it wasn't just that. She stared out the glass with an intensity that made me think of a young girl lost in her own thoughts alone by her bedroom window. No one else on the train stared that way; snow was the last thing any of us wanted to look at, but she must have found it absorbing. After a while, curious about her more than the storm, I began trying to look out too. There wasn't much to see. Hard white tracers left by sleet, sludge-colored drifts close by the tracks, now and then a distant light from a farmhouse window.

A few minutes later the train started lurching forward again, and the men in our car gave a sarcastic cheer. She glanced up at me and smiled; our looking out the window formed a bond, I suppose, and once she turned away from the storm, she became friendly and outgoing. Ilsa was her name, Ilsa Mitchell, named after the heroine in *Casablanca*—her mother's favorite film, back in the days when movies were rural Ireland's only link to the outside world. And that's where she was born, she explained. A small village in the Wicklow Hills. She had left Ireland for Boston when she was seventeen, and this was her first visit back since.

"I hope I can get there," she said, frowning toward the window. "My daughter has her first communion this week, so I only have three days before I need to be back in the States. The village is probably snowed in."

"You'll get there," I told her. "The plows will have no trouble."

"Plows? In Ireland?" She smiled the way people do when they're trying not to laugh.

But I enjoyed talking with her—there was no other decent way to pass the time. She was older than me by a few years, and I felt toward her what I felt toward high school seniors when I was still a freshman—that they possessed mysteries and secrets that made them inconceivably wiser than I could ever be myself. Her face must have been disturbingly attractive for men to look at, back in the fairly recent past, and it was still disturbing enough, with what were left of her freckles clustered close to her nose, and the auburn afterglow of what must have been burning red hair. She could be a poster girl for Ireland, I decided. A poster woman.

I bought her a tea the next time the porter came around, and we laughed over how transparent it was, ice water more than tea. The Aer Lingus representative marched through the aisles telling everyone that because of the storm the airline would put us up at a hotel in Dublin until conditions improved.

For the first time the priest showed signs of animation. "The Gresham?" he said, once she marched on. "That's all right then. Very handsome of them."

The train station, once we arrived, was mobbed with stranded travelers, and even to get off the train I had to put my shoulder down and shove. I had some confused idea about the five of us staying together, but there was too much pushing and shoving for that. There was no sign of anyone from the airline. The Gresham Hotel on O'Connell Street. Fine—but how were we supposed to get there?

It was the priest who finally saved me. "I've a cab!" he yelled, when I broke free of the crowd. "Go halves?" I quickly nodded, shoved my bag in the back before he could change his mind.

We were lucky with our driver—a snowmobile would have had trouble navigating in those conditions, never mind a cab. I'd had this image of Dublin being a laughing, smiling city, but the snow had draped it in darkness, made it sullen. It was like being dropped suddenly in Moscow, the Kremlin, with all these lifeless government buildings that had taken on gray, onion-shaped domes.

The priest paid the driver at the hotel, and I watched to see what he would tip him; when I realized it was nothing, I reached into my pocket and gave him what he deserved.

"Thank you, sir. A cheery stay for you, mind that ice!"

At this stage, I'd been up thirty-six hours straight. I started a bath, pulled the phone off the end table, stretched out full length in the tub, tried remembering the time difference, dialed Carol at work.

"You made it!" she said, through a very bad connection.

"You won't believe what's going on here," I said. "The worst snowstorm to hit Ireland in over forty years."

"It's snowing here too. The weather channel says four inches by morning. The weirdest thing happened. You'll never guess who I ran into, literally into."

That's when the full weariness hit me, when she said that, so it took a real struggle not to drowse off.

"Ted Kennedy! I tried getting a cab on Commonwealth Avenue, they were all being jerks, and he was getting in, saw me having trouble, and he made a little bowing motion and let me have it. Ted Kennedy!"

We talked, she had some wedding details she wanted my opinion on, but the bad connection made it seem slush had gotten into the wires and slowed up our words. I woke up once during the night. The old hotel was shaking like the plane had shook, and the rattling of the windows and howling of the wind made it seem a mob was stoning the windows—an angry, determined mob.

I got out of bed, went over to look. The Gresham is a famous hotel, but I had drawn the room with the worst view—toward the back into an alley. An old piece of clothesline sagged from a wall on the other side, thick enough to carry a few inches of crusted snow. Something tattered and flimsy hung from the middle—it looked like a lady's knickers that had been forgotten

there decades before. Straight out from my window there was
nothing, but if I bent my head down I could see the snow slanting through the cream-colored light from the lower windows,
so it seemed like a storm that began thirty feet in the air.

I watched a long few minutes, tired as I was. The worst
snowstorm to hit Ireland since World War II. I felt there must
be something of significance in this, but though I tried understanding what, I couldn't see much besides how pretty and innocent the snow looked. White, soft, fluffy. Nothing more than
that. Nothing I can easily explain.

The snow stopped in the morning, but the city was slow in
getting back to life. At the Gresham, down in the lobby, things
were busy, as all the stranded travelers lined up at phone booths
or harassed the desk clerks or tried to get moving. Some didn't
bother with any of those things, acted like a party was in progress, and being stranded was an absolute blast. One of these
was Kitty. I came upon her leaning against the wall outside the
bar, and she gave me a big hug. You felt that way with everyone—that we were all in this together, and even the slightest
connection counted for a lot.

I saw Ilsa too, though we didn't talk. I saw her first outside
the breakfast room talking on the telephone, then a half hour
later standing in the only cleared spot on the sidewalk, her
hands primly holding a little carry-on bag, with the attitude of
someone waiting, none too optimistically, for a ride.

O'Connell Street, wide as it was, seemed oceanlike under
blowing drifts. I didn't have a coat that was warm enough; my
shoes were soaked through the minute I started walking, but
I hadn't come to Ireland to mope around the lobby all day. I

decided to walk toward St. Stephen's Green, visit the art galleries, do all the museums, stay indoors as much as possible, then round off the day in a pub.

A good plan—it fell apart almost instantly. There were no cars out on the street, no buses or cabs, and walking turned out to be exhausting, the snow shin-high at the curb, deeper if you stepped off. Nothing was open. Not the shops, not the restaurants, not the public buildings or museums. Yes, I was seeing Dublin under unique and remarkable circumstances; yes, a funny, exaggerated kind of battle story was certainly forming, but it was frustrating, even lonely, not to see anyone, not to be able to drop in somewhere for a drink and a chat. I was panting from effort by the time I reached the Liffey—it ran gray and full, with a wild, tumultuous power it couldn't have had very often—and I only made it as far as Trinity College, which turned out to be just as barren of life as the rest of the city.

In Boston, plows and sanitation men would be out shoveling. I didn't see any evidence of this here. Dublin had surrendered to what had happened; the only signs of life were shadowy, whisking movements near the blinds and curtains as people peeked timidly out. The snow, the lack of traffic, made for a remarkable quiet, though once in a while I'd hear a car alarm go off, fooled by the weight of the snow on its hood, or church bells chiming the wrong hour.

It was late afternoon by the time I trudged back to O'Connell Street. I tried visiting the post office where the Easter Uprising had started, but like everything else, it was closed. I didn't want to go back to the hotel, even though dark was coming on, and when I did stop, it was at the only public space open: a Burger King, its steamy window blazing with light.

It was crowded with tourists who had nowhere else to go. A crayoned sign over the counter announced they had run out of coffee and fries, but people seemed huddled there more for the warmth and companionship than for the food. I ordered a cheeseburger, had started weaving my way through the tables, when I caught sight of Ilsa Mitchell sitting in the frigid zone by the entrance. She sat with the erect, formal posture you see in people who end up in these places and don't really want to be there. She smiled when she saw me, pulled her coat off the extra chair so I could sit down.

"I thought it was you," she said. "Across the street, looking like a lonely polar bear. I was hoping you'd come in."

I plucked at my jacket. "I came upon some little kids back by the river. They were trying to make a snowman, but they didn't really know how, so I helped them. You didn't get back to your village?"

She shook her head. "I called my cousin. He said the snow is much deeper up in the hills, and he couldn't even get out of his driveway. I tried cabs—there's none at any price. So—" She waved her hand, "I've spent the whole day here."

Her eyes seemed smaller than they had back in the train, her expression tighter, more anxious. She wore a black wool turtleneck that made her look wonderful, or should have, with her red hair, but again, she had been staring out at the grayness for hours, and it colored her expression.

I think we were genuinely grateful for each other's company. We talked, little things mostly, more about Boston than Dublin. I noticed that whenever the subject came around to Ireland, rather than growing nostalgic as you might think, she seemed irreverent, even sarcastic, which didn't really square with the rest of her personality. I mentioned I was hoping to hear some good Celtic music while I was there, and she contemptuously shook her head. "Celtic music? I despise Celtic music. All that is, is just fiddling in the dark."

She glanced down at her watch, wondered out loud what her daughters and husband were doing just then, and we were slow in getting back to what was really on her mind: finding a way to visit her childhood home before she had to fly back to the States.

"Can't you add on some days, change your ticket?" I asked.

"Isn't that expensive?"

"Blame it on the weather. Blame it on their having gotten you here late."

"Kate's first communion is coming this week."

"Yes, I remember you telling me that. Well, maybe it will get warm and all this will melt."

"By tomorrow?"

"Your visit has to be tomorrow?"

She nodded, nodded vehemently, as if this were just the point. "They're tearing down my grandmother's house, the one I grew up in. They're tearing it down tomorrow afternoon at three o'clock sharp."

"In this weather?"

"The snow won't stop them. Tom said two big bulldozers are already waiting there ready to go. This is for a car park. There's a computer firm building their headquarters."

"Back in the hills?"

"They're not hills anymore." She smiled, tried making it a joke. "The hills are shrinking. They say it's become New Jersey."

"We could get there by then. There will be buses running tomorrow probably. Can a bus get pretty close?"

"In my time, no."

"Now?"

"Maybe. Yes, probably. It's not very far from Dublin. If they're running."

I glanced out the window at the cold, turned back to face her. "Would you mind my coming along? I haven't seen much of Ireland yet, and there's nothing to do here. I think it would be fun."

"Fun?" That oddly sarcastic look came back over her face, but it was gone in an instant, and she was smiling, nodding— yes, that would be great, she said; there was no telling what obstacles she would encounter, and it would be good to have someone to help.

I wanted to ask her for a drink back at the hotel, but I sensed that was going too far with it, too far in a lot of respects. We agreed we would meet for breakfast at seven, walk to the bus station, and see what was what.

There was a big change in the morning. The army was out, the Irish army. They lined either side of O'Connell Street, friendly men with pickaxes and spades, working toward each other as they cut at the drifts. They seemed pretty casual in how they went at this. There were more pedestrians out than there had been the first day, and the soldiers were more interested in bantering with the girls than they were in snow removal.

"I didn't know there *was* an Irish army," I said, when Ilsa and I crossed through their line.

"Army?" I don't think she had noticed them until then. "Well, you never know. Someone in Ireland may have a good idea and the authorities have to be ready to stamp it out. My father was in the army. He spent the war guarding Dingle Bay. He shot a shark once out of boredom. A basking shark I think he said."

Even with the soldiers' effort, the streets were difficult, and we had to hurry to get to the station in time. It was exciting, I'll admit that—to be walking across Dublin with an attractive woman, on our way to what promised to be a great adventure. The sun shining off the brassy railings, the fresh bite of the cold, the way our shoes crunched against the snow. Exciting, and though we weren't, it felt like we were walking hand in hand.

We made the bus in time—apparently there was some doubt about whether it would be leaving at all. Our driver was a boyish man who looked like a jockey on a horse that was far too big for him. From the moment we pulled out of the station he was wrestling with the wheel, tugging it this way, then that, trying to compensate for what the ice was doing to the tires. Farm trucks or emergency vehicles had been using the highway, so there was a semblance of tracks. "Hold on byes!" he yelled at one particularly treacherous curve. A mile from downtown, and we could have been in Alaska.

At a place called Bray we changed drivers, and this new one seemed more competent. What's more, he brought his own cronies along—four men whose faces were red from cold or whiskey or both. They sat right behind him, kept up a steady stream of advice, applied body English as the bus swayed from side to side.

"What time is it?" Ilsa asked, for the fourth or fifth time.

"Nine on the button. I'm sure we'll make it."

She must have been excited, seeing us get closer. Here she was going back to her childhood home after an absence of many years, all the rich memories that must be waiting there for her to seize, the remembered textures, the sweetness, the funny incidents and stories, the half-remembered images. Yes, of course, this would be tempered by the sadness of seeing it had all changed. I'd noticed the wistfulness in her manner from that first moment staring out the window on the train, but if anything, I envied her. There was nothing in my childhood worth going back to; I had nothing but the same homogenized blandness as a million other suburban kids.

I would have enjoyed hearing her reminisce, but she seemed filled with too much to permit that kind of thing. "This is the way they drove me to Dublin when I left," she said, when the road began climbing up from the coast. Other than that, she hardly said anything, except to keep asking the time.

The snow lay deeper in the hills, and the tires sent up a wake just like we were a speedboat. Some kids in black jackets threw snowballs at us, but no one else was out. We came to a village that was the first place resembling the Ireland I pictured—neat little cottages, a crooked High Street, the smell of burning coal. We stopped here while the driver and his cronies walked around the bus inspecting the tires. "Conditions!" the driver yelled when he straightened back up. He pointed toward a pub. "Tea!"

We filed into a restaurant decorated with waxy old paintings of horses and collies. The owners acted as if we were survivors of an avalanche, went around pouring us hot mugs of coffee, pressed sweaters on us, did their best to make us comfortable. "A step up from Burger King," I said. Ilsa smiled, or tried to. I noticed she sat where she could face the clock. Three o'clock was the time she had mentioned, when her childhood home would be bulldozed. It was noon now, and we still had thirty miles left to go. I had asked to accompany her on something not much stronger than a whim, but I was caught up in her story now, and I wanted to get to its finish nearly as much as she did herself.

But when we started out again, the road conditions got worse, not better. They were widening the highway here, and the storm must have caught them by surprise, because we could see tools sticking out of the drifts at all kinds of crazy angles. Cell phone towers were being erected every few miles— ice covered, they flared like sharp blue matches in the sun— and the feel this gave was of dramatic, transforming changes the storm had temporarily stalled.

When the bus stopped for the final time, we were still eight miles from Trannob, her village. There had been absolutely no attempt to clear the road here; there was nothing but two ice-glazed tire tracks left by whoever had been brave or stupid enough to try going farther. But at least there was a bit more life here than in the last village; a few of the shops were open, and there was a large pub on the corner, which is where we ended up.

We didn't sit down this time. Ilsa was far too impatient, and I decided that now was the moment to begin justifying my having come.

"Who owns the lorry out there?" I asked the man behind the bar.

He pointed toward a video game in the corner. A teenager

wearing a puffy North Face jacket leaned over it with his hands wrapped around a pint of beer.

"Look," I said, going over. "We need to get to Trannob on a family matter. We need a ride."

The boy's eyes seemed as red as his jacket. "Trannob? Place with computers? Can't," he grunted. He jabbed his glass toward the window. "Look yourself."

"We *really* need to get there. I think it would be worth 50 euros for the man who can do it."

We haggled, I didn't think he was going to say yes, but then Ilsa came over, and that sealed our deal. She might be twice his age, but she was still the kind of woman men wanted to impress. Joe was the boy's name. He led us out to his lorry, put Ilsa in the front next to him, stashed me in back with some undelivered sacks of mail. "Don't say I didn't warn you," he said. He leaned forward to tug his jacket off, turned the motor on, overmuscled the gear shift, started out.

He was a good, nervy driver, and seemed to enjoy the challenge of keeping the lorry on the road. The afternoon sun created a layer of meltwater that made things dangerous. Every curve, every increase in the grade, the tires would lose traction and start spinning, and Joe would have to put it in reverse and find a grittier patch before trying again. He kept glancing over at Ilsa, tried getting her to talk, but she refused to say anything—never have I seen anyone stare so intently out a windshield. At the scenery, I thought. It was beautiful now, low hills that tucked into each other in all kinds of secret folds. Again, I envied her having been brought up in a landscape so deep.

There were some bad curves, almost hairpins, but then came a long straightaway that made Joe too cocky. He increased our speed—and then suddenly came another curve; the tires started spinning, we threw our hands up just like in a movie chase scene, and skidded to a stop three feet from the hardest, iciest-looking drift yet.

Joe and I got out to look things over. This wasn't a drift we could butt our way through. The entire road ahead of us was piled just as high.

"We should have gone around by Flaxen," Joe said. "Easier grade, brand-new paving. We'd be there now warm as you please."

"I wish you had told us that."

He shrugged, made a spitting motion toward the snow. "Should have asked."

It had the makings of a good argument, but I think we both realized how stupid that would be. There was a muffled sound from the other side of the lorry, but we were squatting down examining the tires, and it was another minute before either of us glanced up. When we did, it was to an empty lorry. I looked up the road, saw Ilsa with her scarf wrapped tight around her chin, walking steadily, determinedly, through the snow. I glanced down at my watch. 3:15.

"How far is it to her town?" I demanded.

"Five kilometers. Not far, if it wasn't for this."

"Wait here for us. I'll pay you double if you wait."

Joe swept his hand around. "Man froze here once they say. Back in the Troubles. Gallagher was his name." He looked at me with a boyish leer. "That your ladyfriend?"

It wasn't easy catching up. The snow was slippery, my shoes were helpless, and she seemed tugged by a force that hadn't the slightest interest in tugging me. The highest hill, a horn-shaped one, sliced off the bottom of the sun, so it became much darker. When I did finally catch up, she didn't bother looking at me, but kept on at the same pace. Before, back in Dublin, it had seemed we were walking hand in hand, but this was different now; she seemed to be moving within a separate world. Her cheeks were red from effort, and there were tears or something like tears above the dark line made by her scarf. She rubbed them hard with her mitten, but a few seconds later they were there again. Not sad tears, I decided. Tears of anger and frustration.

We walked for twenty minutes, then twenty minutes more. We walked until all hope of getting there before the house was demolished was gone. We walked—but no, it wasn't walking at all now, it was wading, stumbling, falling. So long as the snow remained knee-deep, we could make some progress, but then suddenly it was above our thighs, above our waists, and with a sudden sagging kind of motion Ilsa was stopping, slumping over, her whole posture, in reaction to all that effort, shaping itself into a huddled acceptance of defeat.

It was dark out now. There were no houses visible, no lights. On the side of the road was a shed that must have been built to keep schoolchildren out of the rain. I pulled her toward it without bothering to be too gentle. She fought me at first, staggered on a few hopeless steps up the road, but then she must have accepted what exhaustion was telling her, because I could feel her resistance suddenly go slack.

"Maybe your house is still there," I told her, once I'd sat her on the bench. "Maybe the bulldozers didn't get around to it yet. This is Ireland, right? Procrastination happens."

I didn't believe this, but I was more than a little desperate—

it seemed, in those first few moments, like she might collapse from hypothermia. But that was underestimating her, underestimating her badly. When I had first seen her on the train, I had been struck by the intense way she stared out the window, but this was different; it was as if I were around on the other side of the glass, so I could see, not the back of her neck, but her face—and the intensity and concentration in her expression made what I had seen before seem trivial. When she started talking, it wasn't to me at all, but to the snow, to the hills, to the distant village. It was an Irish voice—even her accent seemed to come back. A voice without any lilt or sparkle. A dark Irish voice unlike any I'd ever heard.

"She let me have my own room, I'll grant you that. Rose. Everyone called her Rose, and there were people who had once called her Rosie who she never spoke to again, though they lived right next door. It was the first snow I had ever seen. I had read about it in books, but it seemed impossible to me, that it could actually be snowing, not raining. I remember being amazed at how pretty it made everything, and that was the magic part, how it transformed that ugly house, that ugly village, into something so beautiful. I could have watched for hours just that way, staring out from my bedroom window. I was ten and I didn't know there was any power in the world capable of doing anything nice to our town."

Now she did look at me, realized she was in danger of leaving me behind. "Rose was my grandmother," she explained. "My father was a big rugby supporter, though he never supported us. When Ireland went to play England, he took the boat over and never came back. My mother died of diphtheria, at least that's what they called it. Something no one bothers dying of anymore. I went to live with Rose and her three un-married sons, my uncles. Rose was a miser. She built herself the ugliest house in an ugly town, because she didn't want any-one to think she had any money. I don't know what my uncles did for a living; I never learned. They stayed at home or went to the pub and traded hard-luck stories with their friends, and Rose would never hear a word against them, but treated them like they were the most important men in the county."

As dark as the snow was, it managed to cast a dirty gray light, and I could see her face very clearly now. There were no tears, no traces of anger. If anything, there was a rigid immo-bility to her expression, as if she were balancing across a wire and one blink would make her fall.

"One of them was Uncle Gabriel. He was the one who came creeping upstairs and pulled me away that afternoon, when I was staring out at my first snow. And that was always the worst part with him. Not what happened after, the cajoling or the threats. He pulled me away from everything that seemed big and open, and took me away to something very small."

There was more; I could see her drawing in her breath to tell me more, but then suddenly it was as if the wire supporting her disappeared, and it's impossible to describe the vehemence with which the next words came out.

"I needed to see that house destroyed, understand that? It's what I came all this way for. I deserved that, after all that happened there. I wanted to see the bulldozers roll across it. I wanted to see the rafters fall, the walls shattered. I wanted to see that house *crushed*."

Her eyes, staring toward the black mass of the hills, now came toward mine, unthinkingly, impersonally, the way someone falling grabs out at a rail. I took hold of her to stop her shivering, but she didn't need that, she got up from the bench by herself. When we started walking again, it was through the crooked path our stumbling had cut in the snow. It was much easier going down, and she never looked back, not that I could see. After a few minutes we made out a yellow light shining toward us on the back of a plaintive beeping, lorry Joe having kept his promise after all.

It was late by the time we got back to Dublin. The streets were amazingly clear; I was ready to give the army credit, but when we got off the bus it was much warmer, a dense fog having blown in off the sea and erased the snow on its own.

I had a hard time falling asleep, tired as I was. Around midnight there was a brittle knocking on my door, as if someone was tapping it with a bottle.

Someone *was* tapping it with a bottle—Kitty, the party girl. She had a bottle of Jameson in one hand, two glasses in the other, and as drunk as she was, she must have caught in my expression a flicker of disappointment.

"Who were you expecting?" she asked, thrusting out her hip. "The Easter bunny?"

A few months later, sitting on the beach on our delayed honeymoon, I told Carol about Kitty and her midnight visit. She took it surprisingly well. "Was she as pretty as me, as smart?" she asked, putting down her legal briefs, squinting up over her sunglasses. "No," I said, truthfully. "She wasn't, not even close."

As for Ilsa, I've never told Carol about her at all, and as long as we remain roughly even in stories, I'm guessing I never will.

When Baby Comes

THEY WERE ALL at six months, showing, and never had snow draped anything so beautifully. The spotlight from the bank next door cast a beam over the handicapped spot where they were dropped off, making it seem like they were arriving for the Oscars. All wore coats of varying styles, materials, and lengths, and yet all six, in that brief rush across the sidewalk, partook of the same classic silhouette. Their roundness a half step in front of them, leading the way. Their heads a little back from the vertical, left behind in the forward rush. Their arms crossed protectively over their overshadowed breasts. The flakes found the leading roundness first and whitened it, seemed eager and happy to do so, until very quickly they resembled snowmen, pregnant snowmen, a resemblance emphasized by the way their scarves streamed out in the wind. They must have all sensed this, because every one of them, even Tara, their elegant alpha pain-in-the-butt, was smiling breathlessly and laughing when they finally made it through the multipurpose room door.

"Forecasting ten inches!" Tom the friendly biochemist yelled, holding it open. He yelled it six times, then five times more when the husbands finished parking and ran inside. Each time, he added another inch, so by the time he finished, it was twenty-one inches he was predicting, and no one, having just driven through it, could reasonably contradict him.

Andy, the JV hockey coach, helped his wife, Wendy, off with her ski coat, then shook it out over the space heater, making it hiss. "It's hugging the coast," he said solemnly.

"*What* is?" Tara said in the exasperated tone she was so good at. She had shed her coat with a lazy shrug of the shoulders, letting her husband, Steve, gather it up off the floor.

"The storm," Andy said, angry at letting her bug him. The week before she had said something, he wasn't sure what, that had left Wendy in tears.

Crystal, the youngest, shivered, looked frightened, though it was clear now she was safe; she stood there touching her cheeks, as if to check whether they were really as hot and red as they felt. "We went off the road twice. If Jackie hadn't been such a good driver, we'd be toast."

Jackie, her nonpartner, bent over to brush off the thin running suit, which is all Crystal wore. *I'm no lesbian*, Crystal had announced at the first session back in October, when they went around the circle introducing themselves. Jackie, it was given everyone to understand, was just a friend from work. How the baby had arrived inside Crystal was anyone's guess; not even Tom, the biochemist, had quite worked this out.

"Interstate's closed already," Steve said. He raised himself on tiptoes, made a counting motion with his hand. "Eleven? Is that you hiding over there, Rashi old pip? Twelve? That leaves one missing."

"Susan Laver," a tremulous little voice said. "There is no Susan Laver."

It was Wendy who said it, the smallest next to Tom's wife, Betty, the one who was so petite it seemed her belly was carrying her, not the other way around. Her voice startled everyone, pulled their attention from the window. For a moment all twelve wore the same blank look of incomprehension. Susan Laver was so much a part of things it never occurred to them that it was even theoretically possible for her not to be there.

"She's always late," Phyllis said, just before the silence grew ominous. She was the computer whiz, the one who asked the most detailed questions—Miss Perfect Pregnancy, though she never pressed this too hard.

"That's right," Tara added, pointing to the clock. "She's originally from Australia. You know how *they* are when it comes to time."

Everyone nodded, though none of them actually knew how Australians were with time. The truth is, Susan Laver was never late; she was always there setting up the chairs and DVD player when they arrived, promptness personified. But faced with the enormity of her absence, they all quickly believed it—that Susan Laver was always late.

Wanting to be helpful, some of the men began unfolding the chairs, setting them up in the semicircle Susan Laver preferred. Eugene, Phyllis's husband, made a soupy sound that was meant to be a low whistle. "I am *so* impressed with that woman, I can't tell you. I'd love to tempt her across to the private sector. I have an administrative job she'd be perfect for. A hundred grand for starters."

"And take her away from *this*?" Betty said, with peculiar emphasis. On the way there in the car, Tom had fallen into his lecture mode, explaining how, thanks to genetic engineering, sex and procreation would soon be two entirely different activities—boy or girl would be available on order, ditto hair color, likewise supersized intelligence . . . and Betty knew it was only Susan Laver's no-nonsense teaching style that kept him from bringing this up in class.

"I mean, she's fantastic. Who on earth can do this better? We need her. The *world* needs her."

They all agreed with this—there were five minutes general raving about how good Susan Laver was, how patient, knowledgeable, and firm. She ran a tight ship, no negativism allowed, none of that prego one-upmanship and prenatal competition that ruined birthing classes at other Boston hospitals. And yet her compassion was there every second, you knew she cared about you individually, and she made it seem as if having a baby was the most natural thing in the world. Which it was, of course, Betty added, giving her belly an extra pat. Only how much more natural it seemed when Susan Laver was saying it.

"It's her fortieth birthday tonight," Tara told them. "I've brought her a gift."

She reached into the leather boat bag she always carried, waved her hands in a magician's kind of flourish, pulled out two plump bottles of champagne. Everyone laughed at that, even those who despised her most—some of the men actually cheered.

"Where can we hide it?" Crystal asked, with her little-girl giggle.

"Hide it?" Steve said. "We want to *drink* it, my dear! At least we non-fetus-encumbered men."

Tara took an appraising look around the room, nodded decisively, pointed. "We'll put Preti near the lights as lookout. Steve, you can do the honors with the corks. Wendy, you're always so good with refreshments, why don't we let you set up the table? Rash can pretend he's asleep on the chair, just to fool her. The rest of us can hide behind the nutritional charts, and when she comes in we'll pull them up and yell *Surprise!*"

She had it all worked out, the idea had possession of her, and she knew that without her direction all the others would simply do nothing.

"Well," Steve said, loyally seconding her. "What we waiting for, gang? She'll be here any second. Let's boogie!"

The women stared down at their bellies, or gave their husbands meaningful little looks. In the silence came a sifting, scratching noise on the outside wall, like the snow had congealed into sand. It was clear to everyone that a decisive moment had been reached—that after eight weeks of birthing classes they had had it up to here with Tara. Up to here with her bossiness, her jabbing her arm up to answer every question first, her constant sucking up to Susan Laver, her boasting about her ultrasounds, her flirting with all the men.

"Well?" Steve said again.

"*Dumb.*"

It was hard to know who said it—the voice was so faint it could have been one of the babies weighing in with his or her own opinion. The look on Tara's face flashed quickly from surprise to anger to bewilderment—all their hatred for her changed in that moment to sympathy. But she had acted as Queen of the Birthing Class for too long now, and no one moved to put an arm around her or cheer her up.

If anything, the silence grew embarrassing. Andy, who as hockey coach knew about leadership, was the first one to jump in.

"Maybe we should, you know, get started?"

"Without Susan Laver?" Jackie asked.

"It's what she would want us to do," Tom insisted.

Yes, Yes, Yes, three people chimed in—it was what Susan Laver would want them to do.

"I agree," Tara said, nodding vigorously, trying to regain lost ground.

Crystal, who stood closest to the window, raised a tentative hand. "But do you think maybe we should, uh, leave? What if it gets worse outside? We could be stranded here overnight."

"That's a risk we all run," Steve said, patting her on the arm. "We're all taking risks. Having a baby is risky behavior, as risky as it gets."

They swarmed toward the window, squinted and pointed, managed to convince themselves the snow was letting up. Reassured, they took their places for initial warm-ups. This consisted of the pregnant women sitting on a mat in a yoga position while their partners knelt behind them and gently massaged their shoulders and neck.

Of all the men, it was generally agreed that Rashi did this best, with the perfect combination of tenderness and strength. This was surprising, because at the first class, when Susan

Laver demonstrated what she wanted them to do, Rashi had gone on strike. He had never stroked his wife in public and he wasn't about to do so now. Susan Laver had been sympathetic—cultural differences were something she was sensitive to—and during refreshments she had taken him aside for a little talk.

The following week, when the women got down on the yoga mats, Rashi had knelt beside Preti and started right in. What's more, he loved it—loved the way Preti's head tucked down when he rubbed the right spot, just below the lovely indents where her shoulder and neck joined; loved the feeling he was stroking not only her, but their baby. What's more, he loved seeing the other men rub their own women; it made him feel, for the first time in this country, that he was among real friends. "Five minutes more, please!" he pleaded when the other couples began to get up—he and Preti were always the last to stop.

"Show time!" Eugene yelled once the mats were stowed away. "Babies in Brazil! Instant childbirth! Out they pop!"

They arranged the chairs so the DVD player stood in Susan Laver's usual spot, gave it the same rapt attention they gave her. Eugene clicked it on—and damn if it wasn't babies in Brazil after all, the same exact tape they had watched last week, sugarcane harvesters squatting in the fields having their babies during their lunch breaks, with hardly any effort other than an occasional semiecstatic frown.

"That's it, honey!" Eugene yelled. "Push it out!" Andy, who had a vulgar streak, laughed out loud and pointed. "Why, she's taking a dump; that's all it is for her. Just your average ordinary dump."

Wendy looked mortified. There was no way he would have said that if Susan Laver was there.

"Aren't we supposed to learn about epidurals tonight?" she asked, in an attempt to get things back on track.

Phyllis shook her head. "C-sections. Epidurals are week nine."

"Cesarians?" Jackie said. "What's the point of that anyway?"

Phyllis knew what the point was. One-third of pregnancies resulted in cesarian deliveries, which meant at least one woman in the room would likely end up having one. They all looked at each other, even the men. Was there a way to tell ahead of time? This was the question on all their faces, but since there wasn't, everyone's eyes quickly retreated back to the screen.

Outside, the storm was increasing in fury, not slackening. The lights flickered, then came back on. Under the door, creeping low on the carpet, appeared a fluffy snake of snow that Tom rushed over to kick back. Everyone laughed at this, but the mood was growing somber. It didn't seem a normal storm, but a malevolent one whipped up just to keep Susan Laver away from them. Phyllis wondered if it was their overly sensitized nerve endings that were responsible for half the storm's fury. But no—she could see the men were nervous too.

Rather than go on pretending they could accomplish anything on their own, they decided the best thing to do was have refreshments early; then, if Susan Laver still wasn't there, they could form a convoy out to the parking lot and make a mad dash for home. Preti, Wendy, and Tara spread the food and drinks out over the table, decorating it with daffodils Crystal had brought from the flower shop where she worked. There was a tub of vanilla yogurt and a salad of whole-grain pasta and high-carb brownies arranged in a little pyramid. Tara, without asking anyone, added the two bottles of champagne as centerpiece. They looked exotic and arrogant there, set amid the homely cider jugs, the cartons of 2 percent milk.

"I wonder if the boys are hungry yet," Tara said, with a little sigh.

"Oh, my Rashi just ate," Preti said.

Tara glared at her. "*Our* boys. Hers, mine."

Wendy was the only other one in the class who knew what the sex of her baby was going to be. Wendy, Tara's look seemed to say, was the only one who could understand what she meant.

"That's what he has me feeling like, like a cow who has to deliver just the right amount of protein and fat or else he kicks. I'm so sick of it. I've already gained my thirty pounds. Let the little bastard go on a diet."

If Tara meant this to shock them, it worked—negative thoughts were something Susan Laver expressly warned against. Still, Wendy could see that in a backhanded way this was meant to be friendly, Tara opening up to her like that. Maybe the little defeat over the surprise party had humbled her.

"I feel like hell," Tara said, pressing her hands over her temples. "PMS, only five times worse. Didn't our beloved teacher tell us the last trimester was the Happy Trimester? I'm sure she told us that, and that's crap."

"Oh, I don't think so," Wendy said gently. "The middle trimester is the Happy Trimester."

"Yeah?" Tara raised one eyebrow. "Whatever."

"Shall we call the others over? I'm not sure we have enough cider."

Tara spread her hands out, beat them over her cashmered belly like she was playing conga drums.

"You know what I'm going to call him? Not. Not Never No Way Richardson the Third. You know why I'm calling him Not? Ask me why Not?"

"Why? Uh, why Not?"

"Fuckface over there insists he has to come on time so we can use our time-share on Nantucket. I'm determined that he will *not* come on time. Steve wants a nanny, but I do *not* want a nanny; I want an au pair. Steve wants him to go to public school to toughen him up, at least through seventh, but I say he's *not* going to public school, not with all those dyslexic bullies. The only thing we agree on is eventually going legacy to Dartmouth. *Not* Harvard, *not* Princeton. He's going to play hockey; he's stuffed to the gills with jock genes. But I'm *not* going to have another."

Wendy, though she tried listening sympathetically, knew this was all just bragging. She could brag too, if she were that type. Okay, Andrew only coached JV right now, but he was just twenty-three, young to be a head coach of any kind. His team had the best JV record in the state, so it was only a year or two before he would be coaching varsity and then prep school and then inevitably college, maybe even the Ivies, maybe Dartmouth—and then one fine day Tara and her son would show up begging to be recruited, and Andrew would be very polite to them, remember old times back in birthing class, and then, somewhere on the tour of campus, take Tara aside and say, "Hey, your boy's a great kid, just a super nice kid, but I've got no room for him in my program, and besides his grades are a little soft."

This ran through her mind as Tara whined on, every last word of it, so she was able to smile, act sympathetic, and yet stand up for what she sensed inside, all the pride she felt there, not let it be bullied.

Steve, coming back now, spread his arms open and made truck sounds. "Snowplow damn near came through the window! Can't see our cars anymore either. I say it's time we opened the bubbly."

He cradled the bottle under his arm—like a baby, they all thought at once—then, like he was forcibly yanking on its pacifier, pulled out the cork.

"Who's first?" he asked, reaching for the paper cups.

"I'll have some," Eugene said. "Might as well party, seeing how we're stranded."

"A touch," Tom said.

Andy stuck out his cup. "Hit me hard."

"How's about you, Rash? That Koran of yours have anything against Spumante?"

Rashi smiled, wanly, then shook his head. The other four men lifted their cups, Steve was trying to think of an appropriate toast, when someone else held out a cup, making them all stop in midsip.

It was Crystal, their daffodil girl, the one they all wanted to protect. "Please?" she said. "Just a little?"

The women, all but Tara, looked shocked. Tom, always the biochemist, reached over and grabbed the bottle right out of Steve's hand, tapped the label with his finger.

"Government warning. According to the surgeon general, women should not drink alcoholic beverages during pregnancy because of the risk of birth defects."

It was so definite, he read it out with such fervor, that for a moment no one could think of what to say.

"Well," Jackie said, obviously relieved. "That's that then."

Crystal looked over at her—it was clear she depended on her, had no one else in the world for guidance.

"Okay, I won't then. I'm sorry, Jackie."

This was too much for Tara. "Don't be sorry, dear. I read that this is all horribly exaggerated, the idea that one measly drink in the course of nine months can make any difference. If you feel like relaxing, what's wrong with that? I'm having a sip myself."

"Anyone else?" Steve asked. "No? I'll save the second bottle for later. Ladies? Gentlemen? To the physical health and financial well-being of the generation that will replace us!"

Replace us? Tom wanted to say. Speak for yourself, pal. Partner us, complement us, lend us new strength. Delight us with imagination, warm us with love. Still, he downed his champagne with the rest of them, smiled at the thought of what Susan Laver would say if she burst in now.

"Another!" Steve shouted, and it was true, the cups barely held even a shot. He poured it out fast; it fizzed over everyone's fingers and hands, and they were laughing about this, when with a loud sizzling sound, the lights flashed brighter and went out.

One of the women, Tom wasn't sure who, screamed. Another one choked off a scream. One or two gasped. Is this the kind of sounds they'll make when the big moment finally comes, the men wondered? The women in Brazil, the cane cutters, hardly made any sounds at all, let alone hysterical ones.

The emergency lighting went on, with just enough voltage

to turn everything red, suggesting candlelight. But the heat went off, so almost immediately the temperature in the room began to drop. Now, instead of joking about it, the men began discussing what they could do for sleeping arrangements, whether they had enough food, how they could all stay warm. Like gunslingers, they reached for their cell phones, clicked to see whether they still worked.

The women remained sitting around the refreshment table, letting the men—all except Tom, who sat off by himself thinking—form their own circle near the dead TV screen. It was Tara next to Phyllis next to Betty next to Preti, Wendy, Jackie, and Crystal. All of them, even Preti, felt yes, this is how it should be at birthing class—the women alone, the men banished—now at last we can really talk.

There was no beating around the bush, no careful euphemisms. Susan Laver always preached honesty and openness? Well fine, they would be honest and open. Tara, who had already drunk five cupfuls, led things off.

"She treats us like naive little girls. Why doesn't she tell us the truth about things? Why doesn't she mention clamps for instance? They still use them you know. Clamps, forceps, pliers. I have a niece named Heather they used clamps on when she wouldn't come out. It left her retarded; she's been institutionalized since she was three."

"I worry about bleeding," Betty said. "I bleed so much already, just routinely. You get ripped, you get torn, there must be a lot of blood. She never tells us about blood either."

This didn't seem fair to Phyllis, their ganging up on Susan Laver this way. "She's very accepting of questions."

"Oh, she is?" Tara said, raising her eyebrows. "She's employed by the hospital, no? The hospital employs the doctors, yes? The doctors are afraid of lawsuits; it affects everything they do."

"Which is why there are so many cesarians."

It was Jackie who said this—Jackie, who, feeling something of an outsider, wanted badly to fit in.

"I read breast milk is contaminated with mercury," Crystal said. "Should we even do it then? What's that called when your nipples get cracked when the baby sucks too much? Nasty or Masty something?

Betty reached toward the champagne, hesitated, looked over to where Tom, her oh-so-careful scientist husband, sat brooding in the corner, shrugged, poured herself a full cup.

"What I worry about is their dropping it. It comes out pretty fast my sister told me. Who's there to catch it? Our husbands? Forget *that*. Our doctors? Uh, excuse me? I don't think so."

This was Wendy's fear too. "What happens if they drop it? It's slippery, all coated in yucky stuff. I've heard stories where babies were dropped right on the floor."

They talked about this for a good ten minutes, everyone jumping in with an opinion, even Preti, who said back in India babies were dropped all the time. The women had to raise their voices to be heard over the storm, and the men, over in their group, were raising their voices too, so there seemed to be a battle in progress, the fury of the storm versus the intensity of their voices. The cold was getting worse—the women wore their coats over their shoulders like shawls, clutched them tight around their throats. The reddish light made them appear worn and haggard—each woman, secretly shocked by the others' appearance, reached up and felt her own face to see if there were creases.

"Another thing that infuriates me," Phyllis was saying. "That test they give when the babies come out? The Apgar, isn't that what she calls it? Why do our babies have to be tested the very instant they're born? I mean, why don't they just go ahead and give them the SATs while they're at it."

Wendy frowned, drew her coat tight around her neck. "What I wonder about is how in the old days the doctor would go up to a husband and say do you want to save your wife's life or your baby's? Your baby or your wife? Do they still ever do that? Is it because the baby is breach or has the cord around its neck? I'm not sure what my Andrew would say."

She tried to say this lightly, as a joke, but the other women gravely nodded. "I know what fuckface would say," Tara said. "Hell, give me the kid."

Crystal's head swam in the champagne's fizz, even though she hadn't drunk any—the dizziness seemed caught up in the wind on the roof, the excited voices, the cold. The emergency lights must have operated on batteries, because they were running down now, dimming, and the darker it got, the easier she found it to speak out.

"I've always been afraid of dogs, like really absolutely petrified. I scream when I see even a poodle. No dog ever did anything bad to me, but my mother said once when she was pregnant a collie ran up and bit her ankle. I know that's not supposed to happen like that anymore, but can it? Can something that happens to us right now affect the baby?" She lowered her voice, brought her hand up to her face as a partial screen. "This weirdo last week at the 7-Eleven. He saw me at the end of the candy aisle, unzipped, started flashing me. It was so gross, and so I wondered, can something like that harm my baby?"

"Of course it can't," Jackie said quickly, putting her arm around her, really touched. All the women were. There was a general leaning-in motion toward Crystal's chair.

"Why, of course it can!" Tara said. "What does know-it-all Susan keep drumming into us? That every second of pregnancy counts, what goes in comes out. I damn near slipped in the bathtub last night, and I know my brat's going to be terrified of the water." She tapped her champagne cup. "That's why I'm drinking this. I want a party guy, not a nerd."

At the start they all sat up the way Susan Laver had shown them, as straight and erect as West Point plebes. Gradually though, as the talk grew faster, gravity began having its way with them—all of them, even Jackie, now sat slumped like they were in bed. Across the room the men sat like poker players leaning in toward a big pot. From the words that flew out, it was all about gas prices, house prices, the Red Sox.

Someone started talking about how she was afraid her husband wouldn't find her attractive anymore—how she had read that the most likely time for a man to have an affair was when his wife was nursing. That reminded someone else of the Haight-Carsons, the mousy man and the preppy woman who had been part of the class, then had mysteriously stopped coming. Miscarriage, they assumed—but no, Phyllis had seen her at Baby Mart and she was showing bigtime. When she went over to say hello, the woman explained that the mousy man had divorced her to run off with a nineteen-year-old optometrist's assistant. At four months he had divorced her; it could happen even then.

"Would've could've served her right," Tara said, or something like that—her voice was becoming so slurred it was hard to understand. Her arm was thrown negligently over the back of the chair, and but for this one fragile bit of contact she would have slid to the floor.

Preti, when it came her turn to talk, didn't worry so much about the big day, as what would happen after. She was terrified of crib death or SIDS or whatever they called it now, waking up in the morning to find your baby dead. Her grandmother had called from Delhi to warn about this, explaining that cats were the reason—that, jealous, they would steal in at night to suck out a baby's breath. You couldn't just dismiss this as an old wives' tale either, there was a high percentage of SIDS cases in families with cats, and when she told Rashi this, he went and found a bread box, whistled over their beautiful, silky, loving Tami, coaxed her into it, took her away he wouldn't say where.

She sobbed when she told them this—at least three women were sobbing now. Outside, the storm seemed to have intensified, sending enough wind under the door that the papers on Susan Laver's desk went flying onto the floor. Under Tom's chair, the leading edge of snow grew higher and rounder, like a huge white python on its way to eat them.

"Why doesn't it stop!" said Jackie, hugging herself.

"Oh it so sucks!" said Phyllis.

"Somebody do something!" said Betty. "Beat it back!"

"Some sickos steal preemies," whispered Wendy. "That's what they do; they specialize in kidnapping preemies and selling them over the Internet."

"Could've should've," drawled Tara, or whatever it was she was mumbling. She bent her head down as far it would go—she buried her nose into the shelf of her cashmered belly, squinted, made her face as ugly as she could. "Go back to where you came from!" she yelled, with enough muffled clarity they all heard. "I don't want you! *I don't want you!*"

And with that it was as if the snow, gathering itself into one furious column, smote them across the face. The women stared at each other, seemed to recoil a bit in shame—and then the door actually did fly open, suddenly, with a whipping motion that slammed it against the wall. Everyone stared. The men, the huskier ones, jumped to their feet, ready to meet whatever was coming in for them—and then there was a happier, lighter kind of motion; a rosy, round face peering in, decorated with snowflakes; a chortling, purring kind of sound. Into the room came Susan Laver in a floppy Aussie hat and a shearling coat so thick her shoulders seemed wrapped in lamb.

"Sorry!" she laughed. "A bit delayed, but it's letting up now. The good news is that the photocopy shop was still open, so I managed to run off some information on vitamins."

This was met with silence—with vacant, mindless stares.

"Vitamins? You know. Those helpful B-12s?"

"Uh, Susan?" Phyllis managed, speaking for them all.

Susan Laver tore her coat off, flung her hat toward her desk, waved handouts at them—Susan in action was an irresistible force.

"Places everyone! We need to talk about Kegels, building up our floors. And let's start with five minutes of breathing, shall we?"

A second later, the women were all in place staring up at Susan Laver, who had jumped up onto her desk the better to lead them—all of them except Tara, who stumbled off toward the ladies' room to be sick. With her gone, Wendy was able to answer a question about how far dilation should be before you start pushing—and she really felt proud about this, a pleasant flush spreading down from the top of her forehead over her breasts to her belly. Rashi got down behind Preti and started kneading his favorite spot on her neck. Steve whispered a joke to Andy, but a quick glare from Susan Laver immediately shut him up.

Over in the corner, Tom hadn't moved. He tipped his chair back against the wall like a friendly night watchman, sat there appraising them, trying to come up with the word he had been groping toward all night. Bemusement? Was that what he felt? Well, they were a foolish bunch, but no more foolish than any similar grouping, and he was surprised to discover how much affection he could summon toward them—even Tara, even Steve. They were united, not just by what was in store for them in three months' time, but by the mystery they were playing a role in, the randomness that, thanks to work he had a hand in himself, wouldn't be random much longer. They probably hadn't gone very far beyond high school chemistry, let alone done any serious work in biology, so their ignorance of what was developing was hardly a surprise.

He felt—what? Nostalgic? Sentimental? Yes, something like

that, thinking about how old-fashioned it was, this way of doing things. They were a naive, foolish bunch, God bless them.
Over all of them hung the charm of the obsolete.

Pucker Pie

BACH WAS WAITING for them when they crossed the state line into Vermont, the Goldberg variations, the perfect accompaniment to the hills, the greenness, the deep sense of peace.

"Turn that off?" Kim said from the backseat, plaintively, with not enough energy to make it anything stronger. It was the way she said everything now. Dan glanced up in his rearview mirror and saw her cover her ears.

Meg, in the seat next to him, sprang to his defense.

"We listened to your station all the way through Massachusetts, Miss Kimberly C. Metz. Vermont is our reward for the pain this involved. Our reward for everything we've been through this year, starting with having a beautiful intelligent smart darling fourteen-year-old who we love incredibly but don't necessarily understand all the time. If Dad wants to listen to his Mozart, it's okay with us."

"Pain?"

She said it even more plaintively than before, more plaintively than he would have thought possible, a world record of plaintiveness. Looking in the mirror, he expected to see her put the back of her hand against her forehead and fall sideways in a swoon. But no. She fell sideways against her window all right, but only to wedge her headset deeper into her ear.

He turned his attention back to Vermont. It was everything he had hoped for, even here on the interstate. The hills started immediately—there was a red barn set high in a fawn-colored meadow, a hawk or vulture soaring above that, and down to their right a rushing blue brook. Even the pavement was different. Around Washington in summer the pavement was hot, sticky, and sluggish, something that sucked the juice out of you even on the short drive to work, but here it was like an icy, granite ribbon you glided along with no effort, your spirit so far out ahead of you that the car seemed racing to catch up.

"Are you too close to them?" Meg asked, pointing toward her sister's red Toyota. "Why are they slowing down?"

"Suza's probably looking for somewhere to shop."

"That's not all she thinks about anymore. She's improved a lot over the time we went to North Carolina with them, and it's mostly online now anyway. Why is that doing that?"

Dan reached toward the radio, turned the volume higher. "That?"

"It sounds like we're driving through shredded wheat."

Where Bach had been came nothing but static, and not the high, nervous twitter of normal static, but something buzzier, more desiccated. He pressed the scan button, but there was static to the left and static to the right, with an excruciating pulse to it now, like what came on when the emergency people were announcing a tornado or flood.

"Interference," Dan said. "It's too bad, because it was just coming to the variation I like best."

Meg leaned forward to peer out the top of the windshield. "Those hills *are* getting steeper. And remember, this is the boonies now, so I bet public radio is chronically underfunded."

"And there's a storm coming. Look over there."

In the syncline where one hill scooped down to meet another lay a licorice-colored cloud that was much firmer and more organized than a normal summer cloud should be. It was 98 degrees out, they had almost fainted getting out of the car their one stop in Massachusetts, and now it was obvious that the heat was about to break.

"Does our house have a screened-in porch?" Meg asked. "I picture us sitting there overlooking the lake with our books piled high on either side of our rocking chairs and the two of us reading all day long, only getting up for more iced tea."

"Kim?"

"Out on the float sunbathing. It won't rain all the time."

"We can't hide her much longer."

Meg frowned sideways. "What's that supposed to mean?"

He shrugged, genuinely puzzled. "I don't know, it just came out. You notice something besides the clouds? How much traffic there is?"

The cars in the right lane were filled with families, carriers on top for the extra luggage, bike racks sagging on back, the whole vacation nine yards. The left lane carried a faster, more purposeful traffic, young people mostly, in bright new cars that looked fresh, spotless, and stolen. *Mass theft from a Saab dealership*—he was just going to try that line out on her—but now Meg pointed with her thumb.

"Just make sure you follow my sister."

"Follow them? I thought the idea was to lose them. Uh, excuse me. Lose Todd."

"He's my nephew," Meg said.

"He's a creep."

Meg was going to call him on that, he could tell from the way she twisted sideways in her seat, but something seemed to catch her, hold her back. The static over the radio had been followed by a few minutes of silence, but now there was music again, or at least the faintest of rhythmic sobs. He reached to turn it louder. It was rock, not classical. Rock, like a million other stations, but it was enough to make Kim's head suddenly pop up into the mirror.

"No Dad, please?"

Plaintive again, but plaintive like when she was little, on one of those rare occasions she was asking for something she really wanted. He had never been able to resist that tone, and he couldn't resist it now, not when he looked in the mirror and saw the eagerness in her eyes. It wasn't happy, not exactly, but closer than most of her expressions lately. And that from twenty seconds of music that could have only faintly penetrated her earphones.

He twisted the dial to the right to hone in on it, lost it, twisted again, and the music came back, blared louder, faded out. He tried again, hoping to find her a station that was clear. Way on the right was the music that had been there way on the far left, which struck him as a coincidence, until he came to the same song played on three different stations in the exact center of the dial. Was it a trick of topography, bunching things up that way? Some kind of round-the-clock marathon tribute?

He didn't recognize the music, though that didn't prove anything, since he had no notions whatsoever about contemporary rock.

"Good group," Kim said, with a little sigh. Even in the
rearview mirror he could see the faraway look in her eyes
where she seemed to be meditating on some great issue only
discernible to fourteen-year-old girls—a faraway look that had
no time for him, and which he hated.

"Not exactly Morrison," he grunted. "Nor Joplin either."

Meg laughed. "Now you'll be telling us you were at
Woodstock."

"Your Uncle Zack went to Woodstock," he said, talking into
the mirror. "A photographer took a picture of him taking a
bath in the mud for *Life*—this famous magazine? He actually
came back with flowers in his hair."

"Dad didn't go, honey."

"Because I was working three jobs at once, trying to pay my
way through community college."

He had more to say on this subject, but Meg cut him off.
"That's the thing I find most surprising in you, how much scar
tissue is left. But you're too young yet to talk about how hard
you had it as a kid—what's that up there?"

"That splotchy thing? Roadkill."

"Oh it's awful! Don't look, Kim. I mean it, don't look!"

"Coyote. No, fox."

"Don't look!"

Surprisingly, Kim did not look up—she kept her eyes locked
on the radio. Meg, having closed her own eyes, now glanced
up.

"Hey, there they are."

Suza's red Toyota was sliding over to the left and slowing, and there was some kind of movement or signal coming from the backseat that was obviously meant for them. Todd had made a sign on the back of a piece of cardboard and was holding it up to the window.

"What does he mean?" Meg asked.

"What does he ever mean, something peculiar and nasty and precociously Republican."

"He's improved a lot since that camp they sent him to."

"Todd? Are you kidding? He'll always have that repulsively smug young stockbroker's face, that braggart's squint, to say nothing of that cadaverous look he likes to play around with. Why did they bring him anyway? He'll hate Vermont. He's jaded, him and his pals—seventeen-year-olds going on fifty-seven."

Meg leaned across the seat. "What's it say?"

They drove two abreast now, the Toyota and their own car. In the front seat, Suza was making nervous little twisty motions, surely telling Rob this wasn't safe, and beside her Rob looked as handsome, self-satisfied, and clueless as ever, and in the back window, covering it completely, was pressed Todd's homemade sign.

PUCKER PIE, it read. Todd, to give him credit, had very neat handwriting.

Kim had her earphones off now. She waved toward the window as the Toyota zoomed off, then made a clutching motion that seemed intended to pull the music even closer.

"I *love* Pucker Pie!"

Dan wasn't positive, but he would have guessed big money that until that moment Kim had never heard of them. Pucker

Pie? In the rough, sloppy file he kept of contemporary cultural references, it made no connection, but, wanting to keep Kim happy, curious himself, he reached to turn it louder.

As with all her music, the blandness hit him first. It was overly synthesized—it seemed to be mixed, stirred, and packaged in speakers that were barely connected to the guitars ostensibly producing the sound, let alone to someone actually strumming the guitars' strings. It had a bouncy enough lilt, the group understood the fundamentals of melody, but they kept fleeing back to it again and again, as if this were their one and only idea. The lyrics were mush; the only words that emerged were the sharp and predictable ones—*bastard* and *bitch, fuck* and *suck*—which gave the impression of studs deliberately woven into silk to make it seem tougher. He tried connecting it to the music he had listened to when he was Kim's age. The Stones, of course—he could see this group trying to inject enough rawness into their mix to give the feel of honesty and boldness—but at the bottom of the music was something totally opposite to this, a honeyed sweetness that was probably the part that hooked Kim. What had they called this when he was fourteen? Bubble-gum music. Under the toughness, the profanity, that's exactly what it was.

"I like it," Meg said, bouncing her head up and down.

"Which you would," he said, gently enough. "Hey tutti-frutti! Wasn't there a song like that?"

"Before I get mad at you, can we find a place to pee?"

No sooner did she ask than a big green sign loomed up on the right, *Vermont Welcome Center Three Miles.* Everyone was stopping; cars were backed up on the ramp, and when they finally got to the first parking lot, an attendant waved them toward an overflow lot where portable toilets were arranged in a little blue village.

It felt good to get out and stretch. Under the clouds the pavement shone like marble, with mica flecks that sparkled the gray into white. The heat was breaking—from the woods came a smell that was heady with pine. Even the potties seemed pristine, and a man with a truck and hose was pumping them out the moment anyone finished.

"Did you hear that music?" Meg asked, when her sister's family came over.

Rob pointed proudly at Todd. "He knows everything there is to know about them. What they earn, how many CDs they sell. I'd love to move dishwashers in those numbers."

Suza had a map out. "There are malls off Exit 3," she said. "Gloves, which I need badly."

Everyone ignored her. Todd hung back from his parents and stood there fine-tuning his scowl until it combined just the right proportions of contempt and disdain. He was good at leers too, only these he saved for Kim—Kim, who had walked over to the edge of the pavement to stare wistfully toward the welcome center, her arms folded across her T-shirt in a way that made her elbows jut out. The building there resembled a barn, with a high cedar roof and a big black chimney. It was attractive and inviting and probably stuffed full of all kinds of useful and informative pamphlets, and Dan felt a little hurt that they had been exiled to this outlying lot.

Each of them found a potty to line up for. Dan joined the longest line, but before he could get there the man who was pumping them out gave him a little nod and just like that started talking.

"You're smart to pee here. The welcome center? Shambles!" Dan liked the look of him—the lines on his face were expressive and strong and knew how to flex in emphasis to what he was saying.

"You know about Pucker Pie? You've been warned?"

Dan didn't understand. "Warned not to listen?"

"Their farewell concert is this afternoon up in Minkton. Some fool farmer rented them their farm. Why farewell, I don't know, but take a guess at what a ticket costs. A thousand per. A thousand *per!* Take a look at those cars over there. You see any that isn't brand spanking new, right off the lot? College kids, the kind who don't have to worry about spending Daddy's money."

Dan looked to where he pointed. The parking lot nearest the welcome center was filled to overflowing, and there were cars parked on the grass near flattened *Do Not Park* signs. As the man said, each car looked new, and almost all were the same silver-gray color, making it seem they had been dipped in a bath of melted coins. All the windows were open, every radio was on, and the sweet bass thumping that emerged was all Pucker Pie.

"What time did you say this concert was?" Dan asked. He turned around, but the man had run back over to his truck. He was coiling up his hose, looking anxiously over his shoulder. Finishing, he climbed into his cab and took off, not toward the highway, but down a path cut for emergency vehicles into the woods. Fleeing, Dan decided; the potty pumper was fleeing, but fleeing what?

He walked back to where the others waited, uneasy himself now, not at all sure why. "Everyone here?" he asked, counting heads. He felt like the leader of a wagon train; between Suza and her outlets and Rob and his dithering, they would never get to the lake.

"Todd isn't," Meg said.

"Anyone seen him?"

Kim raised a lazy arm toward the welcome center.

Rob slapped his hands together like a football coach, but his voice rose to a girlish pitch. "There's no ambition in him; that's what I can't fathom. He won't do anything except those video games and we're supposed to be visiting colleges, and now the whole summer is total toast and we haven't been to even one and in two months, guess what baby? here comes his last crack at the SATs."

He stared toward the welcome center like it was somehow all to blame. Dan felt angry with him, but only for a second.

"I'll go get him," he said.

"Can I come?" Kim asked.

"Absolutely not."

The satellite area was filled with families, but once he found the gravel path that led to the welcome center things changed very fast. A considerable crowd milled around outside, young men and young women, and they seemed to have decided not to drive any farther but to have their party right there, right now. Many were dancing, and the ones who weren't pumped their fists in the air keeping time to the music or cheering on the ones who danced the wildest. None of the boys appeared to have a shirt on—they all looked slim, suntanned, athletic. The girls, without exception, had skinny little torsos and mother-ly round breasts, so, for a crazy instant, Dan thought of top-heavy stick figures from the same lollipop-shaped mold.

They seemed good-natured enough, which was fortunate, since their sheer numbers were troublesome. Dan could see now that an attempt was being made to cordon the welcome center off. The attendant scooted around arranging orange cones in a line between the parking lot and the entrance, while behind him a solitary state trooper stood smiling at the crowd, but with his hand conspicuously on his holster. A safety issue obviously—but was any of that wise? Two boys, cut off from the toilets, were peeing on a baby tree, and he could hear some girls shouting toward the trooper in a guttural tone that wasn't pretty.

No barriers were up on his side, and he made it to the welcome center without being stopped. The doors were heavy to open, sticky, and the floor behind them was covered with a brownish stain he only slowly realized was coffee. He followed its trail, came almost immediately to an overturned urn with its handles snapped off. *Free Safety Coffee!* read a sign askew on its neck. Beyond it, where the building opened in an atrium, things were even crazier. The racks holding the maps and travel brochures had been knocked over, and the pamphlets made a slippery paper carpet on the floor. The wall displays were all of Vermont—photos of farms, farming tools, maple sugaring implements—but these had all been hacked at or dug into or scratched, so they seemed displays of a Vermont at war.

The smell of urine made him gag, and there was a wet pool near the restroom he just barely found a way past. Todd stood by the sinks in a very odd posture, bent sideways from the waist and twisted half around so his head looked up toward the ceiling. He was prying with his fingers at a little green sign that explained how much water was saved per flush in the environmentally friendly toilets. When it still wouldn't budge, he started hammering at it with the side of his hand.

"Hey, Todd?" Dan said, speaking as quietly and gently as he could. "Time to go now, buddy."

He didn't seem surprised to see Dan there. He didn't act particularly upset. He made his face comfortably smug, zipped up, then turned and walked toward the exit with his hands in the air like a prisoner.

Dan, before leaving, took a last look around. He badly wanted someone to tell him what this was all about, but the welcome center was deserted, and, once outside, even the attendant and state trooper seemed to have fled. The crowd stayed where they were in a huge ring around their cars. More boys were peeing now, and gyrating around the circumference was an extraordinarily tall, redheaded girl who had peeled off her top to wild applause.

To get to his own car he had to follow the gravel path, which on one curve came very close to the crowd's edge. He was walking quickly, trying not to catch anyone's eye, when there was a thumping sound, like a giant hitting a car roof with his fist, and then a boy yelling in his direction.

"Hey mister, where are the cows?"

It was ludicrous—it was like being a small kid yelled at on the playground by a bully, and instantly all the old feelings of shame, weakness, and embarrassment came back. He gave a little wave, but this wasn't enough for them.

"Hey asshole, where are the cows!"

Like when he was a kid mocked that time in school by a bully—but back then, to his own complete amazement, holding his forearm out like a professional wrestler, he had run over and smashed the bully in the mouth. That wouldn't do now. Besides, their attention had already shifted. Kim had found a rock to stand on in order to see better—she leaned forward like a ship's lithe figurehead. The college boys started yelling toward her, waving her over, and he could see a childish curiosity on her face that, given a few more minutes, might intensify into something disturbingly mature. And what was odd, they didn't seem to be calling her because she looked so innocent and unspoiled. She excited them because with her blonde hair and pert figure she matched so perfectly the current model of what they were constantly told was beautiful—the beauty of TV shows, videos, and commercials. Beauty simple enough for morons to understand—and this is what frightened him, made him put his arm on her back and hurry her toward the car.

"Danny boy!" Rob waved his cell phone. "I just got us a teetime for 4:30. The pro said it's sunny up there by the lake, not a cloud in the sky. Hey son, where've you been hiding?"

Todd brushed past him into the car. His mother, folding her brochures, got in too. "Beat you up there!" Rob yelled, and he sprinted over to the driver's side. That left Meg—Meg who stood a little to the side, staring intently toward the crowd.

"What's going on over there?"

"Get in the car."

"YAs we call them in the library when they're making too much noise."

"YAs?"

"Young adults, emphasis on the young. You see the beer they're putting away? And they're going to be driving the same direction we are? Look, that's a cathedral they're building, all out of beer cans."

"Good, it will keep them busy for a while, but let's you and me get in the car."

The rain started as they merged onto the interstate—huge drops that splattered apart on the pavement, creating a mist that made it hard to see—and the traffic was worse north of the welcome center than it had been to the south. On the right, timidly bumper to bumper, were vacationing families like themselves, while on the left, roaring past at three times the speed, were fans going to the concert. The lanes were clearly segregated. No one on the right seemed foolish enough to chance moving to the left—not until Rob, with a sassy little motion from his bumper, swerved that way himself. He did it too slow—there was a furious squeal of brakes and horns—and then he had no option but to accelerate to the insane speed all Meg's YAs drove at. The Toyota disappeared over the next hill—one hand out the front window, Suza's, giving a despairing little wave; one hand out the back window, Todd's, giving them a triumphant finger.

Kim, who was oblivious to all of this, leaned forward in her seat. "Pucker Pie?"

Meg responded before he could. "This is Vermont. Let's just enjoy the pitter patter of rain on the roof, okay?"

"We'll listen later," Dan said. "Just as soon as traffic thins out."

The rain made everyone in the right lane slow down, since it was nearly impossible to see even one car ahead, but in the left lane the concertgoers only drove faster, as if determined to beat the storm north. After another mile, Dan drove past their first crash, a minivan lying upside down on the grassy median, obviously a family, because bicycles had been flung to the side and a red kayak lay stuck in the embankment like a spear.

"Was anyone hurt?" Meg asked, twisting to see. "Why aren't the police controlling things? They knew about the concert, why aren't they prepared?"

She pointed toward a green state police cruiser over in the southbound lane going fast enough to send up a rooster tail of spray. He didn't have his siren on or his flasher—through the grayness they could just make out a square-jawed silhouette hunched rigidly over the steering wheel. A mile farther and another police car sped south, then right behind him another one, then a third and a fourth. *South*, while all the traffic and confusion headed north.

"You know what?" Dan said, speaking softly so Kim couldn't hear. "Those cops over there? They're bailing out. They're running away. They're fleeing Vermont."

It was such a new thought, such an unexpected one, that he couldn't quite get his mind around it. Back at the welcome center he had felt so relieved to be in the country that the implications of what he was seeing were slow to sink in. They had sunk in, but now events were outracing him again, and he knew he would have to demand much more from his imagination in order to keep up. And what was strange, this wasn't an entirely bad feeling, not at this stage. He felt alert in a way he hadn't in a long time, alert as in slightly ahead of everyone else—but to what purpose?

"Do you think they're all right?" Meg asked. "What was Rob thinking, to speed off that way?"

"Maybe Suza knows about a tag sale up ahead. Maybe Todd jumped into the driver's seat and hijacked them. Hey, this is silly! Next exit we're getting off and waiting out the storm at a cozy little mom-and-pop diner somewhere, the kind that serves breakfast all day long. Hear that, Kimbo? Feel like some pancakes smothered in hot maple syrup?"

She was turned toward the left window, so it was hard to read her thoughts. She wasn't sulking—there was something prim and demure in the way she sat—but he almost would have preferred sulking to the yearning he saw on her face, the longing, the expectancy. *Here I am, come and find me*, she seemed to be saying. The rain made steam on the window that she kept wiping off with little circular motions, not so much to see out through but to let people see in.

The exit was just ahead and everyone seemed to have the same idea, because the flash of signal lights made the fog pulse red. He could see the first cars veer off, their taillights sinking, then too quickly they rose again, and there was another red cloud, only this time flashing to the left.

Meg saw it too. "What's going on?"

They were on the exit ramp now, and there straight ahead was the answer. Police, local police, had the exit blocked off with heavy wooden barriers. One man, a fireman, stood waving cars back onto the interstate down a muddy track. Some cars had stopped, and their drivers stood arguing with the cop in charge, but they got nowhere with him. Behind the barricades, like reinforcements ready if needed, were husky men standing outside their trucks in yellow rain slickers—not cops, not exactly, but exuding the same kind of dull hostility. *Vigilantes*—the word came to him from some half-forgotten Western he'd seen as a kid.

"They won't let us off."

The police chief, thickened by a flak vest, yelled something through a bullhorn that couldn't penetrate the drum of rain.

"Why? Because there's a fire or flood or something?"

"Because they're protecting their town." He gestured to the left. "From your YAs. They're not taking any chances with them. They don't want any trouble."

"That's crazy."

"I think it's time we tried the radio again."

Stations were supposed to broadcast emergency information or warning messages from the government, but twist the dial all he wanted, there was nothing on but the same relentless music, the jackhammer beat, the profane, tough-guy lyrics, washed down by the cynical sweetness that made even someone like him, someone who detested it and saw right through it, want to snap his fingers, bob his head. He would have turned it off, but it made Kim happy—she looked like she did when she was little and had dropped a toy and he had picked it up again and put it back in her hand.

The next two exits were blocked off by barricades and pickup trucks like the first one had been, then came thirteen miles with no exits at all. Some families tried escaping across the median to the southbound lanes, but it was too muddy for

that, and none of the cars went more than a dozen yards before sinking. The culverts under the interstate couldn't con-
tain the high water, and some were so blocked with debris that
they acted like dams, so between the northbound lanes and
the southbound ones ran a swollen, gravy-colored moat.

Dan kept staring, waiting his chance. "We need one of
those emergency turnarounds they have for cops and ambulances that will be high enough to be out of the water."

A good idea. Meg nodded, turned to look for a place to turn
around, but it was another twenty minutes before they saw one,
and only spotted it then because suddenly all the signal lights
began blinking left. It meant getting over to the passing lane,
which meant accelerating to a speed faster than was safe, but
he had no choice. He rolled his window down to see, took the
acid sting of rain on his eyes, blindly stuck his arm out, held
his breath—swerved. By some miracle they made it, and then
almost immediately he had to brake and pull off.

Under a sign reading *Emergency Vehicles Only!* were already
a dozen cars, twenty cars, pulled over trying to do exactly the
same thing. None of them moved. Horns blared, people got
out of their cars to see, but the rain drove them right back in
again, and new arrivals kept making the jam even worse. The
brand-new Jeep ahead of them, red as Christmas, had skidded
to a stop, and now lay sideways across the gravel so it blocked a
way around. The two male YAs in front had gotten out to stag-
ger around under the rain, necks craned back, mouths open
chugging down the raindrops, while beside the car, leaning
over the door puking, was a young girl with wispy blonde hair
and nothing on but a bikini.

"She's crying," Meg said. "She looks hurt."

"Drunk is what she looks like. We've got to get right back on the highway or else get stuck."

"She's in trouble. For pity's sake, Dan, she's Kim's age!"

Before he could stop her, Meg was opening the door, running through the rain over to the Jeep. He opened his own door, got out, and stood there shouting for her to come back, shouting so loud it made his throat hurt, the wind whipping his words off to the left where they did no good. Meg hunched over the girl, put her arm around her, leaned closer to say something or listen, so for a moment they seemed like one sodden, sisterly ball of wetness—but then just as suddenly Meg was back again, soaked through and shivering.

"She was crying, I was right about that."

"Is she hurt?"

"The concert's been canceled. She said they drove all day to get here from New Jersey and the concert's been canceled because of the rain and mud and that's broken her heart."

"Which is very bad news for us."

She didn't seem to hear. "Everyone will go home now, so it should be much better."

"You say that very reasonably."

She shot him a look. "What is that supposed to mean?"

"These kids paid a thousand per to see a rock group. I don't think they'll be reasonable. They want their fun."

"Do you want me to try hysterical then? I can do hysterical if you want. I've been sitting here for the last two hours getting my hysterical all prepared."

"Because I think we're in a somewhat dangerous situation,

and I'm doing my best to come up with a plan to get us out."

"Can you keep your voice down? There's no use scaring Kim."

"Then turn the music up; we might as well use it for something. And here, put on my sweater."

"We'll just get back on the highway and drive somewhere safe."

She was back to reasonable again—but maybe that's what it would take, accepting everything that came at them as if it made absolutely perfect sense. More cars veered off behind them, the traffic jam on the turnaround doubled and tripled, but he found just enough of an opening to accelerate onto the pavement again, then cut over to the right. Almost immediately they started coming upon parked or abandoned cars, many half-drowned in the swampy median, but some hardly off the pavement at all, which could only mean they were close to the concert site now, which could only mean that parking was impossible there, and the fans arriving early had given up and decided to walk.

The cars were as new, shiny, and spotless as the ones they had seen back at the welcome center, and any older cars, ones that dated even two years back, seemed to have been deliberately targeted by vandals. Windshields were smashed on some, aerials ripped off on others, and there wasn't one that didn't have a long white scar across the side left by a key.

Car snobs, a gang of drunken car snobs. The pavement was shiny with beer cans and broken bottles, and under the tires, even with all the rain, he could hear the brittle crunch of glass. A road sign announcing the next exit had been pushed back on itself and nearly toppled, and past that, a mile from the exit, was a sign that had been hacked off at its base.

"They must be hijacking bulldozers. You know how much one of those signs weighs?"

Meg closed her eyes. "Get us out of this. Just please get us out of this as fast as you can."

Ahead near the exit stood six or seven naked YAs, waving beer cans around like they were pistols and they were popping off shots. They had an old station wagon stopped, and after making the driver roll down his window, they seemed to be inspecting it, though for God knows what. Booze? It was all in Rob's car. Books? Seeing how many there were in the back, they would wrongly take him for a teacher. It was like a checkpoint manned by gibbering white monkeys with patches of coarse black fur, and in thirty seconds he would be up to it, and he wasn't about to take any chances with that.

To the east of the interstate was a temporary fence made from plastic crisscrosses strung between wooden stakes. The concert organizers must have put it there to prevent people from taking a shortcut before the exit, but if that was so, then it meant that cutting off was at least a possibility. Past the fence was a thin band of pliant-looking birch trees, and past that, even in the rain, loomed something gray and solid enough to be pavement.

He had no choice. He swerved to the right onto the shoulder, then accelerated up a steep gravel bank that threw them back in their seats. "Hold on!" he shouted, but the car was already bursting through the plastic fence, and then with a hard yank on the steering wheel he had them past the band of trees.

The tires spun on mud, their rear end fishtailed, but then the treads found something firmer, and they were skidding over the last patch of grass onto pavement again, a quiet country road that seemed, at least for those first breathless seconds, absolutely deserted.

"Kimberly?" Meg said, when the shock of it began to ease. "When you get your license, *never* do what Daddy just did."

It was as if they had been spit out into the real Vermont, the one they had dreamed of when they called to rent the cottage. There on the right rose a proudly eccentric red barn, with windows tucked in sideways under the eaves and bulb-shaped lightning rods that must have dated from 1860. There on the left was a tidy cornfield and toward the back a silo held together by rusty steel hoops, and then some weathered outbuildings that had the color and permanence of rock. Vermont—and yet it seemed half afloat, with floodwater lapping at the windows of the barn and covering all but the highest tassels of corn, so it was like Holland was mixed in the scene too, Holland with the dikes breached and lightning slamming down in jagged blue bolts.

Chunks of pavement had been chewed off the road by the water rushing along its edge, but it looked solid enough to hold them. Which direction was the safe one to go depended on which side of the interstate the concert was on, over on the west side with the highway and its ramps acting as a barrier, or over on the flatter east side, the side they were on now.

"Try right," Meg said, when he still hesitated. "Get as far away from the highway as we can before dark."

"Canada is right."

"Canada?" By her look, he could have said Peru.

"Because we could try crossing over to New Hampshire, but any fans driving up from Boston would come that way, so it would be trouble over there too. The Canadians know how to handle this kind of thing. It can't be more than five or six miles, we're so far north now. I bet we can find a back road that will get us around all this to a border crossing."

"There's a sign over there."

It was Kim who said it—Kim, who hadn't said a word for the last two hours. She tapped her nail on the window. "One of those historical marker things? It says—" she twisted in her seat. "Indians—uh, did something here. Can we stop if we see another one? I'm going to probably have to write an essay about this for English."

"Of course we'll stop," Meg said. "Any historical markers, we'll certainly stop."

The quiet road ended at a wider one, and he turned north on it straight into trouble. There was another cornfield, only this one had a banner stretched between two trees—*Concert Parking $100* the soggy black letters read. Behind it were rows of Audis and Saabs, with water rising high enough to cover their license plates. A half mile farther came another sign, *Concert Parking $150*, and this time there were more cars, newer cars, in rows where the water daintily lapped at their tires—and then came a third field, a sign reading *Concert Parking $300*, with a canopy of blue tarps the cars could park under and keep dry, so it was obvious that rather than skirting the concert site they were heading right toward its center.

They had no choice but to keep going. On the right was a shabby-looking elementary school with cheap tin siding, and past that a garage that must have specialized in repairing farm tractors. There were three in the deserted yard, turned over on their backs like helpless green and yellow dinosaurs. Past that began the village proper, with a neat town green and a Civil War monument, a soldier on a pedestal, only with his arms ripped off, so where the arms should have joined the shoulders were fresh silver scars. On the far end of the green rose a classic white church, which at first seemed to have escaped unharmed, but then as they were driving past the side, he realized the paint was smeared with human excrement. An iron fence separated the church from the road, and girls' panties were pulled down tight on every spike.

The road forked here—another impossible decision. Dan lowered his window, tried listening. In the distance ahead of them, synchronized to the lightning flashes, came the sound of thunder—thunder from a sky that was hoarse from screaming and couldn't quite manage an echo. It wasn't an unpleasant sound, not when it stayed remote like that, but within seconds it grew louder, heavier, and he realized it wasn't thunder at all, but a huge chorus of male voices trying to imitate thunder, bellowing toward the sky in unison, as if to show the heavens that when it came to power, chaos, and fury, they could do it much better themselves.

The sound was too broad to slip past. "Get down!" he said, but neither Meg nor Kim listened. He could see Meg trying to keep calm, wincing, blinking, the lower part of her face, the silly, joking part, struggling with the upper part, the courageous part, the part that wouldn't let fear get the better of her. Kim's face was as unreadable as ever—she sat staring toward the window as if facing a computer screen she could erase if things got too scary.

Past the first bend, in the center of a little park, they came upon their first Pucker Pie fans—five or six male YAs watching two female YAs as they sat astride an ancient black cannon. They shimmied back and forth, rubbing their crotches against the iron throat of it, really gyrating, as the boys applauded, snapped pictures with their cell phones, egged them on. Hearing a car, they looked up, but only to wave—*Come play with us!* they seemed to be shouting—and they looked so obviously good-natured and friendly that for a moment Dan felt an overwhelming surge of relief. Just good kids blowing off some steam, having fun, partying—what was the harm in that?

He didn't realize how tightly he'd been clutching the steering wheel until his nerves relaxed—relaxed, then immediately locked tight again. Past the park was a hardware store, its windows shattered, then a store called "Green Mountain Gifts," its windows shattered likewise, and then the sidewalk ended at a large open square backed by a brick library, with a post office on one side, a police station on the other. The space in between was filled with a solid mass of huddled shapes—it was like looking at an enormous football huddle or rugby scrum, one that scuttled crablike toward one side, met the wall of the police station, scurried the other way, met the wall of the post office, then seemed to quiver, quake, and boil in the middle without moving at all.

Mob—it was strange how clearly he saw the word form in his mind, as if the scene came with its own unmistakable caption. The center of the mob was thick and uniform—young bodies, hard bodies, expensive bodies, trophy bodies—and it was only along the edges that any detail stood out.

Fires had been set in fifty-gallon drums; YAs dipped furled beach umbrellas into their middles, got them lighted, hurled them like spears toward the library. Other YAs hurled beer bottles, cheering whenever one shattered—and then some of them had a better idea, went over to the jerry cans looted from the hardware store, filled the beer bottles with gasoline, used rags as fuses, lit them, lobbed them skyward. In the copper light cast by the flames, he could see girls being passed along the top of the mob, willingly or unwillingly it was impossible to say, their arms and legs all akimbo, passed quickly toward the front of the mob where they were dropped like stones out of sight, only to be replaced by a fresh supply passed up from the rear. They saw one pretty girl with her top torn off standing to the side, hands over her face crying, and past her were two YAs urinating in tandem on a charcoal grill, only they soon got tired of this, took shovels, dug them into the grill, hurled briquettes toward the library as if they were lacrosse balls, the shovels their sticks. A bucket brigade extended from the looted hardware store to the police station—YAs were passing axes along it, chainsaws, hammers, knives. The noise was so loud it bulged their car windows inward. The mob was imitating thunder now, but chanting what must have been one of Pucker Pie's hits, because even under the beat of it, Dan could detect the signature sweetness, so, judging by sound only, they could have been Boy Scouts and Girl Scouts singing songs by the campfire as their marshmallows turned brown.

The rain on the pavement created a ground mist that partly hid their car, the road swung away from the square, gained a modicum of shelter from an undertaker's and a bank. Even so, Dan felt like he was driving on tiptoes, that the slightest sound

must be avoided at all costs. *We'll slip right past them*, he decided—and then Meg suddenly threw her arm across the back
of the seat, like they were about to be in a collision and she was
trying to keep Kim from flying through the glass.

"Don't look!" she whispered. "Ohmygod, don't look!"

She didn't mean the mob in the square—her face was turned
the other way, peering down at something half-hidden in the
shrubs by the side of the road. Dan couldn't see from where he
sat, and Kim must not have heard, because her rapt attention
was in the opposite direction, toward the mob. Instead of acting terrified, she rolled her window down so she could point
and wave.

"Hey!" she said, brightly. "There's Todd!"

YAs nearest the edge of the mob had created a human pyramid, and near the top, his motions jerky and wild like a spas-
tic monkey's, was a figure with enough cadaverous thinness
that it could easily have been Todd. He climbed in the light of
the burning umbrellas, stomped on backs, pulled on hair—
and there, he was on top now, higher than anyone else in the
square, raising his arm in what seemed meant for a Nazi salute, but an awkward one—a salute that had the hate right and
the stiffness, but messed up on the angle.

Dan slowed down just long enough to watch him, and that
was a second too long, because three YAs standing to the side
juggling beer bottles spotted them now, saw Kim with her head
out the window, and immediately started running after them,
drunk and leering and horrible.

An intersection ahead, a blinking yellow light. Dan turned
right, down a road that cut through the most thickly settled
part of town. Houses lined both sides of the road, old ones

that seemed both dilapidated and proud, their sides painted a spotless white, their roofs covered in lichen and beginning to sag. There were no lights on in any of them, no signs of life. "That one," Meg said, pointing to the left. He swerved that way, got out before the car had barely stopped moving, splashed through their flooded patch of lawn, ran up to the front door.

A face in the window, two faces, male or female it was impossible to say, the bull's-eye glass distorting their features into one smeared blur of panic. Seeing him, they shook their heads vehemently from side to side—"No!" they could have been shouting—and he saw the larger shape holding something vaguely cruciform out before its chest, like a charm meant to ward off vampires.

Meg must have seen the faces too, even through the rain. "We're just a family; we have a girl!"

"Was I supposed to beg? Kick the door in? We'll try the next house down."

Meg shook her head. "No, that one over there."

Under the flashing yellow light appeared the YAs who had chased them, reinforced now by a dozen others—they looked like the foamy black edge of a wall of flood water, temporarily dammed, building higher, ready to burst. Confused, they looked left and right, then, seeing the car lights, started running down the road after them. He drove to the house Meg indicated, wondering why she was so sure that was the one to try next, then, when they got closer, understanding perfectly. It was a proud and shabby Cape like the other houses, with a wing extending back from the main house to a connected tobacco-colored barn. On their patch of lawn, whirligigs of geese flapped their wings under the weight of rain, and wood-

en ducks paddled madly, and there was a cutout of a boy peeing on their flowers, and then a flagpole with two flags, the
American and what must have been the Vermont, and surrounding this, two solid rows of stacked firewood, forming
walls as high as a man's height.

He parked near the wall, got out, ran to the front door,
knocked as loud as he could. Instantly, the door flew open—in
the gloom of the mud room stood a short, stocky man dressed
in green work clothes, a woman standing behind him in a
shapeless dress—and just as he was about to start explaining,
start begging, the woman nodded, and the man stepped forward and took his arm.

"Hide the car first," he said, in a whisper of tremendous authority. "Straight back into the barn."

Dan ran to the car, got Meg out and Kim, hurried them
through the rain to the door where the woman took over, ran
back, drove up the bumpy driveway into the barn. It was larger than it looked from outside, the floor covered with hay left
over from when it had housed horses and cows. Every free inch
was taken up with machinery needing repair—snowmobiles,
wood splitters, outboard motors—and though he wasn't sure
why, the old metal smell acted like a calm hand against his
racing heart.

In the mud room a kerosene lamp hissed out a creamy
light. Meg made a prim kind of nodding motion that wasn't
like her, almost a curtsey. "Dan, this is Mr. and Mrs. Bouchard.
I was telling them what happened, how we were driving up
here for a vacation and we somehow lost my sister in the rain,
and cars were abandoned, and then we came to town and saw
this drunken mob and maybe my nephew is part of it and they

saw Kim and—" She made a choked, sobbing sound, and Mrs. Bouchard immediately put her arm around her, drew her over to a bench that ran along the room's side.

It was Mr. Bouchard's turn now. He grabbed Dan's shoulder with a grip like a wrestler's, pushed him roughly toward the hall.

"Get the girl away from the windows. No lights. No noise. Understand me?"

Dan nodded, took Kim's hand, pulled her through a hall of musty-smelling wallpaper into an old-fashioned front parlor, with furniture that must have been new in 1930 and not very fancy then. In the center was an overstuffed sofa that looked like it would eject you if you tried sitting down, but he planted her there anyway, covered her shoulders with a wool throw draped across the back. Mrs. Bouchard came in with a candle, and it threw enough light that he could see decorations on the wall, pictures cut out of newspapers and magazines over the years, one of Franklin Roosevelt and another of a pope whose name he couldn't remember. Beside the last picture, startlingly three-dimensional, was a mounted deer head with shiny spiked antlers. The room smelled of cooking, stewed tomatoes or something similar, and it was so humid with all the windows shut that the smell seemed to be steaming out of the deer's mouth.

"Take that window," Mr. Bouchard said, shoving him a second time. "You see anything, holler for me; I'll be watching out back."

He stood six inches away, yet Dan still couldn't see his face—the voice, commanding and calm, emerged from green work clothes hanging loose on a thick, stooped-over frame.

What must he have been, eighty-five? His wife was just as old, but all he could see of her was a loose muslin dress hovering fairylike in the parlor's center. A "house dress" he remembered his grandmother calling these. One second it was there, the next it was gone, and then a coffee smell wafted its way across the carpet toward him, so it was obvious Mrs. Bouchard was in the kitchen again, getting ready for a long night.

A drape covered the window, and he pushed it back just far enough to make a narrow loophole through which he could peer out. He could see very distinctly the individual logs that made up the wall of stacked wood, but he was high enough to see over the top. The rain kept things perfectly black in the immediate vicinity, with no lights showing from any other house on their side of the road. There was color in the sky, but it was at the far end of town, and he had to stare for a few hard minutes before he realized what it came from. Fire—and not the kind they had driven past in the square—fun fire, play fire, fire in 50-gallon drums or looted barbecues—but the fire of burning buildings. A pink-red glow made a crescent atop the roofs of the tallest buildings, and above these, piercing the rain, shot arrow-shaped streamers of orange and red. Even through the window he could detect the fire's smell, cinnamony and choking.

The mob's voice ran along the window glass, probed at the sashes, leaked in through the dried caulk—a whooping, high-pitched tone that hurt his ears. With it came a steadier drumming that seemed to answer itself from the totally opposite direction, as if one half of the mob were signaling the other half of the mob, working themselves into a frenzy, preparing now to march.

He shifted his angle, tried seeing out sideways to check how close they were, and in doing so he saw a house burning on the end of the Bouchards' road—it was like a sticky lightning bolt had become glued to the eaves and couldn't get itself detached. He counted—five untouched houses between the burning one and theirs. He had decided to call Mr. Bouchard, had just gotten up from his crouch, when behind him, so sudden and loud it all but toppled him over again, came a desperate, full-throated scream.

It was Kim, sitting too straight and too rigid on the edge of the sofa, covering her mouth with both hands as if horrified at what had just come out. Meg threw her arms around her, hugged her tight, and there was enough light that Dan could see Kim's face; it was the face she had when she was little, five or six, and had just woken up from a nightmare that only he could make go away. He started toward her, but Meg was there, and then Mrs. Bouchard hurried in, the two women forming a protective wall around Kim, who softly sobbed.

His protective instinct, the well he had been drawing upon all day, was strained now, weary, and yet, looking at the two of them sitting huddled on the sofa . . . Meg stroking Kim's hair, gently smoothing out her sobs . . . he realized that the fierce depth of it had scarcely been touched.

"They'll know she's here now," Mr. Bouchard said, looming up out of the dark. "Here, you'd better take this."

The moment Dan took the weight in his hand, felt the solid heft of it, smelled its oily cleanness, he realized he had been expecting this and just exactly this all day—to have someone stick a rifle in his hands. What surprised him was how good it felt, how natural, though he hadn't touched a gun since summer camp as a boy. He tipped it back and forth, testing its balance, brought it up to his face close enough to examine the scope, stuck his index finger in the little metal loop on the bottom, found the trigger. It felt surprisingly warm, with a yielding, tensile strength that was not at all unpleasant. There was something satisfactorily forbidden about touching it, so for a brief ludicrous moment he remembered the first time he ever dared put his hand down his girlfriend's pants.

Mr. Bouchard shoved him toward the place he was to kneel.

"If they want trouble, we'll give it to them. Pick the leader out, wait until his nipple fills the scope."

Dan nodded. "And when it does?" he asked, wanting to make sure.

"You hate him. You wait until you do."

A whooping noise came from the barn, a splintery crash. Mr. Bouchard hurried back to his post, leaving Dan alone by the window. He reached toward the open loophole of curtain, felt for the window's sash, raised it just enough to get the rifle barrel through, then raised it higher for the scope. The stock was supposed to be pressed firmly against his cheek, he knew that instinctively, but the scope was harder to accustom himself to, and it took a few minutes of blinking and squinting before he began to see.

In the middle of the road, not a hundred yards away, stood perhaps a dozen YAs forming an advance guard before the darker mass of bodies backlit by flames. They held garden stakes or metal fence posts, and they brandished them over their heads and stamped their feet, maddening up their nerve. The biggest, strongest one stepped forward and pointed toward the Bouchards' house. In his hand was a torch, not a spear, and it illumined his body with a clarity that didn't touch the others. His face was painted in what looked to be greasy frosting, chocolate on one side, vanilla on the other, and the division continued right down the middle of his naked chest.

Their leader, there was no doubt about that, and Dan centered the sight on a spot over his heart just as ordered. The hating part came slower. He was eighteen or nineteen, a kid, a drunken kid who was probably no more messed up than Todd was—but that was dangerous, thinking of him that way, foolish, fatal. It was easier to focus instead on the faceless mob that backed him up, easier to hate them because he had no trouble finding labels for them, categories, until they represented everything in life he despised. Spoiled rich kids— hedonists, preppies, potheads, jock Neanderthals, frat boys— the labels leaped through his heart, deepened there, stiffened up his nerve. Spoiled rich kids, fascist preppies, yuppie scum, jock Neanderthals, macho frat boys, cynical nihilists, stupid geeks.

That was the way, the hate moved from his shoulder down his arm, steadying him greatly. The boy in front, waving on those behind him, started running forward so his chest filled the scope entirely, then his heart, then his nipple centered within its purplish aureole. With a great yearning motion, he hurled his torch toward the house.

Fine, throw it, Dan whispered, though his voice seemed someone else's. The time for learning was over now. His understanding had graduated. His finger knew exactly what to do.

A Fixture on Main Street for Sixty-three Years

WITH ONLY MINUTES left now, as a kind of rebellion, the waitresses sat at the counter serving themselves lunch. There were four of them, counting the cashier—cigarette skinny, worn to a frazzle, but enjoying themselves immensely, the short-order chef grilling up anything they wanted. Was it their fantasy, to kick out the paying customers before the store closed forever? If so, it was a good one, and Larkin, who was looking forward to a last chocolate milkshake, went instead to the rear of the store, the warm part of the store, where they sold pet food, canning jars, and notions.

Notions. It was the word his mother had used when she brought him shopping—*I'll be back in notions if you get lost*—and he always loved the sound of it, the comforting notion of notions. Safety pins, ear swabs, pocket combs. Here it was a five-and-dime store, and here in this aisle were items that cost a nickel or a dime, and as a boy the fitness of this, the truth, had pleased him no end.

Things had pretty well been picked clean now. Toward the end of the counter a woman with a plastic shopping bag shoveled in everything the first wave of bargain hunters had missed. There was snow on her shoulders, snow on the cracked linoleum tracked in by her boots, and that brought it back too—how his parents pulled him on his sled down Main Street for Friday night shopping. His father, exhausted form work at the mill, would follow his mother up and down the aisles, talking over with her even the smallest purchase, though the only thing Larkin had ever seen him buy for himself was an insulated flannel shirt.

The metal rod where these used to hang was still there, though no shirts remained. The wall behind it sagged noticeably inward, as if the wrecking ball already nudged it from behind, but there were still hangers left, old wooden ones shaped like a broad *A*, hangers his father might very well have touched.

He ran his hand over the wood, wondered if there was someone he could ask about having one as a souvenir. Up front toward the plate glass window paraded a cheerful man who must be the manager, a red *Closed* sign around his neck as a sort of joke. Other than him, the waitresses, and the greedy bargain hunter, the store was nearly deserted. Over by the makeup counter stood an attractive woman about his own age who reached down toward things but never actually touched them; there was something dreamy enough about her manner that he wondered if she had come for sentimental reasons too.

It was his second trip of the day. At noon, he had walked over from the office, but it had been crowded then, people drawn by the TV cameras and their cheap excitement. He could visualize what they would make of it on the evening news—a moment of nostalgia, a bittersweet shake of the anchorman's head, speculation on the site's future, a harsh summary of the retailing facts of life. He could even imagine the phrase they would use—*a fixture on Main Street for sixty-three years*—and he found himself, in a quick chill of loneliness, wanting to say these words out loud to someone, feel the sadness deep in his throat.

Leaving the hangers where they were, he walked toward the front of the store where the lights were brightest and the mustiness was smothered in the smell of french fries and perfume. When he was a boy, the merchandise counters had been arranged horizontally when you came in, making it awkward to get from one to the next, but some time in the last thirty years they had been swiveled ninety degrees and chopped in half. There were still gumball machines near the cash registers, still a counter with the paper supplies and glue he bought as a kid, but only a pad or two were left now, and there on the end tipped over on its side lay a bottle of Old Spice shaving lotion someone must have picked out deeper in the store and, having sniffed it, discarded it there on the way to pay.

Larkin had been a sentimental boy, the only child of older parents, prone to identifying with whatever was solitary and unwanted, and he had always felt sorry for things that didn't sell. Take the Old Spice, the exact kind he would buy his father for his birthday or Christmas. It was sad to think no one wanted it, though its price tag had been marked down to a quarter. As he did when he was a boy, he pictured it being found by someone needy, someone who took it home and splashed it liberally on his face to be cheered by the tangy sting of it, the quick moment of freshness—and then, reaching down but not quite touching it, he smiled to find himself playing that game again.

He finished his circuit around the store's circumference, but still couldn't bring himself to leave, even though it was snowing harder now and the interstate would be treacherous. Forty minutes left until the store closed forever, and didn't he owe it to the boy he had been to stay there right until the end? He owed himself a milkshake at any rate—as important as the store had been, the lunch counter was even more important.

It had been his family's one and only place of celebration. A grudging promotion for his father at work, a respite in his mother's illnesses, the small successes that were all he could ever manage for them in sports or at school. Dinner at the lunch counter! There had been a wholeness to it all—it wasn't just the food. The walk through a downtown full of shoppers, the steamy brightness of the display windows, his parents nodding to people they knew, his father, pulling the door open with a little flourish, waving them in ahead—and then the counter itself, the low row of stools that effortlessly swiveled, the little shelf beneath the counter where you could stuff your hat or mittens, the clean Formica sweep with its miniature cities formed by the napkin holders, the salt and pepper shakers, the condiments—and the similar way everyone sat bent over on their seats as if they were all engaged in helping push the counter on a journey that, to his ten-year-old imagination, couldn't help being magical. "Don't put your elbows down," his mother would say, but he found it impossible to balance on the stool without using his elbows as a brace; in a show of sympathy, his father would plant his own arms down, so powerfully that cups and saucers would rattle all the way to the counter's end.

And now all he wanted from those days was a last chocolate milkshake. It wouldn't be easy—the waitresses not only occupied what stools were left, but had walled themselves off behind the kind of orange cones they brought out when mopping the floors. The booth situation wasn't much better. These were small, and only one wasn't piled high with soggy-looking, derelict boxes held together by string. Would the waitresses even notice him there? Shrugging, feeling stubborn, he started toward the empty booth and immediately bumped shoulders with someone coming up behind him and starting in the same direction.

It was the woman he had seen by the makeup counter, the attractive one who seemed so tentative and unsure. He smiled, made a polite shrugging motion, pointed. She understood immediately, and while she kept glancing back over her shoulder as if still hoping for a space at the counter, she followed him to the booth.

The table was wet with spilled coffee and a glaze of old butter, but Larkin planted his elbows down anyway. "Another American institution bites the dust," he said, as pleasantly as he could.

The woman smiled thinly without fully turning, seemed by this gesture to be deliberately giving him time to read her face. She was pretty, or had been, and there were enough freckles across the high part of her cheeks that he could picture her having once been a blonde. She was dressed in corduroy slacks and a coarse woolen sweater; there were no rings on her fingers, and the only kind of ornamentation she wore was a security pass looped around her neck on a nylon cord, so she must have been from one of the labs out on the highway or maybe the college.

He wasn't very good at guessing ages—people his own age he always assumed were older—and yet she must have been well up in her fifties. She looked like someone who had been lucky early in life, but maybe wasn't so lucky now, though it was hard to isolate where in her looks this sense came from, other than the preoccupied way she kept glancing back toward the counter.

"I don't think they'll wait on us," Larkin said, trying to put her at ease.

She brought her chin down. "Who?"

"They seem to be on strike."

"The waitresses?" She thought for a moment. "It's a hard life."

He pointed toward the napkin holder, the little square it formed with the condiments. "Maybe we could eat ketchup?"

He meant it as a joke, but the effect was exactly the opposite—the woman winced, screwed her mouth up in an ugly gesture that seemed totally at variance with her appearance.

He tried again. "Did you used to come here when you were little?"

"Yes," she said, nodding. "No, not here. Another one, but very distant."

Her voice was slow and lightly decorated, the o's open like someone from Maryland, only lazier, remoter. How distant did she mean?

"I started coming here when I was three or four," Larkin said. "It was the great thing for families like mine, to come to the five-and-dime, only I never called it that; I always called it the fiver-and-dimer, and my mother used to laugh every time I said it. The fiver-and-dimer?"

He expected at least a smile, but the woman stared again at the counter, and this time he noticed her pressing her fingernails into her palms.

"It was forbidden, but I loved sitting at the counter alone," he continued, putting more insistence into his words in an effort to make her face him. "It was the great thing, to be swiveling up there alone like a man. I remember once I got up the nerve to sneak away from my mother—she was over in notions—and I climbed up all by myself and held the menu up to my nose like a mask. 'What will it be, Buster Brown?' the waitress said, coming over. I ordered an egg sandwich, I think it was. I ate half before my mother found me. I don't really remember what happened, but she must have been mad. I think we went home after that."

The story fizzled out before he wanted it to. He was trying to think of a better one when the woman brushed her hand across her mouth, as if what she had to say was so light and inconsequential she merely wanted to be rid of it.

"Do you shop here often?"

It sounded like a pickup line—was that her intention? Her breasts were strong against her sweater. "Sometimes," Larkin said cautiously. "Not lately. My wife likes using the computer to shop. It saves gas you know. It—"

He glanced up, saw irony corner up her eyes, felt suddenly defeated. "We buy too much crap," he said sourly. He wished he hadn't sat down with her, began rehearsing the words of an excuse to leave.

"I wasn't going to come in," the woman said quietly. "Not all the way. I said to myself, I'll go and just look in the window, but then the snow came down harder and I could feel it pushing me in."

Larkin vigorously nodded. "We're supposed to get six inches."

"And that's funny, because what I remember most of all was how hot it always was. You could fry an egg on the pavement, and that wasn't just an expression because I saw Dowd Carpenter do that once right outside the Baptist church as a joke. That's one of the reasons we used to go there. To the store I mean. The ceiling was high and they had fans and when the sun came up above the other side of Main Street they would pull muslin curtains across the window so it was cool and dark like a cave."

"Where was this?" Larkin asked.

She didn't answer, not directly, and when she did start talking again the words seemed addressed more to the store than to him—he could feel them slip past his face toward the lunch counter and the waitresses hunched there over their coffees.

"All we ever thought about was boys, of course. I couldn't be a cheerleader because my voice was too soft, so they made me a twirlette, and twirlettes were only allowed to date boys on the offensive line. All right, I decided. If that's the way it is, I'll choose the center, and he was Dowd Carpenter. I used to go to the store every day after twirling practice, not to meet him because he was always at football, but to buy lipstick and nail polish and everything I could find to make myself into the kind of girl he would like."

She grimaced, applying the irony to herself this time. "And as hot as it always was, that afternoon was even hotter. The thermometer outside city hall was a whole inch above 100. I remember stopping at the colored fountain I was so thirsty."

She hesitated, as if to make sure he understood. "Sure, the colored fountain," he said, and for a ludicrous moment he pictured a spigot that was blue.

"I stopped there," she said, "but it didn't work, so I kept on to the store promising myself an ice cream soda once I got there. It was crowded more than usual, I noticed that right off. Dowd Carpenter was there with the other boys from the offensive line, and that confused me, to see them when they should have been at practice. I don't think they noticed me—they were near the lunch counter under the Coke sign. I walked back to the coolest part of the store where they had lipstick, and I was trying some on the inside of my wrist, stroking the colors next to each other to compare them, and all I could think about was how Dowd Carpenter was right over there by the lunch counter in person and what was I going to say to him if he came over?"

"Dowd's a funny name," Larkin said. "Southern good ol' boy, right?"

"And my uncle was there too, Uncle Tobias. He was police chief in town, a gentle man. 'What you doing here, hon?' he said, teasing me like he always did. 'You go on home now, will you?' His deputies stood right behind him acting nervous and tense, and almost immediately all three of them drifted on away. There was some noise after that. I was suddenly all alone in the back of the store and that got me feeling lonely and tired of waiting for Dowd Carpenter to come and talk to me so I decided I'd go up to him and say hello first."

Her eyes went to the lunch counter, as if directing his to

follow. He noticed it was difficult for her to apply the word *I* to the teenager in her story—that it was something unnatural she had to force. She talked differently too, more in a monotone, so he found it harder to listen the longer she went on. Sexist morons, small town dreams—well, it would be his turn soon to tell his own story, and while he tried to give the appearance of listening attentively, he was making a list of things he planned to tell her about, from Old Spice to notions.

"He was over by the lunch counter with the other football players. There were some older boys too, out of high school, and some men. A velvet rope hung between stanchions like in a fancy restaurant, and they were pressed up right against it, their shoulders touching, so it was like a beefy wall, Dowd right there in the center like he should be. They all wore madras shirts—they were new then and everyone was mad to have one. I pressed up close to see past. There were fourteen stools at the lunch counter and sitting on them were twelve colored boys and two colored girls. They were all well dressed like they were going to church, and they sat there without moving like they were praying. The waitresses stood back against the malt machines, kind of smirking but looking unsure of what to do next. They were little more than kids, the Negro boys. College age, but maybe not even that old. I was so dumb it took me a long time to realize that what they were doing there was waiting to be served."

Some forward motion, some trick of light, brought her ID into focus now. *Katherine Bowen* was her name. The picture was of a much younger woman, and it was hard to reconcile it with the intense concentration on the woman's face.

"It was quiet at first, but then suddenly everyone started

yelling, the football players loudest. They pushed right up to the stools so they stood right behind the boys, and they were doing things like leaning over to bark in their ears, or spraying soda fizz on their necks, or poking their ribs with rolled up magazines. I got caught up in it, the yelling. Here they were keeping me off cheerleaders because I couldn't yell, and so here I tried proving I could yell louder than any of them. I screamed the same word they screamed at the top of my lungs, only the word didn't make any sense to me; it was just something we were chanting, and all I could think about was trying to prove myself to Dowd."

Larkin tapped his finger on the table. "What year was this?" he demanded, but the Katherine woman didn't hear him, closed her eyes to focus tighter.

"I was forced away from the end of the counter, but I pressed forward until I stood directly behind the last stool. A girl sat there. She had on a black dress and it made her skin even darker. She sensed me there—I could tell from the way her shoulder dipped, like she was fighting down the urge to swivel around and face me. It was different, being right up next to her, at least at first. I thought, well, I'll shelter her, prove I mean no harm, but the yelling got even louder then; more people were crowding in from the street, and the heat was like a wave of pressure against my forehead, and I couldn't hold it off. I stood right behind her—her head came up to my chest because she was sitting, so I was looking directly down at her hair. It made me mad, her hair did, the way it so passively lay there. It made me mad because it wasn't long like mine, but short and curly and coarse, and it wasn't bleached like mine, wasn't yellow the way the boys liked. It made me mad she didn't sense my trying to shelter her. There was a little space between where she sat and the boy on the next stool, and I reached forward between them, grabbed the ketchup on the counter, brought it back again, pulled the cap off, turned it upside down and started shaking it on her hair."

Her eyes, rigidly on the lunch counter, moved until they found the ketchup bottle there on the table. He saw it too, made to jerk his hands back, then forced them to remain where they were.

"She didn't move, though I was pouring ketchup on her. She sat on the stool facing forward, holding hands with the boys on either side of her, and all she did was bend her head down like she was praying."

Her voice trailed off—her eyes came away from the ketchup and met his directly for the first time since she had sat down. *My turn* he said to himself, *my turn*, and even as he thought this, he could feel the intense expectancy in her, her need for him to say exactly the right thing in response.

He cleared his throat, made a little clutching motion. "That was a long time ago," he said, ". . . a *long* time ago."

And her expression did change with that, went from expectancy and need to a look of complete and utter scorn. She got up quickly, walked past the lunch counter, past the cash registers, past the grinning manager holding up the *Closed* sign, and without glancing back, disappeared out the door into the grainy black and white blur of the street.

"A long time ago," Larkin mumbled.

Five now. The manager had a little bell and he stood there ringing it, so even the waitresses finally climbed down from their stools and began gathering their belongings to leave.

Larkin, in following them out, had to pass a last aisle of merchandise, what sad, unbought remnants were left. It was canary food and aspirin, the cardboard boxes and cellophane-wrapped bells jumbled together in a sloppy pyramid. Canary food and aspirin, aspirin and canary food. What a pity, he thought, staring down at them. What a shame.

Hills Like White Hills

ANYTHING HIGH might have taken his son. Transmission lines, a cell phone tower, trees. Crows even, migrating geese, though it had been late in the year for geese. Ordinary phone lines for that matter, a church steeple, a bullet sent skyward by a disappointed hunter or a bored kid. Something high had taken him, and so over the course of the year Anderson had become adept at driving with his eyes toward the ground. Pavement, shoulders, roadside grass. This was the flat, expansive safety his son never found, and it seemed that if he concentrated on it steadily enough, kept himself from glancing higher, things might be reversed.

It was harder in these hills. Almost certainly it had been a hill that had done the killing. They rose above the road, pinching in the highway, waiting every time his eyes moved toward the shaded part of the windshield with its matching crescents of frost. Two days before Christmas, this early in the morning, there weren't many cars, and yet negotiating the curves required him to look up and look up often, his own safety at stake. Safety? It made him smile, thinking in those terms. Mission was the better word. He had one last mission left to perform, and then he would be done with safety as a notion that ever need concern him again.

The hills became higher and whiter once he turned north onto the secondary road marked on the directions. He remembered twenty years before bringing Tom up to camp through similar hills, and how they had played the game of trying to make each mountain into a familiar shape. A llama, a roller coaster, an elephant. He remembered—and felt, not the sadness he might have expected, but a weary kind of disgust. Good times to mock the bad ones, life's easy and bitter trick. The hills that confronted him out the windshield refused to be anything but stark white hills, and the deeper he drove into them, the more their literalness seemed to matter, matter hard.

The search had come east, but not this far. Those in charge had drawn compass lines every direction from the airport a distance of sixty miles; where those lines intersected hills above 2,500 feet, the lines had stopped. The hills on his right were that high and more. No one, flying in the fog they had experienced last Christmas Eve, could hope to get past them. The search had been inside the tighter circle, but the search found nothing, the leaves had come back on the trees and then dropped again, hunting season had gone by without anyone spotting anything, and the snow took the woods for a second winter, blotting out with its whiteness the whiteness of the airplane.

And now this man, this Mr. Ayers, with his telephone message and letter, the carefully penciled directions to his store. A woman he knew had heard a plane last Christmas Eve low in the hills. Another person in town, an ice fisherman, had seen a flash in the trees, and if you drew a line east from the airport into New Hampshire, there was a gap through the hills it might just be possible for a plane to have entered before the hills joined ridges and closed back in.

Anderson knew it was a slim hope at best, but this was what he was down to as the anniversary date drew near—following through on every sighting, every rumor, every vague impulse his son's plane had left in people's wondering. If he worried about Mr. Ayers, it wasn't about his being wrong, but about his being a crank. So far he had managed to avoid these, the ones who divined Tom's whereabouts through astrology or dowsing rods or home computers. It would have been intolerable, meeting one of these, listening to them babble on.

Mr. Ayers, from their brief conversation, did not seem like a crank. So it was worth the long drive north, meeting him, listening to his theory, trying once again to find closure. It was the word everyone used in justifying the time and expense that had gone into the search. *We need a finish to this*, the state police said, the fish and game people, the aviation experts sent by the government. *We need closure*, and he had heard the word so many times, pronounced it so often in various appeals of his own, it seemed to have become part of him, a stencil over his heart. When he imagined his son's final seconds, it was always the rushing vertigo, the blinding forwardness, the shoulder straps tightening, straining, snapping—but try as he would, summon up all of his courage, he could never get past that moment, imagine impact, not unless he knew for certain where that impact had happened.

At first the country had been familiar to him from fishing trips, foliage drives when Alice was alive and they had gone north for long weekends, but this changed at the next turn in the directions, and he drove through a leaner, sparer kind of land, the hills leaving only a narrow strip into which were pressed a river, the road, and a few scattered farms. All were abandoned, their yards empty and scraped clean—survivors of everything the last century had thrown at them, only to succumb in the first moment of the new one to forces he could only guess at. The houses came thicker as he neared the village. Fifties-style most of them, erected back in the days when everyone dreamed of the suburban life, weathering horribly now, beyond rescue by paint or carpentry or TLC. Most had some attempt at decoration—a plastic wreath, a string of lights—but they looked like neglected leftovers from earlier years, and it made it seem as though Christmas was a much darker kind of celebration here, something that spoke of sternness and not joy.

The last turn mentioned in the directions came at a rectangular green sign: *Ayers Store 3 Miles.* Almost immediately he passed an obstacle he hadn't thought about before, a rusty steel windmill poking well above the ridgeline, dark vines twisted all the way to the top. He winced, brought his head down, felt again the rushing sensation in his chest. The village, when he arrived, was a grouping of six or seven old houses around the white patch of a common that sloped downhill, with the store and its gas pumps set against the higher end, a small yellow church against the lower.

The store itself was as old as any of the houses; asphalt shingles covered the sides, but the pumps and sign looked new, suggesting a recent infusion of energy and cash. Anderson had no illusions about the current state of country stores, and so the inside was pretty much as he expected. The salty things in one row, the sugary things in the other; the beer in a cooler along the back wall; the lottery tickets there by the register with the nicotine. A stout man wearing an apron was ringing up a customer, and so Anderson waited his turn, standing by the shelf with the candy kisses and M&Ms, all done up in holiday packaging, so it was by far the brightest corner in the store.

"Mr. Ayers?" he said, when the customer had gone. "I'm Tom Anderson. Tom senior."

There was a pause long and surprised enough for Anderson to worry he had made a mistake, and then the man smiled, nodded, rubbed his hands down his apron and stuck one out.

"An honor, sir. A real honor and pleasure."

He was a man in his early fifties, with the kind of stocky good health that made Anderson think of a butcher from the old neighborhood, with the same square and delicate hands. He pulled his apron off, went over to the door, pulled the *Closed* sign down, then came back, the eagerness having burst from his eyes over the rest of his face, making it shine.

"Didn't think you'd come, you know, when we talked and all. But it's like you said there on TV. You were willing to follow the slightest lead and so that's why I wrote that letter, got in touch."

There was a lot of New York in his voice, the inflection and speed. "The city?" he said, when Anderson asked him about it. "Oh yeah, way back when. Up here they thought I was a rapist or something when we first moved in. Now? New Hampshire all the way. Snowmobiles, ATVs, skiing. Hey, this is kid stuff.

Lived in Alaska for a winter, worked on the pipeline saving up money for a place like this. But that's what got me when I saw you talking about how your son wanted to be a bush pilot in Alaska someday, how that's what he was working toward. I could relate to that right off the bat."

Anderson was used to this now, the eager way people approached the puzzle of his son's loss. There was a time when it seemed everyone was looking for the plane, then a time when no one was, and now a hard-core group had taken over, the police scanner boys, the ones who always kept rescue gear loaded in the back of their trucks. It was another reason he had come north again—to head them off, throw a solution at them before things got out of hand. He didn't want Tom's disappearance to go into the next stage, become an unsolved mystery, written up in anniversary articles when the rest of the news was thin, fodder for hacks. Literalness was what he wanted, answers. Hills like white hills. Death like sudden death.

Ayers kept talking as they walked out to his pickup. Ice coated the windshield, and by the time the defroster got going they were already pulling over to the side of the road to an overlook, a wide one. Below them the river wound like a flat shoelace between dark pockets of pine, but in every other direction the terrain was high and blocky looking, the hills so tightly merged it was as if they had been towed there and dumped.

Ayers slapped his hand on the dashboard, then turned sideways in the seat. "Just want to get my facts straight, follow my train of reasoning. Sound good?"

"Sounds good."

"Your son was in a hurry, right? I mean no offense, but he was in a hurry. Rented a car to drive to Vermont, where he was assigned to take a Learjet home to Providence for this rich guy, right? A ferry job, straight and simple. But it's Christmas Eve, right? A foggy day, not so hot for flying, but he's young, he's just started the job, and he's crazy about Lears." He hesitated, reached over for the coffee. "A girlfriend, right?"

"Fiancée. Her name is Caroline."

"Right. So he's in a hurry on account of Caroline. He doesn't fly the direction all those morons from the FAA think. Doesn't follow the river or the interstate or anything obvious. He's really sure of himself, a pilot who knows he's good. So he takes a shortcut across the hills. Okay, that's nearly impossible it was so foggy, even flying on instruments. But there's a gap, you look at the map and there's a gap. Maybe he knows about it and maybe he doesn't, but that gap is five miles west of here, and it leads to only one place." He tapped his knuckles against the windshield. "Those mountains out there. They go a thousand feet up in the course of two ridges. Looming up at him like a wall, a complete dead end."

Anderson listened carefully, keeping his hands around his coffee, very aware of how prim and weak they must look there, cup and hands, motionless on his knee.

"You said on the phone a man had seen something," he said, with less impatience in his tone than he actually felt.

Ayers turned back from the window and nodded. "Bernie Beliveau. He was out ice fishing on Sanderson Pond. Right about—" he leaned forward, "down there. A little deaf, Bernie is, but there's nothing wrong with his seeing. He noticed a flash, something bright enough to make him blink. This would have been 2:30 or so—he didn't have a watch. But it squares with the flight time."

"Has anyone checked it out?"

"Snowmobile club. They haven't found anything, not yet. The ice was pretty thin in some spots. Could have plunged right through down to the bottom."

"Can I talk to him?"

"He's out of town. Quebec, his wife's family for Christmas. Wouldn't you know it. Just when you arrive."

"There's also this woman you spoke of. The one who heard something."

Ayers nodded, vigorously this time. "Sarah Hall. Yeah, that's what I was going to do actually. Drive us out there so you can hear for yourself."

He backed them up, skidded on the snow, then turned down a dirt road that sloped toward the river. It was a short drive—just long enough for Ayers to go over the basics. Sarah was a great old gal, he said. Almost eighty-six now and sharp as a tack. A tough life of course. Born when the hills were emptying out, little money around, meager prospects, not much hope. Lived with her parents long past being a girl, having the care of them when they got sick, running the farm alone, parents dying just after V-J Day, then she got polio, so she wasn't any freer than before. One brother a bum. Niece she loved, took care of, but then the niece went bad too, moved west with a slick, handsome liar, broke Sarah's heart. Lives alone now, helped by a friend or two from church. The last of her kind really. Last one wedded so tightly to the hills.

"My wife's gotten to know her better than me," Ayers said, both hands on the wheel now, the road turning bumpy. "She's a visiting nurse, comes out here once a week minimum. She's the one heard the story about what happened Christmas Eve. It's a little vague, but I think there's something to it. Sarah's not crazy or anything, even living alone for so long. She never makes anything up."

Anderson nodded, trying not to let his skepticism show. He had learned a long time ago that hope had nothing to do with his mission, which was to follow every thread, every possible lead, until it gave out. And that's what he pictured strung along the road ahead of them—a gray, all but invisible thread, in tatters, separating, so when they bounced over a narrow log bridge, turned left on a one-lane road under a hoop of bare trees, it was as if they were following the wispiest corner of the wispiest end of the wispiest strand hope ever spun.

They stopped and got out beside an old Cape farmhouse that was easily two hundred years old. It had no charm, no quaintness. Adjoining it, connected, was a barn that had collapsed long enough ago that a large maple grew out of the wreckage. The house seemed on its way to collapsing as well—the roof was moss covered, hardly distinct from the grassy bluff its eaves nearly touched, and where the peak should be was a mushy sag of rotted shingles.

Ayers tried the door, peered into its window. Behind the house was a large field, the uncut hay sticking up through the snow in slender, flesh-colored bristles. It was flat enough to land a plane on—Anderson recognized this immediately. The pilot would have had to be extraordinarily lucky or extraordinarily skilled, because where the field ended, with no intermission, rose a hill, high and abrupt enough it blotted out the sun.

Ayers waved him over. "Let's just go in."

It took a few minutes for Anderson's eyes to grow used to the dark. The hall they entered was decorated with sentimental old paintings in rough-hewn frames, the kind itinerant painters had once turned out for a night's room and board. Adjoining this was a neatly furnished parlor, dominated by a woodstove so ornate it looked Arabian, and past this a kind of enclosed porch, which by some magic of positioning had gathered unto itself what sunlight managed to filter down from the clouds. The furniture was plainer here, a deacon's bench and maple rocker, and there was a regular gallery of snapshots taped to the wall, pictures of animals, farms, and fairs, the most recent of which looked to have been taken fifty years before.

It was what was in the center of the room that surprised him most: a Christmas tree, and not a small one either, reaching all the way to the ceiling, decorated with paper chains and heavy tinsel. It was fresh enough that the spruce smell was strong and bracing, and yet not so overpowering it could hide another smell he had caught when he first came in. Almond or almond extract, a warm smell, the kind that comes with baking.

Ayers tiptoed and peered around like he expected to find her dead. "Miss Hall? It's Don Ayers, Janet's husband? You know, from Ayers's store?"

No one answered. Ayers had turned to go back into the parlor when Anderson put his hand on his arm and nodded toward the one corner the tree did not completely hide. Sitting there in an old wicker wheelchair was a woman who seemed, in that first glance, little more than a forgotten gathering of wrinkles, with eyes that floated above the collection and calmly regarded it.

Ayers put his hand over his heart. "There you are!"

He went over to the window, pushed the shades up, let in more light. Anderson could see her quite plainly now. Her legs were covered by a plaid wool throw, and her chest was hidden by pillows she clutched as a child would stuffed animals, and yet somehow he got the impression of great strength, or at least strength's shadow. Again, this came mostly from her eyes, which regarded them both in the same calm, even way they regarded her frailty. Her glance moved from Ayers's face onto Anderson's, lingered there, then she brought her hand up to locate her forehead, take a girlish swipe at a trace of white hair.

"Yes, come in," she said, or something like that.

Anderson, wondering how to approach her, took his cue from the house itself, the air of quiet that had been bundled up and secreted away. Ayers didn't sense this and squatted down beside her wheelchair, talking far too loud.

"This is Mr. Anderson come up here all the way from the city just to talk to you. He's lost his son, in an accident. I want you to tell him what you told Janet, just the same way."

"Crows," she said, or something like that. "Watching them, looking for corn out on the meadow before you came. No corn there in thirty years. Joke on them."

"Last Christmas Eve," Ayers said, obviously not understanding a word. "You know, the story you told Janet about what happened Christmas Eve."

She smiled, like she had him. "Christmas Eve is tomorrow."

"*Last* Christmas Eve. What happened then."

Too abrupt of him, not the way it was done, a story on demand for visitors who had likely not eaten. Her reaction was plain enough. She tried to get up, move toward the almond smell, but the blanket was too heavy, and she settled back into the chair with a disdainful, impotent wave of her hand. When she started her story it seemed out of frustration more than anything—that being so weak there was no power open to her other than what she could generate with words.

It was hard understanding her, the odd cadence of her voice. It wasn't just the old hill country accent, the divvying of syllables, but the way she blended the end of one word into the beginning of the next—musically, but a music that had been played so often, for so many years, it had lost all variation in pitch, came out as the kind of hoarse, undifferentiated sound a piano would make if all the middle keys were pressed simultaneously. The deeper she got into her story, the harder Anderson stared trying to concentrate, catching up with her only in the pauses, translating to himself before looking over toward Ayers and translating out loud.

It had been a miserable Christmas Eve. Snowy fog, ground wet, the air too warm for December. Remembered feeling blue herself. The field behind the barn, going out to let the cows in from the river. Dumb old cows. Good-for-nothing old cows. She'd taken to hating them, the only creatures she saw most days, what with no one coming anymore to visit. Leaving the radio on back in the house, loud as possible, gave her some company. Lying awake at night listening to the trains heading south, wishing she were going that way herself. That lonely rumble it put into the air. Nice sound. Thing of the past. Billy Sykes worked on the railroad. His mother was cousin to her mother, though they never saw either one of them after the fire.

Anderson listened, managed to stay with her even in the tangents, but only with great effort. He stared at the firm line of her lips, the one place the wrinkles successfully fought back, trying to get help from the way they shaped and decorated each word. Old age had always been something remote to him, a land glimpsed from a safe distance, but he was close enough now that it concerned him intensely, the hoarse croaking it put into a voice, the way even simple stories had to flutter back and forth before emerging. He must learn all this, prepare himself, before he was tossed beat and ragged on the same hard shore.

"Fast for you?" she asked, aware now of his attention, anxious to keep it. He shook his head, waited for her to go on.

It was about two or so, past lunchtime, when she stopped and looked up. It wasn't a sound, not at first, so much as a slight wavy pressure on the back of her neck. What's this? she wondered, turning around. Still nothing. But then from up back of Job's Hill came a raspy coughing sound like the generator made just before conking out. She bent her head back, shaded her eyes to peer. It didn't bore in or race away like most sounds did that reached the farm, but looped around in a tight circle, echoing, like the hills were playing a game with whatever the sound came from, tossing it back and forth between summits just for fun.

She knew what it was then. Airplane. She'd heard airplanes before—at the fairs, and then once in the city where she'd taken her mother when she first got sick. Knew it was in trouble too. She couldn't see anything because of the fog, but she could hear clear enough. A snapping, sputtering sound, but weak and troubled, so she wanted to put her hands under it somehow, boost it back up over the hills to where it belonged.

Anderson was so engrossed in isolating the words that he didn't pay much attention to the thrust of what she was saying, not at first. He trusted Ayers to pay attention for both of them, but Ayers was shaking his head now, frowning in confusion.

"What year was this, Miss Hall?"

She pulled the corner of her mouth down, stared off toward the Christmas tree, widened her eyes.

"Cows," Ayers said, glancing over at him. "Come on. When was the last time they had any cows here?"

"My parents were away," Sarah said, with a look that managed to be coy and beseeching at the same time, as if she knew a secret and wanted help getting it out.

"What year, Miss Hall?"

"Roosevelt year."

"Roosevelt?"

"Whipped Hoover. Whipped him bad. Father cried."

Ayers put his hand against his forehead. "Oh my sweet Jesus," he whispered. "Nineteen goddamn thirty-two."

Anderson had seen that look too many times not to recognize it instantly. On state police captains putting down the telephone with a grimace of disappointment, pilots climbing down from their search planes, shrugging, turning their thumbs down, volunteers slogging back out of the woods exhausted after another long day with no trace. The look of hope hitting a wall. He was surprised at how disappointed he felt himself, having been so careful. Grasping at threads and here he was grasping one all right, the withered rotten end.

Ayers, not daring to meet Anderson's eyes, went over to the wheelchair and knelt down. "Thank you for your time, Miss

Hall. Janet will look in on you tonight; that's what she promised me. You need anything from the store you call and I'll see she brings it. You have yourself a nice Christmas, okay?"

Sarah fussed the blanket closer to her chin, looked over at Anderson with a peculiar kind of curiosity—making an appeal, though he had no idea what it could be for. Mumbling his own thanks, doing his best to smile at her, he followed Ayers back outside to the truck.

Neither one said anything at first. The truck bounced off the dirt onto pavement, and it was only the heavy jolt of it that made talk possible.

"I'm sorry, Mr. Anderson," Ayers said. "I should have gone out and checked on the story myself. Hey, it sounded good, what I heard from my wife. Sarah's pretty sharp, you'll agree on that."

And Anderson was used to this too, comforting people who had tried comforting him. "That's all right. No, I enjoyed meeting her. It wasn't your fault."

He knew them too well, what words he should mumble. Always before they had been sincere, but whether because of being tired after the long drive, the anniversary rolling around in another day, he felt irritated with Ayers, anxious to be done with him, and it took a real effort to keep this from infecting his tone.

He came into the store before leaving. Ayers was off on a new tack, promising to have Beliveau call him when he got back, talking about organizing a search party once the holidays were over. He pressed a list of telephone numbers into Anderson's coat pocket, insisted they stay in touch. Anderson bought a coffee for the drive, hesitated, then went to the shelf that held candy and bought a box of marzipan fruit, the most elaborately decorated box in the store.

He had been daydreaming earlier, not paying attention, but the tread marks left by Ayers's truck were still easy to make out in the snow. He parked by the collapsed barn, followed their footprints, knocked on the door, and went in. As before, he was struck by the almond scent, the warmth of baking, and this time he investigated, searching the small box of a kitchen for its source. There was a blackened teapot on the stove, a saucepan of water, but the oven below it was cold and lifeless. Even the counter, the old maple cutting boards—they were smooth and clean, with no dusting of flour. Whatever was wafting to him had its origin in the past, a memory of Christmas so remote he couldn't locate it for certain, and it amazed him, to think something so forgotten could still be so strong.

He went in toward the parlor, expecting to find her still in her wheelchair. She must have heard his car, because she was up now, walking in from the sunroom, her right leg dragging behind her in a separate, jerkier rhythm, but otherwise moving with surprising litheness and strength. She nodded, seeing him. "Knew it," she mumbled, or something like that, then waved him with a little curtseying motion over toward the couch.

"This is for you," he said.

She took the package, smiled politely, then smiled for real, her hands going down to fumble with the wrapping until she had it apart. A greedy child—that's what he thought of—or maybe a child who wasn't used to presents, and so couldn't help tearing right in. She unhinged the box, held it up to her face to peek inside, put two fingers in, pulled out a marzipan cherry, held it up to the light.

"For you," he said again. She shook her head, held the candy up to her mouth, made a gumming kind of motion. *Not without teeth*—she pantomimed this perfectly. It was his turn to smile now, but she must have been concerned about hurting his feelings, because she very daintily took each candy from its compartment and lined them up on the windowsill—pink apple, yellow peach, pink banana, their colors brightening the entire room.

When she came back she sat beside him on the sofa, sank in just far enough that her shoulder came against his and nestled to a stop. On the end table were some religious pamphlets, and she handed him one—whether as a gift of her own or because of his loss, he wasn't sure. He regarded it for a decent few minutes, turned a few pages, closed it again, then pointed behind them toward the window.

"What happened next?"

He was sure no one had ever asked her that before, to finish a story. She smiled like he had given her another gift, one she could take her time with. Oh that's a wonderful story she said, in the same blur of syllables. Whether it was because he was alone with her now or because he had grown used to their rhythm, the words seemed much clearer this time and he had no trouble keeping up.

For a while she had thought the buzzing sound was gone, and she felt sad about that, without knowing why. But it came back again, just as she was turning toward the house to finish her chores. This time it was so loud she covered her ears, like a motorcycle was racing down from the sky. It's going to crash—she was sure of this—but then the air suddenly went softer, and she spun around trying to locate the feathery little whisper that had taken the roar's place.

She saw it now, back on the far side of the field and maybe a hundred feet above it, dropping as smoothly and uniformly as could be imagined, so it was less like an airplane landing on the meadow than it was the meadow going up to meet the airplane. There's too much snow, she decided, suddenly alarmed, but then the wheels were kicking through the crust, sending up a wake that crested over the wings and dusted them in powder. The motor came on again and deepened; the black propeller spun madly and slowed, and then the plane was landing on the far end of the field near the apple trees, skidding around and starting back, coming to a stop not ten yards from where she stood watching, clutching her hat.

A little two-seater, smaller even than the planes she had seen at fairs. The fabric on the wings was painted yellow, stretched so tight it glistened even in the grayness, and there was a big number 7 painted on the tail in scarlet-colored shellac that still looked wet. The nose rose much higher than the tail, so it was hard to see anything more than this, but then from the rear seat there was a smooth kind of lifting motion, a leather cap emerging, then a leather jacket, then an actual shape, boosting itself free of the seat's skirted rim, jumping out onto the wing, vaulting down.

"Whew!" the pilot said, wiping his hand in an exaggerated gesture across his forehead. He pointed toward the steep hill at the end of the field, tugged his cap off, and laughed.

She knew at once he was the handsomest man she had ever seen, or handsomest boy. He was her age—she knew that too, right down to the year and season, or how else to explain the instinctive sympathy she felt at once? Between the blond hair that blew down from his cap, the easy good humor of his expression, his flawless, suntanned skin, he was exactly what you would expect to emerge from such a machine. What's more, he seemed to know this, seemed to take an active, innocent pleasure in being so perfectly wedded to the power and grace he controlled.

"What's your name?" he asked, tilting his head as if to see right past her shyness, put all that aside.

She told him and he nodded. "Well Sarah, that little mountain of yours almost did for me. A close shave! Great fun, did you hear me gunning it?" He followed her eyes. "Curtis Scout, a beauty. War surplus, but I fixed it up brand-new. Flying the mail, started yesterday, Burlington to Boston, and I thought I knew the shortcuts, but looks like I thought wrong. You're an awfully pretty girl, know that? No, I guess you don't. Not living out here you wouldn't. I guess I've got to be going, what a shame."

Her face burned, but she met his look without turning away, feeling as if something very important rested on doing this. The pilot pulled his cap on, pushed his cowlick to tuck it under, started toward the wing, then suddenly turned back to her and smiled.

"Ever been up?"

She shook her head.

"Want to?"

She shook her head again.

"Aw, come on. It doesn't hurt. It's clearing up now; you'll be surprised at what it's like."

She didn't know which meant more to her, staring up at the plane or staring at him, but that didn't matter because it was all the same, pilot and airplane, and he must have sensed this in her, knew all along what she was going to say. His words caused a lifting sensation through her entire body, a warmth surging from her toes toward her waist; it was no use struggling, though she did one last time.

"Too many hills," she said softly, teasing him, marveling at being able to tease.

The pilot glanced over the field and squinted. "That puny little thing? Hills thrills! Here, I've got some extra duds in the cockpit. You can sit in front. Up ten minutes, some quick sightseeing, then I'll bring you down again, I promise."

He cupped his hands, boosted her up onto the wing. Inside the cockpit was a leather flying jacket like the one he wore, only newer, and he held it for her while she put it on, then handed her some goggles that turned everything amber. The cockpit itself was tight as a glove, though open on top. He showed her how to fasten the shoulder belts, told her to make sure to grab hold of the bar on the side if he did any fancy stuff, then, after looking at her carefully, breaking into the widest grin yet, scooted around and lowered himself into the pilot's seat a foot or two behind hers.

"Let me know if you get scared!" he shouted, and then everything became lost in the sudden roar of the engine, the propeller's kick, reversal, and whir, the clean, light smell of camphor that streamed back from the pistons and made her dizzy.

He bumped the plane out to the middle of the field, gunned the engine, started out. She had never gone this fast on land before, let alone the sky, and the speed pressed against her breasts, making her even giddier than the camphor, even more than the rush of stone walls and hemlocks that seemed suddenly to have become liquid. *Too fast*, she decided, wanting to scream and laugh both, and then the motion slowed and vanished, the pressure moved off her breasts toward her shoulders, and she realized with an overpowering sensation of delight that what she had heard about, read about, seen in the distance was actually happening—that they were airborne, in the air, *flying*.

She didn't have time to be scared, though she should have been. He had taken off away from the steepest hill, but there were plenty of hills in this direction too. She couldn't see any, not with the haze, but he must have—either that or maybe he didn't care a fig for things like mountains and ridges, thumbed his nose at them, trusted to luck. They banked around and around and ever upward until they were at the top edge of the mist, the last wet tatters streaming against the fuselage, the propeller whirring free of it into sunshine, into a world that had been above her every livelong day of her life, but which she had no conception of, not until now.

They were above the clouds, above every hill and mountain, so there was nothing to be seen except endless white beneath them, endless blue straight above. Never had she dreamed of such flatness and expanse. She knew the word *horizontal*, had learned it in school, but she realized now there had been nothing in her world to demonstrate that property, not when compared to this. Endless—every which way was endless, without walls. As they turned into the sun she had to shut her eyes, even under the goggles, the gold flaring out the white and blue, shredding them into ribbons. Behind her the pilot was banging on the fuselage, shouting something she couldn't hear. *Hold on?* She was already holding on, she couldn't hold on tighter, never in her life had she held anything so tight, the pressure moving back on her chest again as he gunned the plane straight up toward the sun.

Just when it seemed the wings must break off from their throbbing, the plane leveled off—leveled off just long enough for her to feel on the back of her neck above the flying jacket a sensation that was cool and warm both, as if someone had kissed her. A second later she heard a happy laugh, even above the motor—a laugh, and so she knew it had been a kiss after all. The plane tipped over into a dive, powering right back toward the clouds it had with such effort escaped, touching the grayness, dipping into it like a kingfisher dipping into a pond, boring the happiness deep inside where no one could steal it out, then looping back up again to start the whole process over—the momentary leveling, the tender kiss on the back of her neck, the laugh, and then the diving back to the soft edge of clouds.

Four times he did this, five and then six. *Forever!* is what she wanted to shout, but on the seventh dive he kept the plane plunging down into the dampness. The motor began sputtering, they banked steeply to avoid something she couldn't see, banked a second time, then broke free into the transparent gray below the opaque layer—came level over the field, coasted, skipped once, set down.

She was shy, being down. The pilot jumped out of his seat and stripped off his goggles, then balanced his way over to help her onto the wing.

"That high enough for you? That's flying, Miss Sarah Hall. That's flying and you did fine."

It was strange, those next few minutes. He had been so dashing and confident before, but now he seemed sadder, being on the ground, standing next to her, neither of them knowing what to say. He looked over toward the house, up toward the sky, then directly at her—seemed trying to connect them all somehow, not sure how to go about it.

"I suppose you have lots of company, it being Christmas."

No, she told him. She wanted to laugh at his thinking that. Her mother and father were in town and she was alone.

The pilot stared at her, seemed trying to reach a decision. "Alone, huh? Oh boy. Nice warm fireplace too, I'll bet." He looked up and winced. "Won't have much time, real clouds now, not that flimsy stuff. Mail to deliver, all these Christmas letters folks are waiting for. Look, I've got to go before I get socked in solid. But I'll come back, understand that? No matter what happens, maybe sometime when you least expect it, I'll come back."

She wanted him to kiss her and not on the neck this time, but shyness still troubled them, and it wasn't until he was back in the cockpit that he seemed his laughing, exuberant self. "Thank you!" she yelled, over the motor, but she wasn't sure he heard. He taxied around to the edge of the field, following the tracks they had made in landing, then gave her a little wave before starting off, even faster and more abruptly than he had the first time, making her think of an arrow pulled back and back and back and suddenly released.

Nothing left but sound after that, the same lost echo as before. Hills had it, played with it, tossed it back and forth, let it go. Then? The snowy field at her feet with two long grooves down the middle. A bolt that had shaken loose from the plane, sharp end stuck in the crust. Standing there staring. Chores to do. Cows waiting. Dumb old stupid cows. Water to haul. Supper. Radio. Bed.

The entire time she talked, the pressure of her shoulder had been against Anderson's, but now, finishing, she sat more erect and the couch separated them into a formal, stiff position it was difficult to maintain. When he got up he got up gingerly, not wanting to do anything that would cause her to tip back toward the empty side. She had her eyes closed. He walked quietly toward the door, leaving his coat on the chair as a kind of pledge. *I'll come back soon.*

Outside, the gray wore a purple undertone, the preliminary to blackness, and the ground was far lighter than the sky. His shoes squeaked so loud on the snow it scared up a ring of crows pecking at brown apples near the barn. Past it he came out onto the field, or at least near its edge. It was long and rectangular, and it wasn't hard to picture a plane landing, even with the saplings and birch that now had possession of its center.

He took several steps more, then turned to face the steep hill on the north side, the hill her pilot had somehow avoided. It rose much blacker than any other part of the sky, though he could still see the scraggly outline of its trees, notice how they seemed like sutures holding the steepness together. Sutures, like sutures. He stood there a long time, enough for his feet to turn cold, his shoulders to start shaking. He felt the same rushing sensation he had felt all year, the hurtling through space, and he was flying in the center of it, everything falling past him, the sky down his throat, and this time he tried closing his eyes to it, closing them until they matted together in wetness, the shudder deepened, the cold and hardness entered him, turned him over, split him apart in an explosion of tree limbs, shattered him senseless on the rocks.

He opened his eyes. He ran his hands down his sides, blinked to find himself in the blackness, or at least whatever puny stuff the sensation hadn't bothered smashing. He saw Sarah Hall coming toward him across the snow, backlit by what light streamed from the house, limping horribly, punishing herself, but moving steadily on, a wool coat around her shoulders, his own coat borne on her outstretched arms like a king's precious robe. And it wasn't her weakness that he fixed on, not the whole of her, but what she was wearing on her feet—heavy galoshes, the black kind with buckles, the boots he had worn himself as a boy.

She came up to him, let the coat slide back toward her chest, reached toward his arm with a blindness he hadn't noticed indoors, the wrinkles in her cheeks tensing and puckering as if to take the place of eyes. She found his wrist first, then his sweater, the material by the elbow, bunching it, going higher, finally tightening on the old useless muscle of his arm.

Poor man! she said—not out loud, not even in a whisper, but by direct transmission through her hand.

They turned toward the only light visible. In its decay, in its sturdiness, the house looked like an ark set on a cradle of yellow slats. Tugging him after her, helping each other over the icy spots, they followed the openings her boots had plowed through the snow.

In the Maze

HALLOWEEN NIGHT the maze stays open until midnight, but so far no one's lasted past ten. They start off with fake shrieks, the teenage girls pulled along by their boyfriends, or the little kids holding hands with their moms. I hang plastic skeletons from the trees, carve jack-o-lanterns because that's what people expect, pin ghost sheets to the clothesline, and these are what get the screams going before they're even out of their cars.

"No one's ever been murdered here—" Margaret tells them when they buy their tickets. She has her witch costume on, with the horrible fake nose. "Not in the last century anyway." And then she cackles, or tries to, Margaret being the sweetest person for three towns around.

That scares everyone, the fun kind of scared, and they race each other over to the maze's entrance. But then later, getting lost, feeling squeezed by corn stalks that rub against each other with hungry scrapings, seeing the scraggly trees with their clawlike branches dipping toward them in the wind, they let out a scream, a real scream, and that's when I put the cash box under the cooler, close up the refreshment counter, start uphill to find them.

It's been a good night so far. No screamers I couldn't quickly rescue. On humid nights with mist it's easy to get lost in the maze, especially near the bottom where so many different paths diverge. We've sold eighty-seven tickets so far tonight, seven short of our record. There's not much trick-or-treating left in town, the new people who move in are reluctant to let their kids out after dark, so this seems a safe alternative.

"Where do we start?" they say, when you hand them their tickets.

"Right behind you there."

"Where?"

"Follow the gravel path, then turn left at the old tractor."

"Is that a spook house over there?"

"It's where my grandparents used to live."

"It should be a spook house, all those cracked windows. Right at the tractor you said?"

What's pulled in more this year is our contest. If you find your way through the maze to the top, you win a prize of five hundred dollars. Five hundred dollars to the first man, woman, or child who successfully navigates the lower maze, enters the upper maze where the twisting gets tighter, escapes from that to the top of the hill and the little New Hampshire flag planted between two rocks—finds the flag, brings it back to me at the cash register as proof.

One person's almost made it. He takes the search seriously,

he has a method, he's returned three times, so I was sure he would be the one who won. I thought he might come tonight, make one last attempt, but he has kids; he must be busy with them, and so that's that. Am I disappointed he hasn't come? Not particularly. The disappointment isn't any worse than it normally is, and that little hardening I used to feel, that cement settling around my heart, hasn't bothered me in years.

Scattered around the base of the maze, propped in the crook of trees, mounted on stumps are the jack-o-lanterns my third-grade art class spent all week carving. There are dozens of these, hundreds. Usually, when the last person leaves I go around blowing out every candle, but the dampness is doing it for me now, and the ones on the north side of the maze are barely smoldering. The faces were gap-toothed and silly when they were new, but the pumpkins quickly soften, blacken, and now they look scary in a way that's real. Leering monkeys, holding candles to their eye sockets, would look that way. I won't be sorry when the last one burns out.

I had closed up the refreshment counter, poured what was left of the hot cider onto the leaves, when there was a papery thrashing sound over by the maze's exit, as if a giant was beating the corn with a stick. It was laughable really, what a small shape finally emerged. Melissa Zack, who I have in art. The tiniest, most spirited girl in school.

"I did it!" she yelled. "Nearly did it!"

She ran over to me, waving something shiny.

"I nearly did it, Mrs. Carter. I was on the top row and so high I think I had only a little way left to go, then I heard an owl hooting, at least I think it was an owl, and I got scared and ran all the way back."

It's been a long time since I bothered correcting any of them on the *Mrs.* part. *Mrs.* seems natural to them, the settled comfortable look they read wrong in me. Mrs. Carter. Fine.

"Did you find the flag?" I asked.

"No, but I found this."

She held out a glass jar with thick ridges around the top, and a green tint that marked it as being very old. I explained to her that although she hadn't won the contest, she had found herself a real treasure: an old canning jar, the kind my grandmother used to put up winter vegetables, one of dozens she ordered every summer from Sears and Roebuck. I could see Melissa didn't understand any of this—canning, winter vegetables, Sears and Roebuck—but that I was excited by her discovery was good enough for her.

"Can I keep it?"

"Yes, of course you can. Will you bring it to school on Monday? It would be nice for everyone to see. Do you have a ride home? You were brave, going into the maze by yourself so late."

"I walked here. I might have a ride. I dunno."

It's like that with all the kids—so happy and spirited until you ask about their parents or substitute parents, then too often those confused little mumbles.

"Wait under the light and if no one comes in ten minutes, I'll have Mrs. O'Connell drive you home. And here—whoever finds a jar gets their ticket refunded, that's a rule we have, so you won after all."

After she left, it was just Margaret. She was fussing around the ticket counter, making sure everything was organized. She had already taken off and folded her costume, and as we talked she kept touching her cheeks and glasses, as if making sure the real her was back in place.

"Where do you want me to store these tickets, Irene? The cookie jar same as last year? Mice might nibble them otherwise. They get so hungry in winter, poor things."

"That's fine. Have you heard anything new about Melissa Zack? I have a feeling she's living by herself now."

Margaret snorted, or at least as close as she's capable of. "Better off, if you ask me, considering the alternatives there. That her waiting? I'll bring her home. Want me to box the skeletons up?"

"I can manage."

"It doesn't feel like Halloween. Halloween's supposed to make you shiver, not sweat."

She wasn't in a hurry, that was obvious. There's a stool for whoever takes tickets, and she pulled it over now, plumped herself down.

"I was talking to Cynthia Dunn in lunchroom today, and in that quiet way he has, Mr. T. came over and started talking to us. It was about you actually. He wanted to know if there was any way we could persuade you to come teach full-time, not just art, but second grade. You would need to get certified, at least pretty soon. A summer or two of grad school probably."

"Well, that's nice of him. Mr. T.'s a good principal. But I'm too old to go back to college."

"Thirty-three? I don't think so, Irene."

I swept my arm around. "There's the farm to take care of, the maze in the fall. I like teaching art, but there's so much to do here."

Margaret usually softens pretty quickly when you stand up

to her, but this time it was different. She had a severe look on her face I'd never seen before, as if part of that witch costume had stayed glued on.

"It would be good for you, Irene. Getting away from here for a summer. You would meet new people; that would be good for you too."

"People?"

Instantly, the severity melted—she all but blushed.

"Oh, Irene. You know we all want what's best for you. You can't really call this a farm, not anymore you can't, not since your mom and Carlton died. It's changing so fast around here now. I was talking to Bill about that just this morning. There's no use being the last of anything. It doesn't do anyone any good to be that."

"I'm too old," I said—not lightly like I usually say it, but meaning it. For the first time ever, meaning it.

Margaret was going to say more, but something in my expression must have checked her, because she turned away to fuss with the cookie tin, banging the lid down too hard with her hand. The truth is I was eager to be alone now, angry that she lingered.

"Well," she said, when there was nothing left to neaten up. "At least no one won the prize this year. You're five hundred dollars richer. I hope for once you treat yourself to something nice."

"I will, Margaret, I promise. You'll take Melissa home? Here, bring her these apples; she's probably had nothing to eat all day besides candy."

The darkness dropped back very fast after she left. I went around picking up candy wrappers, ticket stubs, the paper cups we use for cider. This is always my favorite part of the night. When we still had cows my favorite part was being the last in the barn at night, turning the lights down, seeing the calves were settled. At school, my favorite part is being alone late on winter afternoons, putting the art supplies away or making murals of the kids' paintings. I can't really explain why this is, my needing always to be alone with things, to close things down. I started on the south side of the maze, then worked my way around the perimeter. In the four years I've done this, the corn has never been so high—twice my height nearly, so walking along the edge is like walking around a castle. It grows thickly too, and you can't slip edgeways between stalks. Even Richard, the three times he's come. He's impatient, which is surprising, given how else he seems. He wants so badly to solve the puzzle he'll try bulling his way through rather than admit defeat—but the stalks are too tough even for him.

Except to go in and rescue people, I've never been inside the maze at night, not alone, not in darkness like this. The maze is mine. I created it, cared for it, made it work, and yet on a night like this it's frightening, the hungry rustling sound it makes, the ovenlike way it holds in the heat, that restless tossing.

I walked around the perimeter once, then started a second time, picking up wrappers, pretending I wasn't scared while at the same time wondering why I was. Melissa Zack could do it—why couldn't I? Two times I walked around. On the third time when I got to the entrance, I turned and walked as fast as I could in toward the maze's heart.

There are other corn mazes besides mine, but they're too easy; people quickly get to their center, and that's when I got the idea of making one that was more of a challenge, where you could really get seriously lost. There was desperation behind this—everything else anyone tried here has failed. The south side of the farm has always been corn anyway, so it wasn't hard to cut out paths. I put an ad in the paper, Margaret went down to the college and stuck up posters, and right from that first moment we had people coming not just from New Hampshire, but from over the river in Vermont.

I remember once when I was four or five, wandering off from the house one afternoon, following the tractor ruts into the corn, getting myself good and lost. A baby, crawling through a jungle of bamboo, couldn't have been more hidden. I remember how much I liked that feeling, sitting in the center of the field waiting for someone to come find me, half hoping they would, half hoping they wouldn't. The sun was low enough in the sky that it poured sideways through the corn, the stalks breaking the beams apart like a prism, so I could reach out and put my hand around a shaft of amber, a shaft of yellow, a shaft of gold. And the smell—all the goodness of the earth was in it. I was lost, I knew that, but what was strange was that I had never felt safer, and my father would always tell the story about how when they finally found me after many hours of searching, I was crying, but only because they were taking me away.

Some of this is what people must feel when they come here—lost, but safe at the same time. Safe from what the outside world brings them. Safe from what life dishes out. When we started, I charged three dollars, and I thought that was crazy, but people kept coming, and so, taking a deep breath, I raised it to five, and that didn't slow them down either, so this year I raised it to twelve, certain that would be the end of things. But I could make it twenty-five and people would still come. Who would have expected that? That there are so many people who feel the need to be lost.

All kinds come, but mostly two kinds. Teenage couples wanting to be alone with each other. Divorced parents entertaining their kids. Often there isn't anyone in the middle. Lovers at the start of things. Survivors at the end. What happens in between we never see.

I was curious about this; there were times I could hardly stop thinking about it, so I did something I'm still not proud of. It was the first week we opened back in August. A couple came on a brutally hot afternoon, asked shyly if we were open. They were eighteen or nineteen. Very pleasant, they talked to me about the corn, asked some good questions, then walked hand in hand through the entrance, the girl tilting her head ever so slightly toward the boy's shoulder. When you first go in you have to make a choice—Lollipop or Roller Coaster—and like most teenagers they chose Roller Coaster. I watched them disappear, and while I know well enough what most are going in there for, there was something special about this couple, the tender way they looked at each other, the sweet innocent way they held hands.

It was so hot no one else had come. I made some excuse to Margaret, then followed them into the maze. Lollipop is for the little kids, but it loops around Roller Coaster, so I was able to keep the couple in sight through the corn, though they couldn't see me. There was no real reason I followed them. I didn't need to see what they did, but I wanted to understand how they had found each other in the first place—but I'm not explaining that well at all. It's always seemed to me that an important part of life can slip right past without touching you in any way. I could understand love's sad end, the divorced men and women who come to the maze looking hurt and bewildered, but the happy-going-in part I never understood, not even when I was a girl. How love ever found people, bound them together. That was what bothered me, that I couldn't even imagine it.

They went halfway up the hill, came to the grassy cutout I made so people can picnic. They smiled at each other, looked shyly around to make sure they were alone. The boy took off his shirt, spread it on the ground, and they knelt facing each other. "I love you, Bobby," I heard the girl say, and that's when I left, feeling no closer to the answer than I had before, only now I felt ashamed and guilty, like I had followed them to spy.

The hot weather kept business slow our first week. Labor Day morning I went to the services for Bernard Thurston, who had the last farm left besides ours. Hardly anyone was there. Bernard needed a lot of medications these last few years; social services wouldn't help him, so he went without medicine rather than beg. I spent the service remembering how he used to clear snow off his pond so we kids could skate. Even in blizzards you'd see him out there with his shovel—and now someone rich owns the pond, the winters aren't cold enough to freeze it over, and no one skates on it at all.

Anyone who's crazy enough to come in this heat I'm going to let in free, I decided when I got back. We have an honor system with a box, and I was surprised reaching in to discover twenty dollars—an adult admission and two kids. And just then I heard giggling, a little girl's musical voice dueling with a boy's shriller one, and then the three of them emerged from the exit, laughing at the sudden way the sun slapped them after the twilight of those stalks.

It was a man with a curly-haired little boy and his equally beautiful little girl. He didn't look pissed at them like so many dads do, or worried about them getting into trouble—for once it was nice to see an adult who enjoyed the experience too. He was tall with a beard, homely from the distance, serious looking, and yet he must have had a silly side, because he had draped corn tassels over his head like a wig.

"We've met before," he said, when they came over to buy lemonade. "Richard Crask? I work for the Valley Land Trust. We came to talk to you last spring about buying development rights here, putting your land under conservation easements to protect it."

"I remember you," I said. For some reason it came out sounding mean.

"You said no, which surprised us."

One of the tassels fell off his head. I picked it up, and crumpled it like litter.

He nearly smiled. "Yeah. Well . . . hey, great maze! We really got lost up there. We were trying to solve the puzzle, win the prize. We followed Zigzag; is that the key? I could see how it was playing around with contour, so you always have to dip down into a hollow before you can find a path leading back up. Am I right about that? Down always leads to up?"

He wasn't as homely as he seemed from the distance—he reminded me of professors who come up from the college, only without the high opinion of himself most of them have. His hair was brown mixed with red, and it went pretty much any way it wanted back and forth across his head.

"Can I ask you what I hope isn't a stupid question?" he said, looking across the counter at me. "Walking around here, seeing how well cared for this land obviously is, we realized that whoever owns it . . . you . . . must love it very much. It surprised us that you wouldn't consider protecting it under easements, making sure it stays this way for future generations. We worried maybe it was something wrong we said in our presentation."

I looked at him without blinking, stared right into his earnest, well-meaning, totally without irony eyes. "Your boy is hanging upside down on my swing," I said.

He whirled around, yelled, "Oh jeezus!" went over, disentangled him, came back with a child tucked under either arm.

"I'll be back to win that prize," he said. "How hard can it be? You go down to get up. You need to backtrack before you hit dead ends. There are knight's moves like in chess, and then maybe two more tricks I haven't figured out yet. Another hour of trying and that maze dissolves."

I remembered him. The land trust people were very nice; they had their facts and figures all ready for me, showing how much I would save in taxes if the land was conserved under their program. They even had papers ready for me to sign. Richard was the quiet one, though whenever there was a technical question they hurried over to get his opinion. We all stood behind the barn where the first fields begin. In April, not much was showing under the snow besides yellow stubble, but I could see him looking carefully around, nodding to himself in satisfaction. He squatted down on his heels, stuck a piece of straw in his mouth, kept on squinting. He sees how beautiful it is under the bleakness, I remember thinking. It surprises me how vividly I remember thinking just that.

School started on Tuesday, so I was away getting my room ready for the kids. When I got back, there was a note pasted to the money box.

Significant strides made. SUCCESS ASSURED! Sorry I missed you. Back next week.

Coming into the maze, I almost made a wrong turn; that's how dark it is tonight, even with the moon out. We have signs for the paths, but teenagers stuck pumpkins over them, so it looks like heads impaled on posts. The cocky ones who are sure they can solve the puzzle all make the mistake of thinking the hardest paths must be the key, so they sprint up Roller Coaster or The Jungle or The Path of No Return, all of which are traps. You have to begin on the easiest path, Lollipop, since it's the only one that has an exit that leads to the inner ring. This was deliberate on my part. The kind of person I want to win the prize is a person who understands even the most complicated maze begins very simply.

Even with Lollipop, you have to make a quick decision. It crosses a damp spot, then two openings appear in the wall of corn, a path leading steeply uphill to the right, a path leading steeply downhill to the left. Most people choose the harder path, the steep uphill one, but Richard is right—the path to take is the one that leads downhill, giving you the sensation it's exiting the maze, when what it's really doing is leading you into the secret of the inner ring.

It's the way I walked tonight. The moonlight, now that the

clouds are gone, seems sticky on the tassels, so it's like walking under a hoop of smoldering torches. Inside the inner ring the effect is even more pronounced, only here the whiteness is harder looking, colder, as if the corn stalks have turned into granite pillars. In the mood that has hold of me, I thought about that—how if you wait long enough here, everything, even the most pliant things, turn to stone.

The inner ring is so narrow you have to walk sideways and stoop. I thought I heard a sound back by the parking lot, I listened very carefully, but it was only two trees rubbing against each other in the wind. Melissa's owl was hooting right on cue, and off in the distance I could hear a truck changing gears on the interstate. Other than that, it was as quiet and lonely as a Halloween can be.

He came back again like he promised in his note. It was the day the first leaves began blowing down from the trees, and when I got back from school, sculpted mounds of red and orange were building up against the corn. Margaret jabbed away at them with a rake, but I could tell she was excited about something, and the moment I got out of the car she hurried over.

"He's almost there! He's going to solve it!" Then, remembering the implications, her expression sagged. "There goes your five hundred dollars, Irene."

"Who?" I said, though I knew right away who.

"The man with the beautiful kids, the one who talked to you that time. He was here waiting when I opened, and he's been in there ever since, but not all the time. Twice he's run down to ask for lemonade, then he gulps it down and races back in again. He's trying to worm it out of me too, even though I told him I have no idea. Lemon Squeeze? he says. Lemon Squeeze to Twister Girl to Labyrinth? It sounds like he knows just which way to go."

She seemed so anxious I had to laugh. "Lemon Squeeze? Not even close."

But she had more to say than that. "He was asking about you, Irene."

"Asking what?"

"You know. *Asking.*"

We turned to face the entrance. The fallen leaves were entering the maze one at a time, the brave-colored ones, the ones that were brightest.

"He's in there right now," Margaret said, with something like awe. "He's probing, reaching, groping . . ."

I liked that image, a bearlike man groping my corn. And yet I was angry too, in a way I didn't really understand. I fussed around the ticket booth wondering why, if I felt that way, I wasn't busying myself in the house where I wouldn't see him.

When he emerged it was nearly dark out, and Margaret had long since gone home. I could see the tassels waving and tossing near the top of the hill, then the sinuous line he made bulling his way back down. He seemed surprised he was out again— he blinked like a man staring into a spotlight. His clothes were covered with dry bits of husk, making it look like he had been wrestling with corn and the corn had won.

He smiled, sheepishly, did his best to brush himself off. "The kids begged me to bring them, but their mother said no. For once I was happy about that—we spared each other our usual argument. It's serious exploration work in there. At times I was totally lost. You should hand out machetes."

"You weren't doing it right if you need a machete."

"Oh, I think I'm getting pretty close."

"Margaret says you tried bribing her."

"By buying out her lemonade? Besides, I couldn't get her to tell me a thing."

"About me?"

That surprised him, judging by the way he squinted. It surprised me too, the girlish, flirty way it came out.

"Not much about you, other than that your parents were sick for many years and you took care of them all by yourself, and that you went to college for a semester in Pennsylvania but then came back again, and you had a farm stand that was the best around especially with perennials, and no one really knows why you never married, other than the fact you were always the pretty, shy one who always kept to herself, even in high school."

"Margaret was talkative."

"She said you were the kind of girl who was born old. She said that twice; it seemed important to her. 'Well,' I said. 'Maybe that's not a bad thing, because once you're through with that the only thing left is to grow younger.'"

Though he was smiling, the words felt like harsh little slaps against my cheek. It made me angry, the way he reeled those things off. I walked around him to turn the spotlight off, stood there a moment looking at the first stars coming up over the maze—stood looking at them too long—then came back.

He still had that same gentle smile on his face. I don't think he had moved even an inch.

"When you came that time, you and your friends? The blonde woman who was in charge made me angry, with all her talk about descendants, preserving the farm for my kids and grandkids. How could she be so blind? Did she think she saw toddlers running around, bikes in the yard, toys? But she's not the reason I said no. The reason I said no is that I become angry sometimes, thinking about how things have changed here, and it's scary how powerful the feeling is. I never knew what bitterness was before, and now I think about it all the time. It's there waiting for me if I'm not careful, so I need something to bribe it away. I need to be able to say to myself, if I don't make a go of this, if the world has changed too much for a place like this to survive, then I can always sell the land to a developer and make my million and say the hell with everything."

"Sell out, in other words?"

"Yes. Sell out."

It's not like me to say so much. I felt the way I do when I lose my temper with my kids in class—angry more at myself than at them, ashamed, embarrassed. The kids sense this, of course, make their faces go tragic just to make me feel worse. Richard, though, only nodded and plunged his hands deep in his pockets, as if weighed down with thought.

"I'm coming to a similar decision about my job with the land trust. I've enjoyed it; they're great people, but more and more I have the feeling I'm working for a lost cause. Environmentalism. Protecting the land. It's a constant battle of course, but you have to realize that the battle can be lost. What do you do with the rest of your life then? Go around pining for the old days? I want to spend my life working at something that can produce some victories, and I don't mean just for myself."

He seemed like he wanted to say more, but just then a car

pulled up, a van full of teenagers, and I had to go turn the spot-light back on and get them started. When I came back, Richard was still there, and, if anything, his expression seemed more serious than it had before.

"The Labyrinth is the last actual defined path, am I right? After that you have to find a secret passageway, and it's some-where toward the top of the hill hidden in plain sight. Am I warm? I think I'm warm. I think when I come back on Halloween I'm going to find my way to the top."

"Lots of people brag about what they're going to do on Halloween."

He laughed, clenched a fistful of air. "I'll be back, Irene, I promise you that. The maze comes unraveled on Halloween night."

It didn't take me long to get this high. The Labyrinth ends in a solid wall of corn, but if you backtrack, you come upon a nar-row opening that leads to Lonesome Lane. It became warmer the higher I went, the breeze felt tropical, making it seem like I was climbing toward the sun, not the moon. I thought about how cold and brisk Halloween used to be, but that seems a cen-tury ago, the memory too vague and distant to cool me off.

The secret of the maze comes near the end of Lonesome Lane. The path slants along the side of the hill, and everything suggests you should follow its thrust all the way to the top. But no. What you have to do is carefully pay attention to what's behind you, not what's in front. The opening is so perfectly blended into the wall of corn, comes in on such an oblique angle, hides in so much camouflage, that if you go by too fast you simply won't notice it. You have to retrace your steps, take

a careful look, decide that yes, it's not an optical illusion but
an actual opening, then slip edgeways through—and if you do
this, the path immediately widens into a grassy meadow that
takes you straight to the top of the hill.

People in a maze never guess that the answer, in the end,
might be the simplest possible. You start the same place everyone else does, full of optimism and energy, and when you get
lost the first time it's no big deal. Annoying, discouraging, but
you quickly get over that, and start off again with confidence,
certain it's only a minor setback. Even with the next dead end.
It's an accident, you decide, not meant for me personally. It's
only later you begin to worry that being lost is a permanent
condition. You grope your way along without ever expecting
an answer, without even finding the hint of one, so you circle
and circle in the same baffling groove, never getting one inch
closer to the end. After enough time goes by you can't even
remember entering the maze in the first place, it seems like
you've always been lost there, and even if someone came along
to help you, you'd pull away from them, go hide, not believing
anymore in the chance of rescue. Everyone else in the maze
knows their way—that's the feeling that eats away at you—and
the ones who don't know the way seem to get to the end anyway, so you decide they must be cheating. Alone, that's what
the maze shouts at you. Alone, get used to it, don't ever think
about finding your way out.

Only one thing can change this. Make the maze yourself,
construct all its windings, hide the secret passages, and you
can waltz through it blindfolded without any hesitation at all.

That's what I did. And that's where I am now, on the hill
near the cairn of stones and the little New Hampshire flag

waving there untouched by human hands. There's a bench, be-cause I decided anyone who solved the puzzle deserved a rest. I planted flowers too. Coneflowers—and here the day before November they're still in full blossom, with no sign of wilting, sending out bold new shoots as if winter's approach is no lon-ger a threat to take seriously.

When I was a girl I would sometimes walk up here to look at the stars. Turning in a circle, you could see four clusters of lights spaced around the ring of hills—the Thurstons, the Mustys, the Ballstons, the Zacks. Now there are a hundred lights, two hundred lights, and they form a vise pattern, the square jaws down in the valley where it's flat, the long screw handle jutting back up along the river. Beyond them down the interstate, the sky is purple more than black, and I don't like thinking about what creates such a light.

It's quiet here—that's the only part that hasn't changed. A few minutes ago I thought I heard a car pull into the parking lot. A car door slamming—I thought I heard that too, and just before that came a quick swerving flash that could have been headlights. And I still can't decide. Maybe it was a car, maybe it wasn't. Maybe it's him that's come, maybe it isn't. Down in the village the church bell chimed midnight. I counted off the numbers with my eyes closed, hoping, trying to convince my-self, but when the chimes reached twelve I didn't particularly care either way.

The woman who came with the land trust last spring hurt me when she talked about descendants. But when I think about it now, I realize that's the only thing I am. A descendant, in the deepest part of me. A descendant to the very core.

When the first Carter moved here in 1769, it was to escape

a Massachusetts that already felt old and petrified, offering an ambitious young man no chance. There would have been nothing here but forest in those early years—a maze far more complicated and tormenting than anything you could devise now. A clearing was made for a cabin, trees hacked down with saws, but the rest of the trees were girdled to die slowly, the limbs burned for potash, the trunks gradually softening until they were rotten enough to topple with a gentle shove. Subsistence farming—there couldn't have been very much—and big families in which every other infant would die of whooping cough, fever or ague.

The second Carter tried wheat, and it grew wonderfully for two seasons, then exhausted the soil forever. Rock walls were thrown up, sheep introduced, and the sheep did well until the railroads brought in cheap wool from the West. The land was too harsh and flinty to grow crops profitably, and if you did coax something from it an early frost would come in and blacken everything it touched.

Carters went away to war and came back again—if any of them tried moving west, there was always something tugging them back. But other men did leave. The late 1800s was the golden age of widows and spinsters—many of these farms were run by women alone. They had fewer dreams than the men had, but if anything loved these hills even more. "Land proud" this was called. Pride with no illusions.

Dairy farming worked for a century; that was their salvation. In the twenties, my grandmother took in tourists every summer, fattened them on milk and cheese, took them berry picking, wrote them Christmas cards inviting them back next summer. Pin money for her, but then when the Depression forced them to sell their cows, it was pin money that kept food on the table, the kids in shoes.

My father, once he came back from his war, did much better, at least for a time, but then milk prices collapsed, taxes went up, and even before he and Mom got sick, we had sold most of our herd. It was my idea for the maze, and now it brings in more money, easier money, than this land has ever brought anyone. The land always was a maze, but generations thought they had the answer, so none of them ever fully understood what they were dealing with; they could never step back from their lives far enough to see. I stand on the same spot that first Carter stood, brooding like him over the future, and what I see is a bigger maze, a maze running across the entire farm, one so twisting and challenging and tormenting it brings in even more people than the one I have now.

Will it ever become too hot here to grow corn? I need to research that, not be outsmarted like so many have been outsmarted before, just because they couldn't anticipate the worst. I hug my arms around myself like I used to from the chill. I think of patterns I could cut, tunnels I could make, twists and turns that even the smartest and bravest won't be able to solve, not in the Halloweens that are coming, the ones that will be too warm and gentle to frighten anyone but me.

The Lucy Coffin

MY FATHER, so long a distinguished member of the Philadelphia bar, was totally incapable of making up a story. His
clients were expected to tell him in simple words what had
happened, and then he would try to shape the plain words, the
unadorned facts, into an argument a jury would find compel-
ling. Imagination, exaggeration, hyperbole—he actively disap-
proved of all three. This was bad luck for me, since I was born
with an oversupply of each, something he blamed on heredity,
a great-uncle who wrote advertisements for Florida real estate
back in the twenties, and who, before me, was the closest thing
to a writer the family had.

So the one story Dad told me I listened to very closely. It
was a fish story of course. Fly-fishing was Dad's one vulner-
ability, the only thing we could tease him about, or theme his
birthday presents around, or, on great occasions, actually share
with him out on the water.

He was good at it; he fished all over the world, and his eyes came alive on a river in a way they didn't even in the courtroom. He never had the usual fisherman's virtue of patience. He despised patience, considered it the most mediocre of virtues, but what he had instead was endurance, getting out on the water before anyone else in camp and coming back far later. And he looked the part too, once he started putting some years on. Wrinkles made him more handsome, not less. People always imagined him with a pipe in his mouth, squinting toward the sunset, though the truth is he never smoked.

That this passion was fueled in part by a rather dry, stiff, passionless marriage should perhaps come as no surprise. There were lots of dry, stiff, passionless marriages in the Philadelphia of those years. My parents didn't divorce; they had old-fashioned notions about what was owed their children, and I don't remember any particular arguments. Mother went her way, Dad went his, at least until her last years, when there was a softening, a drawing together, that surprised no one more than the two of them.

I'm not sure when I first heard Dad's one and only story—there doesn't seem to be a place in memory when I didn't know it. He was just old enough to have served in the last days of the Pacific War, and it wasn't until almost a year after it ended that he was discharged. He went back to law school and graduated quickly—which means the story begins in the late spring of 1948.

He decided that before starting his practice he would treat himself to one grand fishing expedition. He would take a train to Vermont, then spend the summer hiking and hitchhiking through the hills, fishing every stream and pond he came upon, boarding at farmhouses where he could find them, or camping rough in the woods. For three months, he would care about nothing except fishing, think about nothing except fishing, press the summer so deep in his memory it would never shake loose.

And that's pretty much the way it turned out. He traveled north along the Connecticut River, and when he came to a tributary, he would fish upstream toward the west, then strike out cross-country and follow the next tributary downstream to its junction with the big river—a back-and-forth, weaving kind of progression that meant there was very little water he missed. The days of the log drives were over, but there were plenty of old-time rivermen left who were more than happy to tell him where the big trout were hiding—and they weren't often wrong.

Back in the Depression, tramps and hobos had been distrusted, even feared here, but once the farm wives realized Dad was just fishing, and a veteran, he was often given a room free of charge. In the morning, there would be chores he could help out with, and afternoons he would spend chasing the browns and rainbows that lived in the deep pools, or fishing for wild brook trout in the beaver ponds where most of these rivers had their starts, wading in the muck if he had to, sometimes taking all day to build a raft.

Thanks to his zigzag pattern, his lingering on rivers he loved best, it took him June and a good part of July to advance northward sixty miles. There was still a lot of Vermont left to go before he hit Canada, but suddenly, between one tributary and the next, the landscape dramatically changed. The Connecticut veered away into New Hampshire, and the rivers flowed north toward Quebec and the St. Lawrence. The forest, instead of being dominated by maple and pine, was now mostly spruce, with boreal swamps and undulating sheets of pewter-colored rock. The farms were few and far between and mostly failed—this was a land of empty farmhouses where ghostly curtains blew out through shattered glass.

The first part of the story, the background, my father told quickly, with a lawyer's fine sense for how much he could ask of a jury's patience. But he would always hesitate here, take his glasses off and put them back on again, look out the nearest window, smile ruefully, then turn back again, his voice pitched now to a lower key.

"And then something odd happened, something I hadn't counted on. You have to understand that I was pretty cocky in those days. I thought, when it came to fly-fishing, I was the hottest thing ever to hit Vermont. But once I got into the deep woods, the lonely country, things changed. I couldn't catch a fish, no matter how hard I tried. Not a trout, not a sucker, not even a chub. They all had locks on their jaws and for the life of me I couldn't find the key."

It was late August now, hot, with low water in all the streams. He slept in the woods most nights, though when it rained he found shelter in abandoned logging camps set in pockets against the ridges. On one nameless stream, fishing through a tunnel of alders, his leather wallet of flies, his best flies, dropped into the water and floated away, so he was down now to his rejects and spares.

"For the first time all summer, I began feeling sorry for my-self. A thunderstorm hit me that night, so I was a pretty sorry sight once morning came. The only thing keeping me from heading to the train station and home was that the terrain was growing gentle again, with those beautiful open hillsides similar to what I had seen farther south. I'll fish one more river, I decided. Just one more and then I'm done."

He was walking along, drying out in the sunshine, when he came upon an iron bridge with unusually elaborate scrollwork, and past it, a tree with a crudely painted sign. *Hand Tied Flies!* it read. In that lonely countryside, it startled him; it could have said *Hand Cut Diamonds* and he wouldn't have been more surprised. There was an arrow pointing uphill along a road so rough a mule would have turned around in disgust. Figuring he had nothing to lose, he started up it—and that's when he had his second surprise.

On the top of the hill, set under a grove of ancient maples, was a small, white farmhouse with an attached red barn. It wasn't derelict or abandoned like so many of the highest places but well cared for, neat, even prim. Holsteins had trampled the yard up, but there was a garden surrounded by a picket fence, and it wasn't a vegetable garden either, but a flower garden, with tall showy gladiolas that were obviously meant to be cut and brought inside.

There was no one around, at least not at first, but when my father circled behind the barn he came upon a toolshed where a husky young man sat on a wicker chair listening to a Red Sox game on the radio. On the workbench beside him were piles of chicken feathers and Christmas tinsel and small black hooks. It was as if, my father said, the man knew he was coming and wanted to get right down to business.

"I saw your sign," my father said.

The young man looked Dad over. "Fly-fisherman?"

"I try to be."

"Then you'll want six of these."

He handed over a Prince Albert tobacco tin. Inside were half a dozen of the rattiest-looking, most outlandish flies Dad had ever seen. There looked to be muskrat fur in them, and duck quill, and a huge shank of rooster hackle—and Dad's first temptation was to laugh out loud.

"How much?" he asked carefully, not wanting to offend him.

"A dollar for the six."

"Do they have a name?"

"No. Well, sure. The Lucy Coffin. There, I just named it. You try one, fish it up on top slathered in fly dope, and if you use anything else, you ain't as smart as you look."

Those of you who know fish stories can sense where this is headed. Dad stuffed those flies in his pocket, then forgot all about them. The last river he fished in Vermont was the Willoughby. As with all the other places he fished in August, he couldn't find a way to get the trout to rise—until, desperate, he remembered the Lucy Coffin. Tying one on, he threw it out there with a why-not kind of cast—and promptly rose a three-pound brown that fought him stubbornly for a good half hour. Six more fish followed, each almost as big, and when he finally gave up because of darkness, trout were still jumping toward it out of the black. For the last week of his trip, he fished nothing else—and everywhere it immediately resulted in the same kind of triumphs.

That was Dad's story, his one and only. Even as a kid, I wondered about it, not so much whether it was true or not—Dad didn't make anything up, so I knew it was true—but at the sweetness that would come into his tone, especially during the last part about that lonely, forgotten farm. It seemed more wistfulness than the summer really warranted, though obviously, being alone like that, at a time when a place was at its most beautiful and forgotten, had left an enduring impression. I'd like to say that as a kid I never tired of hearing him tell this story, but the truth is, I did get tired of it, particularly when I reached my teens. A magic fly? A fly that worked miracles? Sure, Dad. Right. Anything you say.

And then, from a storyteller's point of view, he made a smart move. The summer I was sixteen, driving me back from a camp counselor job I had in Maine, he detoured over to show me Vermont. We fly-fished several of the streams he'd discovered in 1948; Dad, unlike most men who are experts at something, was more than willing to let me go off and learn on my own, playing dumber than he really was, knowing I would either fall in love with it on my own or it wouldn't take.

We only had four days. On the third, I suddenly woke up to the fact we were now doing more driving than fishing, going off on dirt roads that led away from the rivers uphill. All these detours seemed of the same pattern. "We're low on flies," Dad would announce, then suddenly swerve the wheel to the right. We would drive to the top of the hill where the road gave out into ruts, Dad would get out, look over the abandoned field going back to brush, maybe take a few steps toward what remained of a farmhouse . . . a cellar hole, a blackened chimney . . . then come back to the car shaking his head.

"Well, it was around here somewhere. Things have changed,

all this forest. I was on foot, never bothered with maps. Half the streams I didn't even know what their names were. Being lost was part of the adventure."

I tried to be helpful. "Maybe it was over by that river we fished yesterday? I saw a lot of old farms."

My father considered this, then shook his head. "Well, maybe, but I don't think so, Paul. I searched there pretty thoroughly last time."

"Last time?"

He smiled, shyly. "Oh, I had a business trip to Boston a couple years back. Came over here for a few days, looked around. It wasn't fishing season. Mud season, so I couldn't get very far." He raised himself on his tiptoes, put his hands around his eyes like binoculars. "See that open meadow over there? Let's see if we can find a road, then, if it's not there, we'll do some fishing."

He was quiet driving home. It was by far the best four days together we ever had; it got me started fly-fishing, but I was confused at how silent he seemed, how disappointed. If we hadn't found his fly shop, that was okay by me. The Lucy Coffin? Hell, we caught plenty of trout without it—which is what I wanted to tell him, but he had his lawyer's face on now, his *losing* lawyer's face, and I knew that was something I couldn't dent.

When my mother died three years ago, Dad took it harder than any of us would have expected. As I said, during her last years their dependence on each other kept growing as their friends and colleagues one by one disappeared. Passion Dad had missed out on in life, but at least he had found a quiet warmth, and losing that, at his age, hurt him deeply.

When I first broached the idea of a fishing trip, Dad was

hesitant. He still fished, but mostly in ponds now, trolling streamers from a rowboat. I made it sound like I was the one who badly needed to get away. I had just finished a book; I was worn out, in need of a change, and, though he could see right through my stratagems, Dad wasn't immune to what June was doing to the air, even in suburban Philadelphia. Still he hesitated; there was a meeting at his retirement community he was supposed to chair, and I had to come out with the argument I'd been saving as my clincher.

"We'll go and see if we can find the old place where you bought the Lucy Coffin. Maybe even find the man."

"Dead," Dad grunted.

"How do you know that? You said he was about your own age, didn't you? He could still be tying flies. And even if he's gone, we'll make a real effort to locate where that farm was; that shouldn't be impossible."

"It's vanished. I couldn't find it last time."

"You had me in tow."

"Well, no. The time after that. I searched pretty hard."

"You went back again?"

"Four or five times now."

"Four or five times?"

I'd been on the lookout for signs of dotage, but still this surprised me—he said it in a sly, secretive way, like he'd admitted sneaking off to Las Vegas. I didn't know the story had such a hold on him still. For me, it was nostalgic, going back up there, and I suppose I expected it was merely that for him, a story that sleeps wherever stories sleep in men his age, not something that actively burned.

He was waiting for me in the parking lot when I got there

Thursday morning—the leathery, craggy-looking version of
Dad, a rod tube sticking out from his ancient duffel bag, his
waders slung around his shoulders like a bandolier.

Our drive north was on the quiet side—except for grandkids, none of the subjects we came up with seemed to take
hold. Always before we could fall back on politics, me kidding
him about being a Republican, him teasing me about being
a Democrat, but that kind of teasing isn't possible anymore.
Only once did he broach anything even remotely serious. We
were up in Massachusetts, we had just gone through a long
stretch of malls, and he waved his hand around, as if indicat-
ing, not just what we could see out the window, but the deeper,
more essential part we could only sense.

"Countries are like old men, Paul. They get ugly when they
get old"—and the truth of that, the doubled truth, kept things
pretty quiet until we hit Vermont.

It was much better after that. The long evening shadows cut
across the interstate, there were caddis flies dancing like flames
around the top of the highest birches, and when we got out of
the car at our motel the smell of late-blooming lilac made us
look at each other and smile. Next morning, up early, we drove
into the mountains, and the farther we drove, the younger and
fresher the land seemed. I got Dad to tell his story again, not
the end he always rushed toward, but the earlier part, those
June weeks when he had wandered around the foothills with
no motive in life other than catching rainbows, brookies, and
browns.

We fished some of the same streams. Dad took forever
stringing up his rod and pulling on his waders, but once in
the river he did fine, not shuffling along like an old man in

slippers, but high-stepping like a stork. We both caught trout. They weren't the natives he remembered, they were probably two weeks off the stock truck, but the rivers rushed the same way they always rushed, the willows danced the same dance in the wind, and there were afternoon hatches of mayflies we did very well with, fishing deep into dark. If anything, Dad seemed to have more energy and pep at the end of the day than he had when we began.

"Rhubarb pie," he said, taking a deep sniff of evening air. "I can still smell it. All these farm wives baked great rhubarb pies."

We spent the next day on a little tributary that wasn't on the map. I had to peel the alders back so Dad could enter the best pool, but when he did he caught three wild brook trout, the last, for that water, a real monster, pushing fifteen inches. We admired it for the few seconds he took to let it slip back from his hand to the water. "One to quit on," I said, not really thinking about my words. "Yes, one to quit on," Dad said softly.

That night we found an old tourist home, the kind you wouldn't think existed anymore. *Titus Takes Tourists*, read the sign out front—and Titus turned out to be even older than my father, with a thick mountain accent I could barely understand. But Dad could understand—he and Titus sat up talking half the night. "Twenty bucks!" his wife said, when it was time to leave. She acted embarrassed to ask so much, so, at least in this respect, we were back in 1948 at last.

But it was time to go home now. I had a book signing scheduled in Washington, and Dad still wanted to chair his meeting. I had big ideas about driving it all in one day, so we left early, when the fog still lay clotted on the river. We crossed on an old iron bridge, and instead of a regular paved roadbed, there were thick old beams that made it bumpy. Something about the bumps, or the smell of creosote, or the lacy pattern of the metal got Dad thinking.

"Is there a road up here to the right?" he asked, before we were all the way over.

"It doesn't look like much of a road, Dad." I pointed in the vague direction of Philadelphia. "We've got a long drive ahead of us."

"Is there an old barn? Small, like it was made for miniature cows? Two gables, crazy windows?"

He was looking directly at me when he asked this—he was testing himself by not looking out the window.

"What's left of a barn, yes. There, you look yourself. Underneath all that poison ivy."

Dad nodded without looking, as if I were telling him nothing he didn't already know. "Turn right," he said, with a strange tremor in his voice—and then he closed his eyes, as if only by doing so could he find the right way. "There should be a bog in half a mile, then an apple orchard, then a small wooden dam."

Maybe there were those things—the washouts and ruts kept my attention fixed on the driving. A switchback got us onto an easier grade, and the upper part went under a tunnel of purple lilacs that must have been the last to bloom in the entire state. They don't grow wild; someone had once planted them, so maybe we were on the right track after all—and yet no mental effort I was capable of making could make that thick forest disappear, picture this as ever having been open.

The road ended at a washout that could have swallowed a

tank. I parked on its lip. Dad, without saying anything, opened his door and started striding through the trees. Certainty—his whole posture was shaped to it—and though I was a long way from feeling this myself, I started after him.

I caught up pretty fast. There were some spruce, then a band of dying birch, and I remembered that birch were the trees that grew first on abandoned land, and just when I was trying to figure out how many years this could take, I came into a little clearing in the middle of which stood a house.

It was standing, I'll say that much for it. The tin roof seemed pinned by rusty lightning rods to the simple Cape that stood beneath. The siding had long ago been weathered into bone color, hunters had riddled much of it with bullets, and the windows were starred with broken glass. In front was a porch that had once faced the road, but its supports had collapsed, and the gingerbread trim, algae covered and blistered, lay in pieces in the tall grass that licked the sides.

Dad stood staring down at something, and when I came up to him he pointed, bent stiffly, reached out his hand. Below a broken window the planks had been replaced with fresh, clean pine, making it look as if someone had chosen this spot to begin their renovations. Had they started, but then, faced with the enormity of the job, given up? Except for that and a deflated soccer ball we found near the pyramid-heaped ruins of the barn, there were no signs of recent life.

Some of the debris had been pulled over to where an enormous apple tree had muscled out its own clearing. Dad reached down to turn through the planks. The third or fourth had purple lettering burned into its side like an old tattoo—he held it up to the light so we could read it—but it seemed an advertisement for seed or fertilizer, and didn't say anything about hand-tied flies.

"Is this it?" I asked.

I stood there staring toward the farmhouse, trying to imagine paint on it, a shiny new roof, curtains, flowers. I don't know what Dad saw. Again, as with the forest, the hand of time was too heavy for me to lift.

Dad's voice, when he started, was pitched very soft, like the voice a gentle man uses when someone is sleeping in the next room. And he touched the apple tree while he talked. That seemed important to him, the simple rough contact.

"What I'll never forget is how she was standing there waiting at the top of the road. Not waiting for me—waiting for anyone, their life was so lonely. I remember thinking how the sign for flies was their way of luring strangers just so they could have a little talk with someone besides themselves. If so, it was a good lure—it caught me easily enough."

A brown and shriveled apple, last year's, clung to the branch. He reached his hand toward it, and the motion alone was enough to make it fall.

"There was just the two of them. Her brother was seventeen—heavy, strong, and so round-shouldered he was nearly humpbacked. He could take care of cows all right, and winter he worked with the loggers. Their father had gone off to a defense plant after Pearl Harbor, and that's the last they ever saw of him. Their mother died of cervical cancer a few years later. Lucy had the care of her; there was no one else. The parents or grandparents were either very brave or very stupid to have made a farm so high. The boy's name was Ira and her name was Lucy. Lucy Coffin."

The name, which I expected and didn't expect, seemed to come out of him hard. He coughed, or pretended to, and I followed his eyes back to the road.

He remembered what she looked like that first evening, he said. A young woman his own age standing there with an apron on, staring intently toward the dusk, wiping, with a wonderfully impatient gesture, the curly red hair that fell across her eyes. She was beautiful, of course, though not in a way he had ever learned to see as beautiful before. He thought first of a tomboy, someone freckled and athletic, but she was past that stage now, and the chores hadn't yet roughened her skin. In the brief interval of grace that lay between, he saw a girl so fresh and brave and natural it took his breath away, right from that first moment.

"I ended up staying with them for two weeks—they were absurdly grateful for my company. It was like they lived on an island and I had brought them news of the outside world. It was incredibly hard, the life they led, especially during the war years. It was thirty-five miles to the nearest movie house, and they told me how they would use horses to get down their road, then shovel out their old Ford from the snow, push and shove it to get it going, putting on chains when they got to macadam, then drive all that way just to see a double feature, getting back after midnight so they could tend to the cows. Ira liked fishing, so we hit it off pretty quick. He tied flies, sold a few now and then down in town, but they were cheap, gaudy things, nothing special. He really didn't understand what was happening between Lucy and me. Her bedroom faced the barn, and I remember waking up with her, getting out of bed quietly, pulling on my sweater, walking over to the window and seeing Ira stripped to the waist chopping firewood at five in the morning, and then at night he still wouldn't be finished, all the work he had."

Neither one of them knew much about anything except work. Once a month there were those expeditions to go see Clark Gable or Bette Davis, but except for these their life had few ornaments. Dad explained how he found an old kite in the barn left over from when they were little, but neither one remembered how to fly it, and when he tied a tail on and got it up in the air, they thought he was a magician. And a picnic—they had never thought it possible, to go somewhere pretty and eat outside just for fun. At night, the three of them sat by the radio listening to the Red Sox and then to Jack Benny. When Ira trudged off exhausted to bed, he and Lucy would walk outside together with a blanket and lay under the stars.

They weren't hicks; he wanted to make sure I understood that. Lucy had an energy and directness nothing could stop, except for the one great bafflement that had her in its grip— how to be brave and deal with what life had brought her without her bravery digging a trap for her, making the loneliness even worse. For all the harshness in her life, she had a wonderful laugh, and once started it would run away with her, set him laughing too—laughing so much they cried. And silence— how many other girls her age knew how to make silence say everything? If he could teach her about kites and picnics, she could teach him about sweetness . . . never before had he suspected life was capable of being so sweet . . . and, in the end, what sadness was too.

One afternoon they helped Ira finish his chores so they could all go fishing. Ira fished hard, but without much skill, and spent most of the time admiring my father's little Payne fly rod. After their picnic, he and Lucy walked upstream toward a waterfall. She had borrowed Ira's hat for the sun, a battered old porkpie with flies tucked in the band, and before long, that's pretty much all she was wearing, that floppy red hat. He laughed over that, and she laughed too, bending over a little pool where the water was so thin it acted like a mirror.

My father explained all this while holding on to the apple tree, but now he stepped away, seemed actually to break that invisible cord, and walked slowly back to where I stood in the center of those rotting old planks. He looked old—I was startled at how old he suddenly looked—and maybe it was the dark evening shadows doing that, or maybe it was the contrast with the young man I followed so intently in his story. Time had stopped while he was telling his story, but it was ticking again, and, judging by the way he closed his eyes, Dad felt the rush of those minutes even more than I did.

"I thought about asking her to come away with me—I thought about nothing else that last week. Would she have come? It would have broken her brother's heart. Still, I think if I had pressed her she would have come. Our worlds were so different. When I asked her about her future, she wouldn't tell me about any dreams or plans, but then right toward the end she did. 'I'd like to be in pictures,' she said. Out of all her loneliness, she could come up with nothing else."

My father's voice deepened—it was like he was struggling to recapture his lawyer's tone, get back into that safety zone where words expressed simple, incontrovertible facts.

"Lucy is one day younger than I am. She was born on October sixth and I was born on October seventh, and I teased her about how much younger she was, how much wiser I was. Every single birthday since, I've thought about where she might be, what life has brought her. I've always wondered if we kept pace somehow—she in her world, me in mine. I got up in the middle of the night, being careful not to wake her. I didn't leave a note for her, but I left one for Ira on the kitchen table, along with that little Payne fly rod. I walked down the road in the moonlight, and never before had I seen anything so beautiful, and yet every step was torture. I can feel this even now. Understand that, Paul? Arthritis that young doctor of mine says whenever I go for my checkup. But that's not what a man my age feels in his knees. It's all those times you walked away from someone you should never have walked away from."

I went over and took his arm, since he actually seemed faltering now, and there were roots and rocks to navigate before we got back to the car.

"So there wasn't a fly?" I said. "No Lucy Coffin?"

"Oh, there was a fly all right." He reached into his pocket, brought out his leather fly book, the one he used for his very best flies. He opened it, held it toward the keyhole of light still visible in the West.

"Ira could tie in a clumsy, self-taught way. He gave me some Black Gnats before I left. Six of them. Years when the memory hurt worst, I would take one out and tie it on. I have one left. Here, open your hand."

I felt something sharp and tickly against my palm; I folded my fist tight to make sure it stayed there, that it didn't drop loose. *Mine now.* I didn't say it, but, like a small child accepting a present, that's what I felt.

"Yours now," my father said, reading my thoughts. He smiled—not a happy smile, not a sad smile either, but one that seemed pressed into the thin, permeable layer that lies in between. I could see him stare toward the first stars, sensed him using the silence to set up a line to go out on, like an old experienced storyteller from way back when, not someone who just had the one.

"I fished Ira's fly pretty hard all those two weeks, and never caught a thing on it, but for once in my life I didn't care."

Erin Wetherell

W. D. WETHERELL is the author of three earlier collections of short fiction, five novels, four essay collections, and many other works of nonfiction. He is the recipient of two fellowships from the National Endowment for the Arts, three O. Henry Awards, the Drue Heinz Literature Prize, a Rockefeller Foundation grant, the National Magazine Award, and the Strauss Living Award from the American Academy of Arts and Letters. He lives in Lyme, New Hampshire, with his family.